the fixer

the fixer

a novel

JOHN DANIELL

A catalogue record for this book is available from the National Library of New Zealand

ISBN 978-1-927262-10-8

An Upstart Press Book
Published in 2015 by Upstart Press Ltd
B3, 72 Apollo Drive, Rosedale
Auckland, New Zealand

Printed by 1010 Printing International Limited, China

For Michael Gifkins, who booted it over.

Part One

'Pity the country that has no heroes.'
Andrea to Galileo
The Life of Galileo, Bertolt Brecht

Chapter 1

So much depends upon an oval white ball. It sits on a little orange tee, waiting to be kicked into history. I'm standing there, three steps back from it and two to the left. Around me, forty thousand people. Half of them whistling, honking horns, waving flags and doing whatever they can to put me off as I look up at the goalposts again. The other half are praying or looking away or telling their rowdy neighbours to shut up and give me a chance. God knows how many people in front of their television sets. A million? Five million? In front of me, fifteen men in red shirts dotted around the paddock, most of them hands on hips, all of them silently willing me to miss. Alongside me, a line of fourteen blue shirts ready to chase in case I do.

The full-time siren has already blown. There is no wind and while the noise is terrific I'm aware of it only on the edge of my consciousness, like when you're reading a book in a public place. The ball, the posts and the space between them — forty-five, maybe fifty metres with the angle — are all that interest me. The ball is my slave, and it will do whatever I want.

Most of the time, anyway.

As I shuffle and start my short run in, enjoying the moment, focusing on my rhythm and the spot where I will plant my left foot so my right can swing through the ball, sending it into the band that I'm aiming at, just inside the right upright, I already know what is going to happen.

I know because I'm watching it on a giant flat screen in a sports bar in the middle of Paris. It's a replay of last year's semi-final — the bloke who owns the bar is a sponsor, and he puts it on to cheer us up when we've lost. Free beers too, which probably works better. Funnily enough, he doesn't do that when we've won, but when we've won every bastard in the place wants to buy us a beer and chew an ear off. I'm not sure whether he feels sorry for us or it's just good business, but free beer is free beer. I like to think that it's business.

So: I hit it sweetly and the ball curves ever so slightly right to left just as it arrives level with the posts, straightening and flying over the black dot in the middle of the crossbar with a couple of metres to spare. Just as I'm enjoying the looks on the faces of the guys in the red shirts, Rich barrels up and cracks me on the back of the head.

'You're not still watching that? Mate, it's history — you're a bloody hero. Get over yourself and come and check out these Pommie chicks that Moose's bailed up. They're not top drawer but at least I can understand what they say.'

I swipe my pint off the bar, pour a handful of nuts down my throat and follow him. Rich is an Aussie, a show pony with the morals of a goanna and the sensitivity of a crocodile's back. I liked him straight away. He's been with the club a year longer than me. Moose is a big ox from a small town whose name I can't pronounce a few hours east of Vancouver. He just arrived this year. I think the lights and the swirl of Paris have put the zap on his head. He is clutching a glass of mint liqueur cut with Perrier, has a wardrobe full of too tight T-shirts with slogans — tonight's version is a helicopter with the tagline 'Vietnam: we were winning when I left' — and a homespun philosophy acquired in some goatfucking hillbilly hellhole to justify the relentlessly low bar that makes him lucky most nights ('When a man is hungry, no bread is stale') and the front to pull off pick-up lines ('Hey baby, let's you and me get freaky') that might pass for courtship rituals in Saskatchewan or Lockjaw or wherever it is but should never work here. Still, they do — or if they don't, instead of going down in flames he simply shrugs and moves on to the next option. 'It's just a warm body, right? No point in being picky, we're all going to die alone in the end.' Part self-taught existentialist, part oaf.

As we're squeezing through the Saturday-night crowd, Rich turns to me. 'I've called shotgun on the blonde, OK?' Then one of his dirty little giggles. 'Can't say I fancy yours.'

I'm just tall enough to see over the last few people between us and the little group in the corner. I've been left the short, quite plump straw. I'm sure she's a nice person but taking one for the team has its limits and besides, the local anaesthetic in my ankle is long gone and I forgot to take the anti-inflammatories that normally take the edge off it after a game. I peel off towards the other bar and join up with the Frenchies who've come out, planning to finish my drink with them and head home. One of them offers me his bar stool. I hesitate, then accept. It's only one in the morning but I should probably get off the leg. As it is I won't be able to train Monday or Tuesday but I don't want to miss next week's game and the young number ten who's supposed to be my understudy has been looking worryingly sharp.

If I needed any convincing, the physical trainer, Eric, is there. He's too slimy for my liking — there's widespread suspicion that he's reporting back on our nocturnal habits to the coach, who had a moan about 'professionalism' the other day and started talking about breath tests at the Sunday-morning pool sessions with fines for anyone who's had more than a couple of drinks. The players committee put a stop to that but there's something in the pipeline. He looks at my pint — the Frenchies have their little half-pint vessels — and raises his eyebrows. I tell him it's a shandy, finish it in one and make as if I'm going to glass him with it. For a second he looks genuinely afraid. Prick. At thirty-two years old I still finish second in his fitness tests.

The Frenchies — Jacques, our halfback and Coquine, our big hairy hooker and captain (Coquine is French for 'flirty girl' or something stronger: I think his real name is Edouard) — are talking about the game while Eric looks on. Lineouts. They try to draw me in, asking my advice, and for a while I make an effort but it's not really my bag. Rich appears, shakes his head at me in disappointment, tells me that I've 'changed' and starts in on a spiel about beautiful English girls who want to meet a real Frenchman. Eric looks chuffed as Rich shepherds him off.

I say my goodnights to the Frenchies and look over towards the corner where Eric is being introduced by Rich and Moose is whispering something to the blonde girl who laughs. As I reach behind the bar to pick up my bag — we came straight from the train — a couple of fans who are slightly the worse for wear bounce over and request a photograph with me. I sling my bag over one shoulder and pose, first with one, then the other. They might be on the long list of supporters, none of whom I know, who have tracked me down in cyberspace and want to be my friends. I can't make up my mind: if I turn them down I look like an arsehole, but I don't want them getting too close to my life. For the moment they're sitting in my in-box, thirty-seven of them at last count.

'Big game next week, ah?' says the shorter one in heavily accented English. He must be in his forties, the spare tire of his belly showing in the unforgivingly tight-fitting replica jersey. 'We were there today, in Lyon,' offers the other, younger and slimmer with a hook nose and monobrow. His English is better and I catch the tone of regret at what might have been. I pull a face. I kicked six out of eight, and the two I missed were hard, from the touchline on my wrong side, but if I'd put them over we would have had a draw. In reality the game wouldn't have been played the same way if they had gone over — but I know that's not what these guys are thinking. They're probably thinking we could have won. Maybe they're right. I doubt it. 'It's a shame,' I say in French. 'I'm sorry'. Last year I kicked thirty-two in a row before missing a couple in the final, but it's always the ones you miss that they seem to remember. 'No problem, not your fault. We have many problems in the lineout,' says the one with the paunch, rolling his eyes. 'Anyway, we have the bonus point. But next week, ah, good game?' The question comes with a cheery thumbs up.

'I'll do my best,' and with what I hope is a polite smile slip off towards the door. I'm intercepted again before I reach it, this time by a young woman. 'Excuse me, are you Mark Stevens?' This time the English has only the slightest hint of an accent, and it's not French.

She has brown eyes in an oval face and straight mid-length hair that looks black in the murky light of the bar but might just be brown, and she's wearing a black silk shirt undone just far enough for me to get a glimpse of lace covering a gentle swell of flesh. The sports bar isn't a dive, and there are plenty of good-looking girls, but it has a sticky floor, you can buy shots of flavoured vodka by the metre and the toilets tend to be blocked. This one looks like she's slumming. If I'm the reason, that has to be good news.

'I am. And you are?' I lean in closer, partly to hear better, but only partly.

'My name is Rachel da Silva. It's a great pleasure to meet you.' The handshake is firmer than I expect. 'I'm here in France to do a story on rugby for a Brazilian magazine and, if it's all right, I would like to do an interview with you.'

Perfect. Normally journalists are middle-aged men who I always suspect are hoping to trip me up. 'Of course, no problem. It's a bit late, but we can do it now if you like.'

'No, it's going to be a really in-depth piece and I need to watch you train and play as well as talk to you. Will it be all right if we organise to meet tomorrow and I can tail you this week?'

Better and better. I'll have to let our media manager know. He can be a bit of a drama queen about access to players but he loves this sort of interest from foreign press so I don't bother mentioning it to her. She produces a card with her name on it and 'O Globo' in white letters on a blue background and writes a French mobile number on the back. 'When would be a good time for you tomorrow?'

I eat lunch with the boys and then sleep after the Sunday-morning pool session and then I was going to hook up with Davo for some movies. That can probably wait. 'I'll give you a call at about three and we can go from there, OK?'

'Great. See you tomorrow.' She gives me a quick smile — no more than professional courtesy — and then she's gone. I place the card with the numbers in black ink carefully in my wallet and head out into the night.

Chapter 2

I wake up early on Sunday mornings, even if I've had a really big one — around eight, which is early enough for a rugby player on a day off. When we play night games it takes ages for the adrenalin to run out of my system, so sometimes I have only three or four hours' sleep. This morning, having had six hours, I don't feel too bad: of course my ankle feels like there's broken glass in the joint and is hot to the touch, my right shoulder aches and my left hip and both thighs are sore but otherwise I'm all right. You get used to it after a while — feeling battered becomes normal — and where I play, at first five (fly half if you're a Brit) I miss the worst of it. I'm more of a general than a footsoldier, running command and control, away from the grunt work in the trenches. Still, you have to be prepared to put your body on the line: anyone who looks soft in contact gets targeted, and then things can get untidy. I like to aim my biggest, nastiest runners at my opposite number. It gives him something else to worry about.

I go to the fridge to get an icepack for the ankle, strap it on with a bandage, then mix myself a milkshake with two bananas, two pots of low-fat yoghurt, half a pint of skim milk and a supposedly chocolate-tasting powder that the club gives us to help recover more quickly. Then I go back to bed with the computer, look at my emails, do a little social networking and check out what's happening in New Zealand. Until five months ago, Sunday mornings were when I used to catch up with Dad. He never got used to web-cams — I bought him a computer and installed everything he needed before I left to come over, but he always preferred the phone. After Mum died he found it hard to adapt. She'd always done all the cooking and cleaning, so he seemed to live off toast and baked beans and fish and chips, and newspapers and unwashed clothes would pile up until the cleaning lady that I paid for came round once a week. Mum would have been furious to see the state of the place. It was her work of art, the thing she lived for, along with us kids. We thought he'd get used to it eventually, that a man like him who could fix anything, who liked to catch his own food and who was so proud of his independence would want to take control of his own life again. He used to say he was too old to start over again and too young to go into a home. Then I was living on the other side of the world and there wasn't much I could do except send money and talk to him on Sundays. I didn't feel that guilty about taking the money in France — it had become clear that I wasn't going to play for the ABs again, and the package was worth a lot more than what I was on with Wellington even after nasty French taxes. The club are good at working dodges. Dad encouraged me, I didn't want to end up skint at sixty and God knows what I'll find to do when the clock runs out on the rugby. Guys doing real jobs tell me that it's hard to get ahead. Coaching looks like easy money but there aren't that many gigs around. One of the guys I used to play with is having panic attacks: big mortgage, no job, twins on the way and he daren't talk to his wife about the money situation.

Sometimes we talked for more than an hour. Now I get occasional updates from my sister, Alison, who moved back home straight after Dad's funeral with her dodgy boyfriend and her two little girls, Steph and Sasha. Dad was always annoyed that they both had the same initial, that it would be difficult to tell them apart on message boards at school. Ali said that was ridiculous. She was right, but she could have made an effort. How hard is it to find a name that starts with a different letter of the alphabet? Of course, Dad liked that they were Stevenses, he just hated that their fathers hadn't stuck around for long enough to leave their names.

No news from Ali. I'll give her a call during the week.

At 9.40 I drive the few kilometres to the pool complex where we have our recovery sessions. It only takes five minutes at this time on a Sunday, which is a small victory. I won't start on traffic in Paris. It's a ten o'clock meet, but already half a dozen of the boys are gathered in the large room on the upper floor that we use as a base for these sessions, along with three physios, Alain, the forwards coach, and Eric. I circle around the group shaking hands with everyone as the French always do; unlike the locals I don't do kisses with boys, especially not first thing on a Sunday. Xavier, our centre, is reading the paper. Yesterday's game rates half a page. My French is now good enough to struggle through the whole thing but I try to avoid reading my own press — when it's bad it's depressing, and when it's good you wonder whether journalists really know what they're on about. The French sports pages have a kind of shorthand for saying who played well — your name is underlined on the team sheet — and I am cheap enough to look. My name is underlined, along with three others. Ordinarily it's not worth much — Xavier's name is underlined as well, and he missed two tackles and threw a pass that was intercepted and led to a penalty that cost us three points at the death, which makes it worth even less.

Over the next twenty minutes guys dribble in, and even the doctor arrives, puffing, just after the supposed ten o'clock deadline. The morning drags on: after waiting to see the doc for half an hour, I get five minutes with him while he clucks and prods and twists the ankle. 'Yes, that hurts.' The coach, Christophe, is there by this point and stands in a corner of the small room that is commandeered as a makeshift surgery. I can tell that the doc wants me to take some time off, but Christophe insists that I'm fine. They come to the expected compromise: Monday and Tuesday off, Wednesday a light run, Thursday's off anyway then back to normal on Friday, game on Saturday. I'm getting to the point where I'm a bit worried about the ankle myself — they've already put some sort of gel in it — so I ask the question: am I better off not playing?

The reply is a shrug of the shoulders, a half smile and 'Should a prostitute stop work?' Cheers, doc. A pat on the back from Christophe. *Tout va bien.*

Another half hour before I get on the table for a rub. By the end of it I'm feeling sleepy. Lunch with the boys is starting to look like a chore. An afternoon with Rachel da Silva has been at the back of my mind since I woke up and it would be good to be on form.

Josh, our Kiwi prop, slaps me hard across my bare back. 'Come on, mate, get your gears on. We're off to lunch. Your shout.'

'Can't do it, my friend. Big date this afternoon.'

'Good one. Who'd want to get that close to you? Anyway, you know the rules — bros before hos.' Josh is married with three kids under six. Any excuse to get out of the house — preferably minus the family — is gold as far as he's concerned.

'Nah. You're probably going Scottish anyway.' The Scottish restaurant — world-famous for its burgers — is one of my pet hates. The boys love it. Not that I can throw stones about diet, and I'm not much of a cook, but this is France and I can afford to go somewhere decent. I'm pretty sure the others can too, but unless they've told you, you never know quite how much other guys are on. Although last year someone in accounts got cubbyholes mixed up and Coquine opened his rival's payslip. By mistake, allegedly. Turned out he was on four grand more a month than the skipper even though he's lower in the pecking order and despite — or, more probably, because of — Coquine's being loyal to the club since he was a kid. I know about this because the payslip had a brief spell decorating the changing room. There was a bit of tension.

I think Josh is pulling around ten thousand euros a month, which sounds all right until you take out Paris rent, a mortgage on a place at home, a wife who likes to shop and three kids to feed and clothe.

'Twoallbeefpattiesspecialsaucelettucecheesepicklesonions-onasesameseedbun. Come on, you know you love it.'

'That meat, it's all lips and arseholes. Why do you do it to yourself? And they're destroying the rainforests.'

'Good times, great taste. Your loss. If you're going to brush us off for time with a lady then I want a written report on my desk by tomorrow morning. I don't want you getting involved in anything until Uncle Josh has told you how it works. I've got your back. Don't forget it.'

Josh does have my back. A couple of months ago we played against a team whose number eight kept looking for me with his elbow. I managed to get under it when he did, but you could tell he was going to keep at it until he found me. He had to go off just before half-time after Josh dropped a knee into his ribs while he was lying on the floor at the bottom of a ruck near our line. I don't think anyone else saw what happened. Josh didn't mention it.

* * *

I almost ring Rachel da Silva and ask her what she's doing for lunch but decide that would be overplaying my hand, so I pick up some sushi and eat it in front of the internet. With the help of my finely tuned relaxation technique, I manage a forty-minute nap then wake up and take a shower.

I make the call bang on three o'clock. This kind of longer-profile piece is always good press, and normally I would invite the journalist round to my place, but for some reason it doesn't feel right so we agree to meet at her hotel which isn't far away.

The hotel is one of those big, business-like affairs, all white marble and minimalist chairs. There's a gaggle of Asian tourists in the lobby either checking in or checking out and Rachel is striding towards me. She's wearing knee-high black leather boots, a grey skirt and black blouse with her hair — it is black — pulled back in a ponytail. The firm handshake and a quick, tight smile — nervous? — flicks across her face. In reply I cut off my big cheesy grin so it ends up looking like a grimace, but she doesn't notice as she's half-turned and pointing towards an area over by the bar, a structure in dark wood trying to look like an English pub in the middle of all the marble. 'Is it OK if we do the interview over here?'

We both order coffee, she sets a little tape recorder on the table and explains that she wants to follow me through the week building up to the game itself on Saturday night. 'Rugby isn't a big game in Brazil but now that it is an Olympic sport we want to know more about it. You played for New Zealand — they say that your team are the Brazil of rugby . . .'

The interview rolls on for about an hour covering pretty standard ground, although there is one uncomfortable moment when she asks me how my wife feels about the risk of injury and I have to explain that I'm single. The grey eyes widen. She looks away and flicks her hair. The eyes come back to meet mine, softer now: 'I'm sorry, I didn't mean to get personal.'

'It's fine. No big deal.' Suddenly, I don't know what to do with my hands. They come up to my face, which is ridiculous, so I slide them under the table. Safely hidden, they clench into fists.

'Of course. I'm just surprised. You look like that man Cooper . . .'

'Quade?'

'Bradley. And you're living here in Paris . . .'

I might be blushing. My fists unclench. 'I broke up with my girlfriend last year.' The information lingers over the table. 'This isn't going in, is it?'

'No.' The flicker of a smile kicks her lips up as she looks down at her notes. 'I want to talk to you about money.' It's my turn for the eyes to widen. 'I saw a poster of you and some other players on the way here. You will be playing at Stade de France soon, probably full, the television audiences are big, and yet I understand the average wage is only fifteen thousand euros a month. I'm sure a guy like you is making a lot more.' (Twenty-one thousand euros a month, plus car and bonuses, so over the course of my five years here more than my old man made in forty years of slog but the only people who know that are my agent and the club and I'm not sharing it with Brazil.) 'I guess thirty, forty thousand a month — but it still isn't very much. Footballers here in Paris make ten times that amount. How does that work?'

'Rugby only went professional quite recently.' Thirty or forty thousand — *ten* times as much?

'Yes, but the French competition is supposed to be the richest in the world, attracting the best players. And the football here . . .' She rolls her eyes.

'That's just the way it is.' Unloved, maybe, but I had never felt underpaid.

'And there are no problems of corruption?'

'Like what — throwing games?'

'It happens in football. Why shouldn't it happen in rugby?'

'It's just not in the culture. I can't think of anyone I know who would do that. And there are too many people in a team — you could never keep it quiet.'

'And referees?'

'You'd have to ask one of them. I can't see it.' Some of the refereeing over here is pretty ordinary, but I'd always give them the benefit of the doubt. I can remember Dad reffing when I was still at primary school. He liked to be able to go to the clubrooms for a beer feeling that he'd done something. He would have preferred to still be playing, even in his forties, but he couldn't risk it with his job, and his knee was bad enough already. He would play touch with us kids sometimes, showing us the little tricks of the trade: how to slingshot someone into a gap, or how to defend against an overlap. Sometimes when he was running his knee would just give out and he'd fall over with no one even anywhere near him which I found a bit embarrassing. Sometimes I would try to get him to stop. He never did.

We move on to kicking — 'As you know, Brazilians love to kick the ball' — and my role as a goal-kicker, then finish up agreeing to meet the next morning at the ground just before training so I can introduce her to the media manager.

I walk away with a bit of a bounce. It should be an interesting week with Rachel da Silva. She must be about my age, bright, no wedding ring, foxy as fuck. And the match-fixing idea reeks of a dirty mind.

Chapter 3

I am ten minutes early for the meeting on Monday morning, but so is Rachel. We go and get a coffee at the café across the road from the stadium. I've already explained that I won't be doing much training for the first couple of days — it doesn't seem to faze her. The boys will pile in as soon as they get a sniff so I want to make sure my territory is well staked out before they do.

'So, seeing as I've spent all this time talking about myself, how did you get into journalism?'

'The usual way. I studied hard, I worked for free for a long time after university then I slept with someone important, and now I have a good job in Europe. I speak four languages as well, which helps.'

This last bit about languages doesn't really register. While I like to think of myself as being worldly, the other information is a slap in the chops. Noting that her words have had the effect she — presumably — was after, Rachel follows up. 'English, Portuguese, Spanish and French. Oh, you mean the other thing, right? He was the son of the owner of the newspaper. He was supposed to be learning how to run the family business but he spent most of his time running after girls.' A shrug of the shoulders, followed by a pout. 'We went out for a while. Of course, it was never going anywhere. He got what he wanted and so did I.'

She looks me straight in the eye. There is a silence that could be qualified as awkward. 'That's very impressive.' More silence. 'Perhaps I should have played harder to get for the interview.'

Finally, a laugh. I tried a few gags on her yesterday and didn't get more than that slight curve in the cupid's bow of her mouth.

'What do I need from you now? Besides, I am working. And,' looking at her watch, 'it is time for us to go to work.'

We go up to the office complex and I introduce her to Benoit, our media manager. In fact, she has already arranged things with him and he's all smiles. A photographer will be joining her for Friday and Saturday. He looks a bit uncertain when she says she wants to follow me around everywhere — changing-room access is out, and she will have to ask Christophe if she can sit in on the video session, but otherwise she has the run of the place.

It's nearly nine as we get to the video room where the whole squad is gathered. Christophe is writing up notes on a whiteboard next to the video screen and barely looks up when I tell him a Brazilian journo is going to sit in. Then he catches a glimpse of long hair, does a double take, snaps upright and introduces himself. By this point there is some catcalling from the back of the room. I lead Rachel down the back and find her a chair and one for myself. We sit down to applause. Rich introduces himself to Rachel. 'You're a journalist? You'll be wanting to interview me then, I guess.' He produces a business card that I've never seen. 'I'm free this evening.'

She takes the card. 'That's very kind. I'm afraid I don't know very much about rugby.' A charming smile. 'That must be why I've never heard of you.' The hooting spreads across the room as the exchange is translated for the Frenchies. Someone brandishes a red folder in Rich's direction.

'Just trying to help.' For all the slick projection of plumage and weapons-grade yap, Rich is someone who got himself into such a fever about his first game in the hallowed green and gold that less than two hours before kick-off he told the staff they needed to get the other guy to play. He knew he could walk out onto the park and have a go, he just got so wound up about it that he was pretty sure he would get the first few minutes wrong, and that wasn't going to be good enough. His whole life had been working toward this moment and now he felt he would let everyone down, so he told the coach he should put him on the bench. So they did. And, as you'd expect, he never got off it, never got asked back again. When he told me the story, he said he dropped his balls, but that wasn't really the case. Sure, you can overhear yourself think sometimes, and it doesn't usually end well, but he'd been around long enough to know how that worked. He just put the team's interest in front of his own because he thought that was the right thing to do — even though he knew what it would mean.

Obviously he still makes an arse of himself from time to time.

Christophe calls us to order. He runs through the upcoming week — the only thing that deviates from the already established timetable is a suggestion that the forwards might want to look at the tape of last week's lineouts as a group before their own session. Coquine tells him they've already got it organised and will be looking at it tomorrow afternoon.

Then we do forty minutes of video. They're selected highlights — and more particularly lowlights — of Saturday's game. If we watched the whole thing we'd be there all week, so he picks out problem areas and one or two good things that we need to develop. I don't agree with all of what Christophe says — at times he's very astute, at others you wonder what planet he's living on. Still, he's the boss, so it's worth paying attention. I have to defend myself at one point over one of what I consider to be Xavier's missed tackles. Christophe reckons it's my fault, but Xavier followed the ball carrier out of his zone, allowing him to slip a pass to a player cutting back on the angle. It's a schoolboy error, but because I was coming across in cover and managed to get a despairing hand on the cutter, I superficially look like the guilty party. Christophe is saying I should have worked harder to close the gap and it was up to me to make the tackle. Fuck that. I am all ready to get quite worked up about it — I do miss tackles, but he's not pinning this one on me — when Xavier backs me up immediately, which is pleasing. He has played a couple of games for France and is already being talked about as the next big thing at twenty-three. This won't do him any harm, but he might have found it convenient to shut up. You'd like to think you can trust the guy standing next to you, but it isn't always the case.

At the end of the video session the group splits: Saturday's fifteen and reserves who played more than half an hour have a light morning playing touch and soccer to sweat out the bumps from the game; Eric takes the leftovers and flogs them with drills and fitness. I go to the gym and spend twenty minutes on the winch, a kind of bicycle for the arms, followed by half an hour of light upper-body weights. Titi, our flanker who used to play for France, has a corked thigh and is with me in the gym on the bike. So is Rachel, watching. I work a little bit harder than I might have if she hadn't been there.

It wasn't so long ago that I pushed myself to the limit at every physical training. It was a good habit. I caught myself cutting the corner running round the field at a warm-up the other day and realised that somehow I've let it slip over the last few months. At my age, all I really need is maintenance — I'm not going to get any faster or any stronger — but it's a worry when I'm not looking for an edge. Even if my game isn't all that physical, if I'm just doing the same thing as everyone else then I'm on the slide. I used to train twice on Christmas day, just on principle. Last Christmas I started on the booze before noon and I was pissed before lunchtime. I don't remember what time I stopped.

Rachel is playing with her mobile phone by the time Eric arrives to check up on Titi and me. He's brought pads and boxing gloves and we have a short, sharp ten-minute session alternating crunches and bagwork. Even though it's impossible, I enjoy trying to hurt his hands through the pads. Titi, with his thickly muscled pipes and barrel chest, puts it in as well.

Afterwards, Rachel takes me to lunch. 'Expenses.' Difficult to refuse. A women's magazine is still sitting on the table when we are seated, and she picks it up and flicks directly to the horoscopes. Her tongue touches her white teeth as she looks up and smiles. 'Do you believe in this?'

'Not really.'

'They can be interesting.'

'Go on then.'

'So what's your birthday?'

'November twenty-six.'

'Sagittarius, then. "Venus is working her magic but don't get carried away with something that looks good. Attachment may be fleeting. You're a nice person, not everyone is."'

Hers is a peach: 'Capricorn: Not exactly love at first sight but one of those prolonged flirts that you so enjoy. It should be fun. Try not to hurt him.' I can't help laughing.

Once we've ordered — steak and red wine for her, respect — she goes off to powder her nose. I flick through the magazine to re-read what the stars are suggesting. In fact, Sagittarius says, 'Juggle diplomacy with your desires. The past is in the past.

Communicate openly with those around you.'

Hers says, 'The wind is getting up so drop your sails. At the same time, don't give up. If you're feeling off-balance, that's OK.'

* * *

Ali texts me that night, asking for a call-back.

'Hi.' She sounds mopey. I'm not that interested — she sounds mopey most of the time.

'How you doing? How're the little rascals?'

'Hellish.' That's funny, Mum used to say 'hellish'. 'Look, I can't talk for long, Sparky. I just wanted to say that I was clearing out the last lot of Dad's stuff yesterday and I found some old cassette tapes that look like they have something to do with Granddad. Are you interested?'

'What are they?'

'I don't know. My old tape deck is bust and I'm sure as shit not about to buy a new one just to listen to these. They've got "Oral History Archive: Benjamin Stevens, April 2, 1980", handwritten on the side. Three C60s. If you're not interested I'm going to bin them — there's so much crap piled up here.'

'Of course I'm interested. I can't believe you're not.'

'Well, you can tell me about it once you've had a listen. I don't have much time for myself these days, in case you hadn't noticed. I'll send you a package as soon as my pay cheque clears.'

'Have you got through that last three grand I sent you already?'

'I had to get the car fixed. It costs money to run a family. I'd send Sasha out to work but apparently there are laws against it.'

'What is that useless prick Darrin doing? He's living at home, he should be putting something in, at least be paying rent.'

'Darrin got laid off from the works last month, I told you that.'

'Jesus. All right, I'll send you some more, but it has to last for a couple of months this time. Tell your boyfriend to get off the couch and get a bloody job. And send me those tapes fastpost — the last thing you sent took a month to get here.'

'Thanks, bro.' I can hear her smiling now that she's getting her cash. 'I'll send them tomorrow. Gotta go. See ya.'

'Tell Sasha she can call any time.' She's already gone.

Chapter 4

The old man's funeral was its own special kind of weird, as you can imagine. Ali had done a lot of the organising by the time I got home so I left most of it to her but I couldn't deal with the cheap coffin she'd opted for.

I upgraded him to a high-end casket and paid for it myself. There wasn't much in the will. Ali wanted a new second-hand car and she's got feet on the ground besides her own so I wasn't going to get sticky.

After a little calming down, I was able to see the kicker: I was — am — next. But there was a flipside. The world belonged to me now.

I didn't have to answer to anyone and I would do whatever I wanted without the fear of judgment behind me. God was already long gone; Mum had always been able to make me feel guilty about anything that wasn't 'right'; now even the old man wasn't around to make his chippy remarks about me being overpaid or overrated or overseas. I could do whatever the fuck I felt like and who could say I was wrong? True, in thirty or forty or — hopefully — a hundred years I would have to start coming to terms with wherever my decisions led, but in the meantime I was my own man. Free. But when I got home, Ali handed me a sealed envelope. The scrawl looked even more spidery than I remembered.

Sparky,

Sorry not to see you before I go. I hope you win that final but if you didn't it really isn't a big deal. Otherwise I hope that everything is good with you over there and that you will find the right bird, settle down and have a couple of kids of your own. They are a bit of a pain for a while but then they turn out alright. Your Mum and I have always been so proud of you, mate. We couldn't have wished for a better son. Look after your sister and the girls. Going to that school you did would give them a good shot. Sorry about the writing it, was never very good!

Love,
Dad

* * *

I got a sports scholarship to the local private school when I'd just turned sixteen. Didn't even need to apply — they just came and got me, stuck me in the first fifteen. According to the parents it was a no-brainer, so I pitched up on the first day of school and found myself already in some sort of training camp, months before the actual rugby season got under way. I didn't realise it then but it became clear that I was part of some sort of marketing deal. The kind of people who could pay for their kids' education liked to think they were going to a school that could hold its own on the rugby field — which they barely could without ringers like me.

The rugby was ordinary. A few decent players but it seemed to me that most of them made a lot of noise so the girls would know they were out there doing their bit. A few days after I arrived the old man came and picked me up after work. One of the boarders, a first-year kid, told me the next day that our family car used to belong to his family. It was the kind of coincidence that would have tickled me at his age too, but when I thought about it I didn't like it. Still, I could see what the olds were on about pretty quickly. In between the sport I had to do some academic work and the old dear running my history class — we were studying the French Revolution — got me into a situation where I looked silly then got me out of it. 'How do you explain the way in which the Parisians took up the Terror?' I didn't put my hand up but she asked me anyway so I said that I thought it was like the way crowds got caught up at a game. Snickering. 'Why do you say that?' So I stumbled through a thought process and said that we like to think we're objective but as soon as you bring in any kind of group mentality into a face-off, we like to find a reason to come down on one side or the other. Once that way of looking at it hardens, if most people pick the same side they get a rush and if there are no limits things can really kick off. More laughter from the expensive seats. Ms Woods' response cut it off. 'That's a pretty sophisticated piece of thinking. He's told us what he thinks and why. And he may well be right.'

I started to see the usefulness of putting effort into schoolwork, the payback in understanding things that until then had appeared beyond my reach. I had played up to the expectation that I would be a boofhead because I could play sport. At the local we used to go to school more or less to eat lunch and talk shit before having a run around. My mates at the new school were all going to university — even the farmers — so I figured I'd do the same.

I had already played in the rep team at age grade level with a couple of the guys from school, and I got quite tight with a bloke called Davo. We would go round to his place — tennis court, swimming pool, old pictures and a new kitchen — and hang out when we had some time. Mr was a classic: tall and athletic still, he did something in real estate — industrial or commercial, not residential; somehow it would have been too low-end for him. Mrs was a good sort too, well-groomed and smiley, always pleased to see you. Not at all brittle or fussy in the way Mum could be in company. Davo's sister, Mary — blonde bob, green eyes and a walk like a man, couldn't-give-a-shit attitude — was the cherry on top, but she was only there when she was back from studying for her law degree.

The first time I went round I made up a four to play tennis with Davo and Mr and Mary. It was all very relaxed, bare feet and shorts on the immaculate grass court. Mr took one look at my serve and started sledging: 'Typical rugby player — all piss and wind.'

Afterwards we had beers by the pool before dinner and I was too nervous to talk to Mary. Davo fished something out of his nose and went to stick it on her dress. She yelped and threw her drink at him. Mr ignored the whole scene and asked me what I was reading and Mrs saved me by arriving with the food, a whole salmon. We'd always gone out for paua or snapper or crays with the old man and Uncle Phil, but I'd never seen a whole salmon for dinner. After getting up to try to help I sat down and pulled myself too far into the table, my knees hit the stays and the bottle of wine fell over. Everyone — apart from me, who went fire-engine red — laughed, even Mrs, who'd copped some of it on her dress.

A couple of weeks later Davo came round to mine. We had sausages. He was very polite. Mum loved him. Neither of us said anything. We ended up hanging out at his place.

* * *

I've saved up a bit of money. Two rental properties at home that still have fourteen and seventeen years' worth of mortgage to pay respectively, worth about ninety thousand taken together. Seventy thousand in the Caymans. A hundred invested here in France. About twenty grand on long-term deposit at home. Theoretically I own half of the family home, but I can't sell it out from under Ali and she'll never have the money to pay me out, so that's a write-off. She'll probably keep bleeding me. Less than three hundred thousand euros, about five hundred Kiwi, give or take. A bit less, even. My old school fees run at about twenty Kiwi p.a., five years of that for the two girls is two hundred K or nearly half what I've made. Baby Jesus, that'll sting. I'd planned to buy a place for myself outright but the Kiwi dollar is flying against the euro and the bloody prices keep going up so as it stands I wouldn't get much of a house if I ring-fence those school fees. If I can put aside a hundred euro a year for the next three years that might be all right. I need enough to reinvent myself, see what turns up. And a little 'fuck you' money would be nice. No one wants to go back to the bottom of the pile.

* * *

It fell to me to make the speech at the funeral. I kicked it around on the flight, but what do you say? That he was a kind man, he was a wise man? Shit, I didn't even know if that was true. I wanted to honour him, but if people know it isn't true the whole thing turns into a joke. We'd had our moments, father and son, good and bad. I thought about that time at Christmas when I was playing cricket with my cousins on the flat down the hill behind Uncle Phil's farmhouse. I must have been about twelve. Richie and Pete were a bit older than me but not much and not very sporty so I had been skittling them out with my bowling. They got a bit arsey about it and one of their mates who was sitting watching started taking the piss. He was an idiot but I was only twelve and he must have been fourteen and it really started to hurt: 'try-hard', 'greaser', that kind of thing. Maybe there was nothing in it but I confess to taking a certain satisfaction talking to Richie at the funeral — I hadn't seen him for ages — and discovering that his mate had been fired from the cops a couple of years ago for being useless. He hadn't had any news since then.

Anyway, the old man must have been keeping an eye on what was going on between bottles — the ancestors had a couple of crates going, it was a sunny afternoon — and walked down the path, put himself into bat and told the others to field or push off. I was never all that fussed about batting, I preferred to bowl. I had all the stress of goal-kicking already in winter: I didn't want to be ruined just for one small mistake when the weather was good. The old bastard took half an hour away from his beer and made my summer.

'That's a bloody great ball — where did you learn to do that? Listen, Sparky, you're good. Jesus, Hadlee himself would be proud of that one. No, that's too short, pitch it up more and make me play. Well bowled. Now if you hold the ball like this, across the seam — this is only a two-piece, so you should get plenty of swing if you keep one side shiny but it will cut back as well. There you go!' The two of us beaming at each other like idiots across a makeshift pitch that we had turned into the Basin Reserve for the afternoon. Just thinking about it makes me want to cry but that isn't going to happen.

I got in at six on the Wednesday morning. Ali picked me up. The funeral was Thursday afternoon. 'If you don't feel up to it, Uncle Phil will do the speech.' No chance, though I still didn't know what I was going to say. Ali showed no sign of emotion until she came and sat with me after I had shut myself off in what used to be my bedroom but was now some sort of cemetery for neglected paperwork. I had been trying to work on my laptop but the thing felt bloodless so I started to write down ideas on blank sheets, most of which had ended in the bin.

'How's it going?'

'Average. I haven't got a clue. I spent the best part of a day and a half thinking about this on the plane and I don't have dick to say.'

'You could always say he was a dick.' I know — lame, right? But suddenly we were both laughing then she was crying and I would have liked to join in. 'My first ever memory is when he came and got me and we went to the SPCA to pick out a dog and he let me pick Rosie.' Rosie was the family dog who died when I was six or seven, I don't remember. 'She came and put her paws up on the wire and . . .' All right, enough of that. It felt awkward, hugging Ali on the bed, conscious of her tits crushing themselves into my shoulder. My sister. The same flesh. 'No one else is ever going to do that for me.'

How do you translate a dog and a cricket session into a eulogy? I don't know. I ended up with some short-winded blah about how he was an example to me, a friend to others and a source of inspiration to many. The first two are true, I don't think the last one is but you have to say something high-minded. I kept feeling half-terrified, half-delighted by the idea that I was going to burst out bawling as I was speaking but it didn't happen and everyone saluted my courage afterwards so I guess I played it the way I was supposed to.

Chapter 5

I hadn't known how sick he was. I'm pretty sure he hadn't known how sick he was either, at least not to begin with. Pancreatic cancer can be misdiagnosed as stomach ache, old age, pretty much anything to do with your gut. 'I'm a bit crook, but the nurse is here, she'll see me right,' was the line. I gave him a prod, without wanting to know too much: 'Just getting on, mate. Nothing anyone can do about that. Plumbing is a little tricky.' I wasn't that keen on finding out much more about his plumbing. Ali hadn't twigged until the last couple of weeks, and he made her promise not to tell me, so I can't blame her for that. When I thought about it afterwards I could remember her getting weepy once but I've heard her cry wolf before, so if I thought about it at all I thought she was milking it.

On the other side of the world we had made the quarters, then the semis, then the final. I was still coming round from Sarah leaving and had thrown myself into the games and preparing for them. When I think back on the phone calls — I didn't overdo it, because you don't — but he must have been able to tell I was chuffed, was looking forward to whatever happened next. I could just hear him: 'It won't make any difference to me. You let him enjoy himself. He's had a rough time lately.' It would have made a difference to me, though. And I'd like to think it would have made a difference to him as well. I should hope it would have made a difference to him. And he should have told me.

I should have picked it up, though. More missed signals. Difficult to say how much I fucked this one up. I got the call at about two in the morning the night of the final. We were at the town hall, pissing it up even though we had lost. I couldn't hear what Ali was saying, or thought I couldn't, with all the noise, so I left the vast room, went through one set of doors then another before I could be sure that I had heard what she was saying. I stood on the flagstones saying, 'What?', pushing the automatic plate-glass door closed, only it didn't want to close at my speed, it would close in its own good time. There had already been a lot of French hugging so I just left, walked back through the city, crossing singles and couples and hating them for the ease with which they kept on with their lives, enjoying the warmth of a June Saturday night. A couple of drunks were fighting on the quay by the Seine, pushing each other and flailing away between insults. I thought about stepping in just to let off some steam.

When I got home — really home — the nurses had left a little notebook, outlining the state of the patient and the treatment administered. I flicked through it, just three weeks from start to finish. The dose of morphine got bigger with every day, then leapt tenfold at the last entry. Even I couldn't miss that. How could they do that? And why the fuck would they leave the evidence? So I sat and thought about it for a while. I guess they figured that he was surrounded by his loved ones — daughter and granddaughters — and the rest of the old crowd who trooped in to see him, were there at the funeral, were the ones who told me I did all right. So there wasn't any point in drawing it out. Maybe he asked them for it. Maybe they left the notebook there for me to see. But if they did, what was I supposed to see? That they had done the right thing by him? Or that I was a graceless, selfish little shit who should have been there and not cocking about on a footy field on the other side of the world when my old man was breathing his last?

Physical pain, in my chest. I screw my face up to encourage tears, hold it like that for what feels like minutes. Hope for a release, the flow of saltwater down my cheeks into my mouth. No, nothing except the pain, a dull, dumb ache in the middle of my chest.

So I kept thinking about it for a while. My first thought was to kick up a stink. He died the day after the final. If they'd waited another couple of days I could have been there before the end. Might have been there before the end. Perhaps I should just go and see them, find out what happened. And I thought about how that might play out. Embarrassment, excuses, tears. A nasty lawsuit. Or a cool, even stare from a business-like woman who knows, who just knows. Who might ask whether I have any idea about the kind of pain he was dealing with. About each second of living with that.

I left it alone.

* * *

At training the next day the boys insist that my hot date come out with us. Tuesday-night drinking has become something of a tradition. Rich has worked up a spin on his public humiliation: 'I know she wants to bite — she's just playing hard to get. I'm going to play her for a bit and then reel that baby in.' I think he's joking.

Josh has his own take. 'I'm just pleased to see that it's a lady. I swear I caught you cock-watching in the shower the other day.'

We have a G7 meeting — seven key players — with Christophe after lunch and then I'm off for the day. I grab a couple of DVDs of Saturday's opposition and watch them at home before a snooze and a scrub-up.

A text arrives. Rachel's in for drinks.

* * *

'You must be chuffed about this.'

'About what?' I place four beers on the table.

'Mate, tell it to someone else. How good's Miss Brazil? Don't try to play it cool with me. All those romances you've been watching, you'd have tennis elbow by now. How long's it been?'

Sitting down I look over Rich's shoulder, towards the door. Again. I suppose I said nine-ish. It's only twenty past.

'Stop looking so bloody desperate. They can smell it.'

'I'm just trying to be polite. And she's just doing her job.'

'Hey, Rich, give the dude a break. Not everybody thinks with their dick.'

'Got me where I am today.'

'Exactly.' The clink of glasses.

Josh's phone, sitting on the table amidst smears of beer, quacks. He looks at it — 'Jesus, bloody journo' — and refuses the call.

Rich is dismayed. 'Fuck me, it's all go. First Sparklehorse, now you. I'm a media void. I need some profile work.'

'Nah, it's Diesel and I don't want to talk.'

Diesel is an Aussie who used to play here about a million years ago — before my time, anyway — then went freelance after he hung up his boots.

'What's he into you for?'

'Somehow he got hold of that deal we did at the World Cup. Alfie must have spilled his guts.'

'And?'

'He wants me to tell him all about it.'

'If he already knows what happened, why does he need you?'

'He wants it all on the record, reckons they won't run his story otherwise. I guess Alfie wouldn't be that dumb. Don't know why he thinks I am.'

Moose: 'What was the deal?'

'You might as well tell him. Everyone else knows.'

Josh fiddles with his phone, thinks about it.

'It'll go straight to the vault, buddy. Scout's honour.'

'Couple of years ago, World Cup time, I got the call up, for the Manu. The hitch was that it meant I'd miss the start of the season here. The club were going to be down a prop — Mika was going with the Frogs — so they told me they wouldn't pay me if I went but they'd bung me if I stayed.'

'So you stayed.'

'Yep.'

'How much did they bung you?'

'Not as much as fucking Tino. Prick opened a clothes shop in Milan on it.'

'Duh. He's white.'

'Rich!'

'That's cold, bro.' Josh is trying to laugh it off, but what hurts is that it's true — the Italians have decent coin for their players, so the Fibber had to make it worth their while to stay. The Samoans weren't getting much more than bus fare, so they were over a barrel if the club wanted to screw them.

Moose, ploughing on: 'So how much?'

Josh has another think. As a rule, money is not something we talk about, but put on the spot he can't dodge it. 'Twenty.'

'Fuck that. Twenty grand? You should have told them to shove it. How old are you?'

'Thirty-four.' Josh gets up and goes to get beers.

'Moose, just drop it.'

'There's no way I'd miss out on the World Cup for twenty grand. He won't make the next one. That dog won't hunt.'

'You don't have kids. What's he going to do when he finishes? And they weren't going to pay him for his time away so he would have been down thirty or forty. So really you're looking at more like sixty-odd, up or down. Which is a bit of a luxury for a couple of games of code.'

'Mate, it does him good to talk. Sure, he's filthy about it but feed him a bit of shit, have a laugh, he gets it out of his system. Confession, absolution.'

Josh returns with a tray of refreshments, parcels them out.

'Thing is, Diesel reckons it goes all the way up. Says he took it into the paper and they got quite excited.'

'How's that?'

'Apparently it's quite a big deal. Club could be relegated if they got busted.'

'What?'

'I don't know how it works, but he's pretty fired up. Been on at me for weeks now. Fucking IRB this—.'

'The IRB?'

'World Rugby my friends. There's been a reboot.' Rich is an early adopter.

'World Rugby, whatever. Diesel reckons he got in to the paper with this story, they're all over it but they shove him in a room in isolation — he's not allowed to talk to anyone, not even allowed to put it into the computer in case someone finds out. He talks to Vili who's too dumb to know any better, he talks to Christine, who put the payments through — she's sharp, not having a bar of it — but he's got enough from Vili and I guess Alfie to call the Fibber. So he puts the call through — he's got the editor with him listening in — and gets his head ripped off: "This is all bullshit, I'll see you in court." He puts the phone down and straight away the editor gets a call from the Fibber. Diesel can't hear the whole thing but the guts of it is that if the paper runs the story he'll pull his advertising and sue the paper.'

'I've shot better men than that for a dollar fifty a day.' Heads turn, slowly, to look at Moose. 'It's just an expression.'

'So the editor is in reverse, right? But Diesel says they should try the IRB' — Rich rolls his eyes, but lets him get on with it — 'see if they want to stick their nose in, they've got enough for that just on the grounds that we refused selection. So he puts a call in to the head honcho who says this all sounds terrible, something must be done, let's have an inquiry. Diesel thinks that's all right, the IRB say they'll let him know what they propose, he's got his big story. Next day the IRB are in reverse as well. The big dog is saying it's not possible, they don't have enough to go on, Samoa haven't laid a complaint, print your story and we'll see what falls out.'

'When was this?'

'Weeks ago now. Anyway, the paper start tiptoeing around, they're not that keen. Not enough to go on, can't afford to get involved with a big hitter like this in case he lawyers up. So Diesel goes to the Manu, says why don't they lay a complaint?'

'And?'

'Turns out they did. But no one wants to know about it. Not the Frogs, not the IRB. Everyone wants to let it slide, except bloody Diesel who's on his high bloody horse by now, trying to get someone to give him the nitty-gritty.'

'So what does he want from you?'

'He keeps going on about the money trail. Reckons he can run the story if he can show bank accounts. Not from me.'

'Yeah, why would you want to do that?'

'Exactly.'

'Hello? Because you got fucked over?'

'So what? They going to play the World Cup again? I don't think so. The club going to shit on me? Yes. The taxman going to start looking into my accounts? Probably. Where's my upside?'

* * *

'I'm blind. I'm going home.'

'What are you talking about? You can't declare yourself blind — the blind call has to be external. Basics. And you're not blind anyway, you're not even swaying. Your round anyway.'

My phone buzzes. A little lift, but the text is from Ali. 'Thanks, bro.' That was quick. I throw the phone down.

'So you're a dud root. It's not that big a deal.'

'I don't get it. She said she'd come.'

'Maybe she was faking?'

Chapter 6

It's nearly seven years since I played in black. I had only half a dozen Tests, and three of them were off the bench — I warmed it three more times without getting on — so it's not as if I was a legend, but I'll take it. Anyway, once you've worn the jersey it stays on you for ever and ever, amen. And not just on the field but in the stands, at the pub, wherever you go: London, Cape Town, Whangarei. In Paris it's just as big a deal as in New Zealand, maybe even more so because there aren't that many of us around. The upside to everyone wanting a piece of you is that most of them want to impress you, so they can't do enough for you. You get introduced to someone at a do and the guy making the introductions adds those two words and you can just see the kick it gives them. Particularly the big dogs — they like to show you what they can do as well, so quite often it's 'Come and watch PSG in my box' or 'Madonna's coming round for drinks. Why don't you pop in as well?' It's not all hard yards.

The bitch of it is the feeling of responsibility: you have to live up to it, which cuts both ways. I didn't realise how much being a part of it meant to me until I got shut out. Sure, it's a big moment when you make it for the first time. In the weeks coming up to the announcement you try not to think about it too much to avoid disappointment; when the press start throwing your name around you start wondering whether they have some sort of inside run; then comes the phone call, then the announcement, then all the other phone calls from your mates, your old coaches, rellies, the lot. I wasn't taking it for granted, but all along I had the sense that it was a natural progression, that it was right, and that it was going to be like this for a long time. I'd played for New Zealand through the age grades, then the Juniors, so it felt like I had been on the conveyor belt for years now, that this was where I belonged. The higher up the ladder you go, the easier it is to play — even if the opposition are better, the game faster and the intensity higher, the guys around you are quality too and everything clicks and you're flying.

I felt bulletproof. The next bit sounds pretty obvious now. The press were saying I looked set for a long spell in the number-ten jersey, everyone thought I was a great guy and the only way to go was down. It didn't happen on the field. I wish it had.

It was the night before our Tri-Nations game in Wellington and they'd decided to use Max as cover for ten so I was a dirty dirty — a non-playing reserve. I wasn't that chuffed about it but some of the other boys were going out and one of my mates was in town from overseas so it meant I could catch up with him. We went out after dinner. I don't think we actually told the management that we were going out on the piss, but they must have had a fair idea. Anyway, they had other things to worry about.

I met up with JT at the Cross. He was there with his younger brother — it was his brother's birthday — and a bunch of varsity students. They must have been there for a couple of hours already and they were all pretty liquored, playing drinking games. It got quite loud quite quickly and the other dirty dirties shot through after a while. I had a couple — nothing serious — and joined them for a couple of rounds and I could see they were getting messy. Everyone was. At ten on a Friday night in a Wellington bar you don't see many people you'd want driving you home. The place was crowded and one of JT's brother's mates — Sammy, a skinny little kid with a smart mouth — knocked the glass out of the hand of a guy in a group behind him when he stood up too quickly on his way for a piss. The guy shoved him, Sammy said that he was sorry but he didn't need to be shoved, so he shoved him back and pretty quickly it was all on. The other guys were a bit older and didn't look like students and I stepped in, trying to do the right thing like an idiot. I was wearing civvies but I was easily recognised and one of them wanted a piece of me, pushing me first then flailing these big loopy punches when all I wanted was to stop the others. He must have connected — afterwards I had a puffy cheek which looked great in the Sunday papers — and I guess I reacted on instinct. I'm not much of a brawler but I'd done some boxing training over the summer just to mix up the off-season a little and I'd learnt how to throw a punch, rotating the arm as it uncoiled in a jab. It just shot out like it had a mind of its own. I was all ready to throw another one but he'd walked into it beautifully, leading with his nose. The whole scene happened in that super slow-motion that you get when the adrenalin tears through you. He went down like the sack of shit that he was and even with the buzz I realised that no matter how sweet the punch, this was not a good thing.

I'm not sure what everyone else was doing but I was on my knees straight away: 'You OK, mate? Are you right? Sweet as, eh? No worries.'

A woman came over and started in at me. 'You bastard! Who the fuck do you think you are, you wanker? Oh my God, he's bleeding!' JT was pulling me off and getting in between us and the crowd had gone so quiet the music was quite clear. (Hendrix:

'Hey Joe'.) My hand didn't hurt as much as I would have thought; I'd hit him right in the fleshy part of the nose. The bouncers arrived, a big Samoan guy, quite young, with a ponytail, and a smaller white guy, older, with a moustache. There was a little circle gathered around us by now and the guy was still on the floor but at least he was sitting up. There was a bit of blood, not that much, and he was wearing a black T-shirt which helped. As soon as she'd worked out he was going to be all right, she started in again: 'You motherfucker, I know who you are.' She was spraying little flecks of spit. 'I'm gonna get a lawyer and we are going to fucking crucify you.'

'Whoa, lady, let's just settle down. Shit, we don't need any lawyers. Let's see if your man's OK and then we'll take it from there, right?' The guy with the moustache was good value. 'Now, are you all right, mate? How's the head? Yeah, there's a bit of claret there. Can you walk? Bring him in over here to the office. You too.' JT and I followed. I couldn't see Sammy or the other guy who kicked the whole thing off. The woman, who was wearing an orange skirt, came too. Nobody else said anything. 'I can look after this, Mosi,' said the moustache to the Samoan.

I could see the guy's nose had a nice lump in it and he gave me a dirty look, I think more because his girlfriend had seen him get smacked than anything else. He wouldn't have been as old as me, twenty-three, twenty-five tops. There wasn't much he could say unless he wanted to lay charges. He didn't look the type to want to get the cops involved, but I could see the chick scheming away. The guy with the moustache was having a look at the nose. JT pulled me over to the corner and whispered, 'How much cash have you got on you?'

'What for?'

'You're going to have to bung him. How much?'

'You're kidding. I'm not paying that cunt for having a go at me, that'd be plain wrong.'

'Grow a fucking brain, Sparky. It's the night before a Test against the Boks and you get caught in a ruck in town. If it gets out you're toast. Here, I've got eighty bucks and some shrapnel, maybe ninety. You?'

'I am not giving that prick my money.'

'I think it's broken,' said black T-shirt to moustache, tipping his head backwards under the instructions of the girlfriend.

I took out two fifties and a twenty. 'That's all I've got.' JT put it with his.

Moustache gave black T-shirt some paper towels and pulled his head forward. JT went over to them with the money: 'Look, sorry about that, it was an accident. Here's something so you can, ah, buy yourselves a drink. OK?'

Moustache looked at me, eyebrows raised. I walked over and held out my hand to black T-shirt. 'Yeah, sorry, mate. No hard feelings.'

'Good one. You're not getting out of it that easy.' This from orange skirt.

'Shut up, Sal. It was my fault. Fair enough.' A handshake.

For a while, I really thought I'd got away with it. I had the same sort of light-headed feeling I'd had after walking away from a crash that totalled the car I was in. I got some cash out and tried to give it to JT, who wouldn't take it — he felt nearly as bad about the whole thing as I did. We walked back to the hotel and I went to tell Rosie, the team manager. He was in his room. He'd already heard — someone had rung the night desk at the local paper and the journo had rung him for the details. Rosie, caught short, had tried to cover for me, saying they should wait until it was clear what the story was and that the team wanted to concentrate on the game. I told him the whole story and he was pretty good about it but I could tell he was worried.

I hardly slept that night, or for a lot of nights afterwards. There was nothing in the papers Saturday morning but some smartarse had put something up on the internet — most of it was exaggerated but it was close enough to the truth for it not to make any difference, so it got regurgitated through the press and they milked it to the point where people were talking about it in Parliament, there were editorials about role models and high wages all mixed in with the pride of the nation. Luckily we won. To be fair to black T-shirt, he didn't say a word and neither did orange skirt. But the fallout was enough. It might have been different if someone had videoed it; it would have obviously been self-defence. A few people took my side to defend me in public, but only a few. I was summoned to a meeting midweek with my agent and the management team laid it out: having a few beers wasn't a crime, and they might even have overlooked the 'incident', as it was now referred to — no charges were laid, so the cops never got involved — if it had gone under the radar but for political reasons they were going to have to stand me down for the rest of the Tri-Nations and they'd come back to it for the end-of-season tour. The door was still open for the World Cup squad but the way it turned out my replacement went all right so that was it. I signed a new contract for a couple of years, backing myself to make it in again. It didn't happen.

I hadn't done myself any favours by having a big night out when I'd first got selected. A couple of seasons earlier, our coach had come up with the bright idea of breath-testing us on the morning after the game at our recovery sessions. They weren't too touchy about what you actually blew apart from the two or three times a season when we had a short turnaround or were travelling and wanted to make sure we were going to recover all right for the next game. On those days, you had to blow zero or you'd be out of the starting line-up. The rest of the time, predictably, it became a bit of a contest — at the second session, one of the props blew a thousand, and from then on, the back seat of the bus was reserved for those of us who made the thousand club. After my first Test, I thought it was the done thing to have a few. I got a bit carried away and copped some dark looks the next day from the staff when I didn't turn up to the press conference. I hadn't thought much more about it, but apparently it had gone down as a black mark.

Dad just said, 'Never mind,' and got on with it. Mum was tougher, and for a while she would pipe up with little digs about pretty much everything. I couldn't load the bloody dishwasher — that I had bought them — without a sigh and a shake of the head at how useless I was. I would have liked to have cried about it but I haven't managed that since I was a kid, not even afterwards when they died. Ali had just had Sasha so she had other things on her mind.

Anyway, I kept playing. What else was I going to do?

My form might have dipped a bit.

Chapter 7

'Where were u last night?'

Too possessive. Delete.

'U around?'

Rubbish. Delete.

'I want you.' I seriously think about sending this for at least five minutes.

Delete. At least I dodged that bullet.

Can I turn to someone for advice on this? I can just hear Rich: 'If it walks like a moose and it talks like a moose, you've had a fucking moose.'

JT would be sincere. 'Just tell her how you feel.' Bless, but even less helpful. His woman is not someone I'd have chosen.

Call her. Find a reason, shoot the shit and you'll have a better idea where you are.

'I just wanted to know if I have to organise anything for you this weekend.' Sounds all right. Her phone rings foreign. Like at home. London, presumably. Three rings. She would have my number on her phone.

Four rings. Is she looking at it, wondering whether to pick up?

Five rings. Or is it buried in the bottom of her bag?

Six rings. Fuck.

Answerphone in three different languages. Showy cow.

If I don't say anything it'll look weird. She'll know I rang.

'Rachel, hi, it's Mark Stevens. I just wanted to know whether you needed me to sort you out this weekend for tickets. Let me know. Thanks. Bye.'

That is fucking silk.

The morning of the game we meet at ten for a stretch at the ground. The usual round of handshakes. When I get to Rich he claps his hand to his chest: 'Strength and honour.' Friday night the boys came round to mine for pasta and a DVD. Moose's missus is back in Canada for a couple of weeks, Josh got a green card on the grounds that the film is 'game preparation' and Rich is single anyway. Sarah went back to New Zealand last year after we broke up. Rich made us watch his copy of *Gladiator*, getting it past us on the grounds that it was the director's cut. ('Mate, it's fucking art — this is the real deal.') Then he said the lines just before the actors did, and eventually got pummelled.

The stretching takes place in silence, and we can hear the sound of passing cars. I can smell the grass. It's too early to get wound up — I try to avoid it, anyway — but the tension is there, just under the surface, always. Afterwards the backs run through a new move that we're planning to use against their rush defence while the forwards do a couple of lineouts, then a shower, when the mood lightens and the chatter increases.

We leave our cars at the ground, take a bus to the hotel and go straight into lunch, the whole team in tracksuits and polo shirts. Blazers have been left in the changing room for after the game. There are two tables: forwards and backs. Some of the forwards already have headphones on which always strikes me as a bit much four hours before kick-off. The hotel is functional, one of a three-star chain we use everywhere we go — light wood, dark carpets, Monet prints on the walls. The food too is standardised, unremarkable — just fuel, really. I must have had the same meal of grated carrot, tinned corn, tomatoes and ham followed by chicken and pasta followed by yoghurt and fruit salad a hundred times since I got to France. If we have beetroot it's an occasion. Our game is at 2.30 and I had breakfast at nine so I just pick at the main and grab a couple of bananas that I'll take to the room. Around the backs' table there is gossip of who is likely to be coaching next year — Christophe is at the end of his contract — and I prick my ears up. There was talk of a foreigner but sadly this looks less and less likely and the general theory now is that he'll get another couple of years, perhaps with Coquine coming on board because it's his last season as a player which will mean the other bloke will get the arse. I've barely heard him say a word, anyway. He's really there as a fuse so Christophe can push him out first if things go haywire.

Jacques, our halfback, is my roomie as usual and he always goes for coffee and a cheeky smoke after the meal. I go straight to the room, which means I get the double bed. I flick through the TV channels until I find BBC News. I get five minutes of it before Jacques arrives and as usual heads straight for the toilet and, leaving the door open, takes a dump.

'Honestly, that is a habit you have to change, my friend. It's not civilised. There are toilets in the hall. Or just close the door like everyone else.'

A snort from the bog. 'Every time you say the same thing and, you know, every time I feel a little bit closer to you. You know that we have to keep the channels between us open, that we must not have any secrets. I wouldn't do this with my wife but with you, I can really be myself because I know how close you are to me. We are truly intimate. It is a bond that no one can break.'

I put my head under the pillow and pull it tight. (Jacques is Catalan. Perhaps that explains it. A mate of mine who plays in Perpignan told me how they have an extra character in the Christmas crèche in Catalonia: you've got all the usual suspects, three wise men, sheep, donkeys, cattle, Mary, Joseph and little baby Jesus — and a guy in the corner taking a dump. The Christmas shitter. Something about man's bond with the earth. I'm not sure what he was supposed to have been doing in Bethlehem, but there you go. Life's rich tapestry.)

We have only forty minutes before the doc and the physio arrive and it would be nice to get a little sleep. The toilet flushes. Jacques grabs the remote. 'No, there'll be no foreign languages here.' He flicks around, tries to fiddle with the blocked porn channels in the vain hope that by some freak of chance they'll work without having to pay for them — this has never happened, despite numerous attempts — and settles on a game show.

I close my eyes but don't get to sleep, instead running images through my head of the plays I will be using during the game, the guy I'm marking, the first contact, first tackle, the different kicks. I touch on them lightly, reassuring myself, like a tradesman checking his tools before a job to avoid any surprises. Don't overdo it. Positive imagery can be a bitch: if you tell yourself that this is what is going to happen then you cock it up, suddenly your confidence isn't where it used to be. And it is a slippery fucker to get hold of once you've lost it. It's like the teacher's curse — 'could do better' — a twisted prophecy that takes you closer to the edge than you need if you're struggling to believe in yourself. Walking along a metre-wide passage is easy, but if you're dealing with a two-hundred-metre drop on either side things are a little more complicated.

I allow my mind to slacken, to choose its own direction: Sasha, my niece, and the picture I have on my fridge of a stick figure kicking an oval ball through a capital H with a huge orange sun smiling down on the scene from a corner. This slips into thinking about those school fees, a couple of hundred grand for the two girls would sting like hell, but no point in worrying about that now. Slide naturally into Sarah, who wanted kids; Rachel, the big brown eyes and 'What do I need from you now?' Not for the first time I wonder what she will look like naked. I gave her my ticket to the game. Benoit will have given her one too and she could probably sit in the press box but there's no one else to give it to anyway.

The TV is still on — the game show over, polar bears are now starring in a nature documentary. Jacques is snoring lightly. There is a knock at the door. I get up to open the door for the doc and Paul, one of our physios.

'You're early.' Once I'm strapped, I'm locked into the game and two and a half hours out is further than I would like.

The doc is defensive. He gets quite a lot of grief, one way or another. 'There's a lot of guys who need strapping, and your thing always takes a while.'

My 'thing' is a dodge we've cooked up. It's a precaution, really: the bone spurs in my ankle hurt without — apparently — doing any long-term harm. I'll need an operation in the off-season; until then I just have to grin and bear it. Local anaesthetic gets me through the games. The catch is that, strictly speaking, I'm not allowed to play with local anaesthetic. So the doc cuts me above the hairline and puts a stitch in it now, and when we get to the ground he jabs me. That way if I get pulled up for a test there's an explanation for the local — we just say that I got cut during the game and stitched up afterwards. The chances are it will never get put to the test. I almost wish it would because it would make the whole palaver seem worthwhile. Getting stitched up when you're hot from the game doesn't really hurt, but when you're stone-cold and sitting in a hotel room it's not so much fun. And I had bloody well better not go bald — I now have a row of tiny scars that will make me look like an outcast from some obscure African tribe if my skull ever gets exposed.

So I sit patiently while the doc does the deed. Paul straps Jacques' knee. Outside in the corridor Xavier and François, our reserve first five, are fucking about making a racket and laughing. A door bursts open, there is a thud and the wall shakes ever so slightly. Coquine's deep voice rumbles, the pitch too low for me to hear what he's saying. The noise level drops off. After the doc has finished, he moves on to his next patient and I eat the first of my two bananas while Paul straps my other ankle. Jacques and I watch the polar bears and wait. I eat the second banana.

With just under two hours to kick-off we assemble in the team room. Chairs are arranged in two broad semi-circles. I take a seat at the back. Christophe is pacing up and down in front of us, scowling and rubbing his face, as guys arrive. Any conversations now are in a low whisper; few people speak. Written on a whiteboard, an outline of the game-plan; at the bottom, underlined three times '*Gagnez les duels*'. Beat your man. It's not rocket science.

Rich pulls up a chair next to me. Josh is sitting with the front row — Coquine insists that they do everything together on the day of the game, even to the point where the three of them room together. It drives Josh nuts. Christophe starts on his spiel. There really isn't that much to say: all the work has been done and if we're not ready now we're screwed. He says it anyway. Part of the ritual, I guess. The first bit, at least, is logical, going over tactics again, targeting their weak points and reminding us of their danger men and where they will look to strike. Then he starts in on his motivational chat, with some over-ripe lines comparing it to battle. This kind of thing always leaves me cold. I keep a clear head, and I'd prefer the guys around me to be the same. Rich whispers, a little too loud, 'What we do in life echoes in eternity.'

Christophe finishes by asking if anyone else wants to speak. Coquine stands to look at us. He's not much of a speaker, but at least he's brief. 'We play for each other, OK? We play for each other.'

As the chairs scrape back, Rich gets the final word: 'On my signal, unleash hell.'

* * *

The police escort is waiting for us at the reception desk, talking to the receptionist. '*On y va? Allez.*' The pair of them ride out in front of us stopping traffic so that we get to the church on time.

Headphones go on. Everyone wears the mask. We get wired in to ourselves before getting wired in to each other. On the bus, I sit alone and stare out the window at cars and buildings, looking without seeing. Joy Division over the headphones ('They carried pictures of their wives/And numbered tags to prove their lives'). I like bleak. It makes me feel determined.

Chapter 8

We arrive at the ground an hour and a half before kick-off; the bus drops us at the gate. The crowd of flag-waving supporters decked out in club colours parts and with their encouragement in our ears we walk in single file down the corridor to the changing room. While we have been away jerseys, shorts and socks have been hung up on our respective pegs. Handing jerseys out individually is only for the big games. I change quickly and, in bare feet, pad through to the physio room for my jab. The doc draws the transparent liquid out of the glass vial, taps the syringe, squeezes a short squirt and, satisfied, swabs the instep of my heel with antiseptic before pushing the needle in a couple of centimetres. As it breaks the skin I tense my leg. His thumb presses down on the plunger until nearly all the liquid is inside me. I never get used to the needle but it does the job. Paul straps the ankle to make a pair with the right one and by the time I stand on it the dull ache that would otherwise rise to a biting, crippling pain when I run and twist and jump on it has gone, and I am aware only of the tight white bandage supporting the joint, limiting flexibility and pulling at the stubble of the hairs I keep shaved there.

Back in the changing room the smell of liniment cranks me up another notch. The referee is there, talking to the front rowers while the touch judges move around the players checking sprigs to ensure there are no sharp edges. I look at mine — sixteen millimetres: the ground is soft in Paris — to make sure none of them are loose, then put socks and boots and tracksuit top on and go out to warm up. Denis, our fullback, Rich, who plays on the wing, Thomas, our other winger, and François are already outside, kicking. In twenty minutes the others will follow and we'll run through the warm-up together. More than an hour before kick-off the stadium is still virtually empty, the punters clustered around the bars or struggling through Saturday-afternoon traffic. I jog a lap around our half of the pitch — the other lot are warming up in their half — and spy Jamie, a Kiwi whom I know from home. It's his first season in France. From what I've seen in the paper he spends more time on the bench than I suspect he was planning on. He trots over.

'Howzitgoing?' A bro-style handshake and a friendly smile on the halfway line. He's playing centre. At home he had a reputation for being more glitz than grit. Christophe reckons he is vulnerable on his left shoulder. We'll see.

'G'day mate. How're you finding it?'

'Sweet. Bit of a shambles sometimes but the club's been good. They try hard, anyway. The missus is in a bit of a state about the baby but it's always the way, isn't it. You around for a beer afterwards?'

'We've got some stuff with the sponsors but I'll catch you at the after-match. You guys staying up?'

'Nah, we're flying back tonight. They don't want to pay for another night at the hotel.'

'Tight bastards. I'll see you after then?'

'Cool. Have a good one.'

'Same with you.'

I run around underneath the goalposts and stretch. The sky

is cloudy but the forecast is for no rain — as a rule they're pretty reliable. There's a bit of wind coming across diagonally from left to right. Alain arrives to tell me that we've lost the toss and will be playing from this end, slightly downhill. It's our kick-off.

I start by hoisting a few up and unders for Denis, then some line kicks with François and finish with goal kicks from forty metres — far enough to need to kick it but not so far that I have to force it. I make six out of six. The ankle feels fine.

The rest of the team arrives and we run two laps of our half, the first one slow, so tightly bunched we can touch each other, the second quicker, loping. Eric runs us through more stretching. Coquine barks short, sharp sentences about us being at home. I ask him what zone he wants the kick-off to go to. Deep. Then passing drills, building up to a full sprint. Two balls go down, which is a bit average, but it would be a mistake to draw too much from it — you can never tell with the French. Then press-ups, sit-ups and boxing on the pads, held by the reserves, before finishing on tackling drills on the pads. Up in a line. Seven tacklers, one noise. The first thud on the shoulders. Again. And again. And again. The clock on the big screen in one corner of the stadium shows 2.15. We go back to the changing room.

Inside, the intensity goes up again. The forwards gather in the showers to wind up. Josh hates this bit, when the Frenchies start shouting at each other and head-butting. I can't help thinking it's window-dressing — the ones with the wild eyes don't seem to do any more when they get out there. I don't think it's as bad as it used to be. In my first year one of the boys had his eyebrow split open when one of our old props was a little over-enthusiastic getting into character. Anyway, I give the fatties a wide berth in these last few minutes. A few weeks ago I overheard Coquine having a friendly chat with his opposite number before the game as we were checking out the pitch. When the time came to get changed, he said, 'Well, I'd better go take out my brain.' We ran out onto the field that day each holding the hand of a kid from a local junior rugby team. The kids must have been eight or nine years old, all dressed up in their rugby gear for the big occasion. As Coquine let go of his little mascot he bent down and tenderly kissed him on the head. Two minutes after kick-off he had a dust-up with his mate. Who knows what goes on in these people's heads?

Thomas comes over to me. He's marking a big Fijian winger today and he's a bit edgy about getting steamrollered. He's anxious that I give him plenty of warning if I'm going to kick behind the defence so he can come up quickly and not give his man a run-up if they recover quickly. Thomas has one of those strange anatomies that comes from too many upper-body sessions and not enough lower-body work: he looks like one of the Roman legionaries in *Asterix*, a huge torso on chicken legs. It wouldn't surprise me if he'd been at the magic potion at some point. I reassure him. Communication is important, particularly in a team that speaks three different languages — we have an Argie flanker as well, Freddie, although he's been here a few years now. He's on the bench today. He's sitting next to me, thighs hanging down like dewlaps. His English is pretty good, too. I hear it's chaos with Georgians.

Eight minutes to go. I bounce a ball off the floor, hitting the end so it comes back towards me. Moose heads to the toilet and throws up. Funny to see such a big bloke have nerves, but it happens most weeks. Even though I'm sweating and my pulse must be at 120, I feel calmer now than I have since the doc came and cut me more than two hours ago. I know this, I know what's coming and I know I'll do it well; it's what I do. Life in the real world is complicated: you can get lost up your own arse trying to work out how to live it. Out there it's simple: make a decision and execute. Most of the time your instincts make the calculation for you. Jacques raises his eyebrows at me, looking for a pass. I flick him the ball and he flicks it back. I stand up and jog on the spot, sprint for three, jog, sprint for three, jog. Hit myself on the chest with the ball. Flick it to Jacques. Then some reverse press-ups on the bench.

A knock from the ref. Five minutes. The reserves make a tour of the room, slapping backs, tapping bums and murmuring encouragement before moving out into the corridor. The rest of us form a tight circle, arms around each other's shoulders. Coquine is talking about clearing out; someone else reminds us to stay on our feet. The words are almost meaningless now, just there to fill up the seconds; the next useful information won't come until after the ball is kicked. I look around at the faces. When I came back after Dad's funeral, each of them had something for me, even if it was just a kind word. Josh and Moose and Rich of course, but the Frenchies too. Jacques' missus baked and cooked enough food for a month. Coquine brought me three boxes of his brother's wine. Thomas actually insisted on coming round and cooking a meal for me and we got pissed together, just the two of us, talking. And so on. Don't get me wrong, I'm not going to tear up here and I'd rather I was looking round at a bunch of guys wearing black.

And it's only a game, and in all honesty I couldn't give a shit about the jersey.

But for now, these are my guys.

The ref knocks: two minutes. Time to go.

We line up behind Coquine by order of numbers on our backs. French superstition. Paul and Pompon, our bagman, stand by the door holding tins. Vaseline, Vicks, wax for grip. The forwards lather their ears with Vaseline; I put Vicks under my nose. I don't trust the wax. The click of steel sprigs on the concrete floor. The reserves clapping us on the back as we move out. The sound of the ground announcer calling out the team sheet comes down the corridor. A cheer greets each of our names. Indian-file down the tunnel, until we're standing next to the other team. Jesus, they're big. I wink at Jamie; he grins. The referee checks both teams: everyone's here. Jacques, just in front of me, crosses himself leaving the tunnel. We run out over the running track into the big green rectangle.

The crowd, as they say, goes wild.

Chapter 9

Afterwards, standing in the ice bath set up by the showers, water up to my waist, I can feel my gear retreating north into the warmth of my body. Coquine is in the one next to me, splashing freezing droplets onto anyone who comes in range, laughing.

How did the game go? The same as always — team A played team B, one of them won, one of them lost. True, occasionally it's a draw, but not today. Who really cares? There'll be another one along in a week. You've seen it a hundred times, a thousand times, ten thousand. Beforehand it seems anything is possible, and maybe it is, but when you come off the field it feels like somehow the blank sheet of paper already had lines traced on it, and you were just there to colour them in. Not that it was literally predetermined, just that when you take into account all the different factors in play — the work done in preparation, the individuals involved, their motivation, the conditions, the referee, everything — the likely outcomes were finite, tiny in comparison to the theoretical possibilities. If you could break it down to its smallest component parts it would become obvious. None of us can, so commentators and journalists like to talk about 'critical moments', but they have to say that, it's how they make their money. Every moment is critical, none more than another. Some games look like they turn on a hair, the bounce of the ball, seem to be won and lost in the final minute, the final second. But that's because they're presented that way. Outside the tyranny of linear time, maybe it was the extra kicking practice someone put in — or that they *didn't* put in — on Friday, maybe it was the extra kicking practice someone did when they were sixteen, maybe it was the lineout work the forwards did on their own, maybe it was because it turned out that Jamie *is* vulnerable on his left shoulder and maybe that's because he's been carrying an injury for a month but their doctor can't pick up anything on the scans he's ordered, maybe their number eight hasn't slept all week because his one-year-old son is teething and he was too tired to get back to cover so their fullback got turned over in the thirty-second minute because he was on his own when the high kick arrived a split second before Rich and Xavier, or maybe he's just lazy. Or the ref likes giving out yellow cards for one thing but not for another. Or we just have better players because we have more money. And on and on and on. What really decided the outcome? All of the above. The trick is to master more of the variables that make a difference than the other lot. God is on the side of the biggest armies, and when he isn't it's because the biggest armies fucked up, got too cocky, didn't do their homework. 'Luck is what happens when preparation meets opportunity.' There's a lot of bullshit management-speak formulae floating around sport these days but that one you can take to the bank.

We won; we were always going to win. It was 44–18, and a bonus point for attack. I kicked eight out of nine, even managed a little dot, total points tally twenty-four, earning myself man of the match, no less. And don't worry, I'm enjoying it. I worked hard for it. A good day at the office. They aren't that gutted, either — I spoke to Jamie afterwards on the field, fresh from the slaughter, and I could see it in his eyes: 'Oh, well.' No point in letting it hurt. Unless you use the pain, and the fear of it happening again as a spur. Then it becomes useful, flips you into a new cycle, makes you work harder, get better prepared. Unless next time you get out to play you're paralysed by the fear. That's not so good.

Anyway, as I say, who cares? I'm going drinking with my mates and with a bit of luck I'm going to bed a beautiful bouncing Brazilian. I hope she was watching, and I hope she's picked up enough over the last week to know that I played well. Playing well always impresses girls, it's just that most of the time they aren't the right ones. I wonder if this one is?

This ice bath is fucking freezing, and I'm getting out.

* * *

Blazer, white shirt and jeans. It's a bit old school, although mercifully we don't have to wear slacks. We are supposed to wear a tie but hardly anyone does — they're a sickly-looking duck-egg blue. The president likes us to look smart: it's good for the image with the sponsors. 'Professional' — the same word in English and in French, though with a slightly different twist depending on who's saying it, and the way they say it. Apparently there are ten different intonations of '*voila*', each one with its own specific meaning, but fucked if I can tell the difference yet. Every so often the manager, Didier, gets wound up about the tie situation because the president's been at him and we get fined twenty euros for not wearing one. I can take the hit.

First stop, the press room. There was a time when journos could come into the changing room but that's long gone now. Then we used to go straight there after the game but guys weren't getting ice onto injuries fast enough or doing the warm-down so we changed the set-up. This means the hacks get edgy when it's a night game — if it's a nine o'clock kick-off sometimes we don't get out until midnight and they want to get their stories filed. I can't say I go any faster to help them out.

It's a funny relationship we have with the press. They follow us around so much, ask for interviews that take up our time and earn their living telling the world what we do, so we can't help feeling that they owe us a bit of loyalty. They're parasites, we're the host, it's only polite. When anything bad happens — we lose, play badly, someone gets themselves in the shit off the field, whatever — we want them to run damage control. Instead they put the boot in, and look like innocence besmirched when we get shitty about it. If we're honest we wouldn't want to read papers that were just PR but it just feels like bad manners, so we always view them with a bit of suspicion. Rachel doesn't count. I go into the press room on my guard. My frame of mind is sunnier as we've just had a win and I've collected man of the match, but still.

Christophe and their coach are already there, each with their little swarm hovering around. Coquine is leaving as I arrive. 'You're moving fast tonight,' I say.

He grins. 'There's a beer getting lonely without me. See you at the after-match. Enjoy.'

The PR woman we had in told us that we should view our dealings with the press as an opportunity to talk about ourselves, our teammates, the coach, the club and sponsors in a positive light. The hitch is that none of this comes naturally — talking yourself up is the kiss of death; most of the time we're bitching about the coach behind his back; saying nice things about the club looks like serious arse-kissing; and most of us have only a vague idea of what sponsors do — apart from the essential. What do we know about telecoms or construction or light industry?

Beer should be easier, but you can hardly say, 'If you want to get pissed, drink this. It works for me.' So: a shout-out for your teammates, avoid anything that might sound controversial and get out as quickly as possible. The club make you do it, but they don't really care what you say as long as it doesn't reflect poorly on them.

Some of the questions are pretty curly; you have to think on your feet, make sure you don't say anything that might make anyone look bad, particularly yourself. It's like an American cop show: 'Anything you say may be taken down and used against you in the court of public opinion.' A mate of mine got stitched up with a throwaway line about the rigours of professional rugby, how you weren't having a runaround with your mates any more. The next day's headline was 'I'll never play with my friends again'. Doing it in French adds spice, especially as the version you pick up on the field is closer to the gutter than the classroom. I got taken out to a smart dinner about a year ago, sponsors, politicians and associated bigwigs. Someone made an interesting statement and I wanted to say, 'Really?' In fact, I told him he was an idiot who was taking the piss. It goes over all right in the changing room but there's a nuance, apparently. You should have seen the faces.

The press room isn't a big conference hall with tables and so on, just a small, windowless nook with a few perfunctory chairs where people stand around in clumps; there's a sponsors board in front of which we have to stand for TV interviews. I get my own clump as soon as I walk in. Christophe, left totally deserted, looks a bit put out. My hand is pumped by several of them, who smile their congratulations: I've had a beer with some of these guys, all off the record, and they are human beings. I guess I'd be the same if I was in a rush to get it done and needed some filler.

I can't see Rachel. Perhaps she's getting into her nurse's outfit. Little minx.

The first question is typical: 'Did you think it was going to be such an easy game?'

To which I could reply, 'Let's face it, they're pretty average. They've won once away from home all year and that was three months ago, their kicker has a success rate verging on fifty per cent, and they didn't even put out a first-string side. We're lying fourth in the championship, they're eleventh. An outbreak of cholera in Paris might have given them a chance.' Actually, this is more or less what I told Rachel, on the basis that she wouldn't print it, and even then it felt dangerously like counting unhatched chickens. Instead, I give it the dead bat: 'We were coming off a loss last week so we had something to prove to ourselves and to our supporters. We were lucky at times. I guess it was our day.' Cue scribbling.

Same thing for the next one: 'You must be pleased with your game?' Possible reply: 'Yes I am, and if I don't get laid off the back of that there's no justice.' Printable version: 'The forwards played very well, they really set a platform for us and gave us some great ball going forward which we were able to use. And I thought our back three were phenomenal.' Rich, you owe me a beer.

'Your kicking was superb.' The man of the match permits himself a modest smile. 'Just doing my job.' Where is Rachel? She should be getting some of this down.

'In a few weeks you've got a big game in the European Cup against the form team in the Celtic league. Are you ready for them?'

'We've got a couple of injury worries but we'll certainly be doing our best. We'll have a look at the tapes, work hard over the next two weeks and see how we go.' Honestly, what am I supposed to say? 'Yes, we're planning on kicking the shit out of them'? That'll look good on their changing-room wall.

'Have you worked out a strategy?' Hold on, I've got my notes somewhere — would you like to publish them? 'As I say, we'll have a look at the tapes. They don't seem to have many weak points.' I try to look thoughtful. Can I go now?

The joke is that tomorrow I will read a dozen other people saying the same thing, and come away thinking I've learned something.

One of the journos who has been talking to their coach oozes over, all smiles and congratulations. Journalists are like referees — you don't really pay much attention to the good ones: the job gets done without fuss. Among the English speakers on the team this one is known as 'the child molester'. He must be in his late fifties, sports a comb-over, thinks he invented the game and constantly misquotes us. I hate talking to him because whatever I say he'll write what he wants. If he does an in-depth piece we ask him to send it to us first so that we can check it. The captain of the other team walks in and my camp followers desert, leaving me alone with the child molester.

Then the cavalry arrives. Rachel and her photographer, an Asian man in his forties. We exchange two little henpecks; the photographer stands back to take a couple of wide shots. I speak to her in English but the child molester won't take a hint and stands by my elbow until he can get a word in. 'So, did you expect it to be such an easy game?'

Christ.

Chapter 10

It's nearly six by the time we get out of the stadium to head over to the after-match, but there are still a couple of dozen supporters hanging round outside. I sign a few autographs while Rachel stands to the side and her photographer captures the moment. When we get to the long, low-slung building that houses the clubhouse there are more backslaps and congratulations, most of them from old geezers wearing club blazers. Even after three years I don't know most of their names and have no idea if they actually do anything useful. When you're young you wonder what the hell these sad old bastards are doing — surely a man's life gets bigger than a rugby club? Recently I've realised that I might just become one of them.

There's a meal for the players in a separate zone, roped off from the crowd. More pasta — rice, too — and this time with beef or fish. Behind the rope, sponsors and assorted hangers-on graze contentedly: nibbles, free booze and a solid home win. The adrenalin is still draining out of my system so I'm not hungry but I've had enough bad experiences to know that it's worth making sure I eat. As I make my way through the crowd, I stop to say hello to Coquine's wife. Kisses on both cheeks. She has a round, friendly face and a couple of kids in tow. The eldest, a boy, is about eight or nine and fat as a house. Coquine is explaining why to a sponsor: 'He wants to be big and strong like his father, so whenever I have pasta, he has pasta. I eat a lot of pasta.' Mrs Coquine smiles in a long-suffering way. Coquine gently grabs his son's cheek. 'But you have to run as much as papa as well. Otherwise you'll end up in the front row and your mother doesn't want that. I've already told you: PlayStation isn't a sport.' The sponsor changes the subject and I move off.

Rich joins me with a beer in his hand and we walk towards the food. 'Have you seen the size of that kid? He's got bloat. Back at home we'd go in with a knife — a handspan in and a handspan down — and all the gas'd come out.'

'He is quite solid.'

'Kids, mate. Don't need it. What a hassle.'

'There must be something in it. Everyone keeps doing it. Biological instinct — genes and that.'

'Not everyone. We're not animals. The George Clooney gambit. That's where my money is.'

'The George Clooney gambit?'

'Everyone's favourite bloke. Chicks love him, guys want to be him. The man has a plan.'

'You're not George Clooney.'

'Close enough. Here we are.'

The boys have kept us a couple of places, so Rachel sits down with us — her photographer has slipped off — and Rich takes the opportunity to introduce himself. 'Hi, I'm Rich.'

Moose: 'You've got to stop using that line.'

Rachel grins at Moose and stands up to kiss Rich. Her shirt rides up as she leans over the table, exposing a couple of inches of flesh. 'Now I know who you are. I'm Rachel.' I can see an ornate tattoo sprawling across her lower back; her lips brush Rich's cheek. At the base of my belly, something lurches. Moose swoops, gets a kiss as well and I try to make out the tattoo, a chaotic swirl of bright colours — a baleful yellow eye, perhaps, and blue and red scales.

Jamie, who's sitting with us, doesn't want to be left out so he gets some too. Josh, still sitting, interrupts his dinner briefly to hold out a hand. 'Josh.' He points at her bum. 'Nice tat.'

She's turned towards him so I can't see the look on her face, but I can tell she's smiling by the sound of her voice. 'Thanks.' She pulls her hair into a bunch and then shakes it out. I don't know whether it's a nervous tic or she's deliberately trying to look like a shampoo advert but the last twenty seconds have convinced me that my own interests will be best served cutting her out of this herd so that we can set up on our own.

Rich confirms this. 'Would you like a drink? There's some wine here or would you like champagne or a beer?' His good manners are only ever a cover. Mates: sometimes they're more like hyenas.

'Champagne would be great, thanks.'

'Very slick. Grab us five beers while you're there.'

'You really are going George Clooney, aren't you?'

Rachel: 'George Clooney? Interesting role model — he's gay. That's very enlightened of you. Or is it all true what they say about the showers?'

Rich, stunned: 'George Clooney is not gay. I have no problem with it, but he isn't.'

Rachel: 'Come on. He dresses well, he must moisturise three times a day, he's involved with humanitarian work, he's always talking about the women he's been with. It's obviously a front.'

Rich: 'I'm not buying it. Moisturising is not grounds for that kind of accusation.'

Rachel: 'Tom Cruise?'

Jamie: 'Yeah, Tom Cruise maybe. But Clooney — really? He's married.'

'So was Oscar Wilde. And he had kids.' A sacred cow bleeds out on the floor in front of our eyes.

'So, where are we off to tonight?' It's important that I know this so I can make sure we don't go there.

Rich has an itinerary planned. 'The Frenchies are keen for Bob's as usual so we can show our faces there for one or two and then I thought, in honour of our distinguished guest from Brazil, we might go high end. There's that cocktail bar round the corner, the Zinc or something. They have a Long Island Iced Tea that works like magic. Sound all right?'

Moose has reservations. 'Bob's has gone a bit *Star Wars* lately.'

'How's that?'

'The bar full of freaks where Luke and Obi-Wan Kenobi meet Han Solo in the original.'

'True. Sponge and his mate — you know, Coquine's personal trainer — keep showing up for a chat. Fuck that.'

'If you want something fancy, let's hit that new joint off the Champs Elysées straight up. I've been there twice and both times it was knee-deep in quality.'

Rich shakes his head. 'Too early. No one goes to that sort of place before ten. Anyway, we have to do a little mingling with the Frenchies. Team spirit. We're out of Bob's by eight-thirty, nine, then cocktails and we can see what happens after, OK?'

I just want to see more of that tattoo, and everything that goes with it. 'Works for me. I'll drop the car home and get a taxi in. Rachel, I could drop you at the hotel and then we can get a cab in together?' I read in some men's magazine that a man should always have a bottle of champagne in his fridge, just in case. I've got one that's been sitting there for the best part of a year, but it looks like it might be just about to come through for me.

Rich returns with a half-empty bottle of champagne, two

glasses and no beer. Josh grunts disappointedly and gets up to do it himself. 'Call yourself an Australian. Bloody disgrace.'

* * *

Jamie's team take off and Rachel goes to find her photographer, saying she'll just be a minute. Diesel, the journo whom Josh has been avoiding, is looking mismothered, fiddling around with his phone on the edge of the crowd.

'Don't quote me,' I say, 'but Josh was telling me you're trying to get a story out of him.'

'Mate, the whole thing reeks. They peddle this big lie about values then airbrush anything that might upset their raking it in.'

'How's that free beer?'

He looks at his glass, looks at me and grins. 'Fair call.'

'Not a big fan of the president myself.'

'He's just following his instincts. You can't tell a great white that baby seals are off the menu.'

'So who are the bad guys if it isn't the Fibber?'

'Everyone who knows he's out of line and has the ability to stop him doesn't do anything about it. The French Federation, the IRB . . . Honestly, don't get me started. You know why he's called the Fibber?'

'Because his pants are on fire?'

'Yeah, that does work, doesn't it? But it's short for Fibonacci.'

'Fibawho?'

'You went to uni didn't you?'

'Busted. So who's the man behind the Fibber?'

'Fibonacci is the bloke who brought numbers across from India to Europe — twelfth century, I think. Hold on, I'll look it up.' He starts fiddling with his phone.

'Anyway—.'

'Before him it was still all Roman numerals, people using an abacus, fingers and toes, whatever. The guy changed the way people do busincss.'

'What, the Fibber read *Moneyball*?'

'Josh!'

'Mate, I'm not talking to you.'

'Good call. Deep waters, my friend. Grown-ups are talking here.' Josh stops to listen. 'He's talking about how the Fibber got his spots,' I explain.

'It was just because he was all about the numbers. When he arrived, everything changed.'

Josh: 'Don't think he's the only one — plenty of boys can tell the same story.'

Diesel: 'The one about how you get fucked over by the rich guy but don't want to do anything about it?'

Josh walks. Now that I think about it, I don't want to be seen talking to Diesel for too long either. 'Free beer?' He looks at his glass, shrugs, and we move towards the bar. 'So what are you going to do about it?' I ask.

'I'm a bit buggered if no one goes on the record. Papers have all run a mile anyway — my editor was passing all the information I was giving him to the club, then the fuckers paid me off not to print the story. The Fibber swings a lot of weight around here. It's doing my head in, to be honest. I used to think that because the cameras were focused on us we were the whole show and what happened on the field was what mattered, that the blazers were just hangers-on. In fact, they're the ones with all the power, we're just the footsoldiers, the gimps. But what really gets me is how the guys who run the show keep trading on the bullshit about discipline and integrity and respect, then they rort the system when it suits them. It's marketing for monkeys — doesn't really matter what the product is, as long as the packaging looks good you can flog it. And the money is an invitation to go feral. The big countries divvy up the lion's share of the coin among themselves because the voting system is rigged in their favour. If any of us got caught doing something like that we'd be crucified.'

* * *

Outside, it's started to drizzle, so I take my jacket off and offer it to Rachel as we trot towards the car park. I know she's not going to take it — and she doesn't — but Rich isn't the only one who can look gallant when the situation calls for it. I even open the door for her.

'So, do you think you have everything you need for the piece?'

'More or less. There are one or two more things I'd like.'

'What's that?'

'Oh, you know, just follow-up stuff. Sometimes a story doesn't become clear until you start to write.' She bunches her hair and does the shampoo-ad routine again. I still don't know if it's deliberate or a tic. She smiles. 'I'll let you know what I need from you.'

We drive in silence for a while, until she says, 'Actually, now that I think about it I don't really have to go to my hotel. I've got everything with me.'

'You don't want to get changed?'

'You don't find me presentable?'

'You'll do. I'm just going to get changed and maybe we can have a quick drink at mine?'

I park the car in the garage that I use, fifty metres from the apartment building. As a general rule I prefer to play away on the first night — if you find yourself wanting to chew your arm off to avoid waking her up the next morning because you've exercised poor judgement the night before, there's less danger of being doorstopped in the future. And my place is a bit spartan: it's a big flat, and Sarah did it up beautifully — she had a ball buying stuff in the flea market where we used to go on Sunday afternoons — but I let her take everything with her when she went home. All I have left is a poster of Wonder Woman in the kitchen, one of Sasha's drawings on the fridge, some books and the furniture that was already there. When I look at it the way a woman might, I can't help feeling it's a bit dull. Perhaps I can get away with minimalism. In any case, it's too late to worry about now. I'll have to trade on the bachelor image and champagne. And I don't mind getting doorstopped by Rachel. As far as I'm concerned she can move in tomorrow.

The lift is tiny. Rachel is so close I could reach out and pull her to me without even moving my feet. She catches what must be my hungry stare, holds my look for a couple of heartbeats, then looks away with a little smile. My gut is tingling and I am annoyed to realise that my palms are sweaty. It's terrible, the things a beautiful woman can do to a man.

I let us into the flat, drop my bag just inside the door and grab the champagne from the fridge. 'We have cocktail glasses or wine glasses — no flutes, I'm afraid.'

Rachel takes the bottle and looks at the label. 'This I could drink from a mug, but it would be a shame. These will be fine.' She places two martini glasses next to each other on the bench. I tear off the gold paper and the wire casing around the cork, then twist until the pop, which always comes as a slight surprise. Cold air drifts from the mouth of the bottle. The liquid splashes and bubbles up to, and even over, the rim before settling.

'Cheers, then.'

'Cheers.' A clink that resonates through the apartment. I offer her a tour; she declines. 'Maybe later.' She spots Sasha's drawing on the fridge, big yellow sun in the corner, livestock spread over a paddock and someone — me — kicking a rugby ball through the posts. 'You have children?'

'My niece. She's very cool.' Last time I was home she ran up and leapt on me, put her arms around my neck and said, 'I love you, Uncle Mark.' It was so pure, I actually teared up. How does the hymn go? 'The love that asks no question . . .' We walk through to the living room. There are two sofas, but we both sit on the same one.

'Sorry if this is a little personal, but I can't help wondering what a guy like you is doing without a girlfriend.'

'What do you mean, a guy like me?' Yes, I'm fishing.

'Good-looking, reasonably successful.' Only 'reasonably' successful?

'I could ask you the same question.'

'What makes you think I'm single?' Fuck. I didn't see this in the script.

'Well, no wedding ring.' I take a big slurp of champagne, then have to resist the temptation to burp.

'I'm only teasing. Yes, I'm single. But I asked you first.'

'Long story. I brought my girlfriend over from New Zealand when I came — nearly three years ago now — and like I told you we broke up last year.'

'And there hasn't been anyone since?'

'Not really.' Technically speaking, this is a bit of a grey area, but I'm pretty sure this isn't the moment to get into details.

'You must be out of practice.'

I bristle, then register the look on her face, the gleaming eyes and the wet lips. A tractor beam pulls me towards her. As

I clamber aboard, my teeth connect with hers and a gurgle of laughter emanates from beneath the softness of her breasts. I probably am out of practice. I used to think I was pretty good.

Chapter 11

Living the dream. It never lasts for long, you adjust to it so quickly that you hardly have time to enjoy it before the effect has worn off and it's just a new reality about to become routine; the thing you really want next is hovering just outside of your reach so you have to set about getting organised to get there. You're like a kid who wanted an ice cream with a burning intensity springing from the certain knowledge that when you got your sticky little paws on it, your whole existence would take on a golden, happy glow. Then five minutes later, it was over. Or, worse, you didn't pay attention, the scoop melted in the summer heat and your glittering prize was suddenly on the pavement being licked by the bloody dog. So for that short, blissful period when you're king of your own little world, you might as well get your money's worth. Lying panting on the wooden floor of the living room, sweaty and half asleep, my belt buckle digging into my shoulder and Rachel's head weighing agreeably on my chest, I have just finished my treat and it was delicious. The best news is that the ice-cream lady is sticking around for a bit, so I can have some more. I plan to make a pig of myself.

Rachel sits up. 'Is it OK if I smoke?'

'Sure.' I get up and ferret around in the cupboard for a paua shell that I plucked from the rocks on the east coast last time I was home. The iridescent blues, pinks and greens of the interior have barely dulled with time. I put it on the table in front of her then pad through to the bedroom, put on a dressing gown and pick out a white shirt for Rachel. I love women wearing my shirts.

She is sitting on the sofa, naked, pulling on a cigarette. She puts on the shirt, buttoning it up only halfway. She looks even better with it on than she did naked. I lie down on the sofa opposite her.

'Why did you break up with your girlfriend?'

'I guess we didn't want the same thing.' This isn't my ideal after-match chat but I suppose we'll have to get through it at some point.

'What do you want, Mark?'

'Is this the follow-up stuff you need for the article?'

'No, this is just for me. I want to know what you want.'

'World peace. And a six-pack. It's not easy, though — I can't seem to get rid of this last little bit. My metabolism isn't what it might be.'

'Come on. I want to get to know you better. What do you want?'

Now I'm starting to feel uncomfortable. Sarah asked me the same thing. I found it easier to tell her what I didn't want. 'I don't know — the same as everyone, I suppose.' Why do I not have a better answer to such an obvious question?

'"The same as everyone"? You can do better than that.' She has crossed her legs, and is swinging the top one impatiently.

'I guess I don't spend a lot of time thinking about it.'

'You don't trust me enough to talk about this? Am I being pushy?' She looks hurt.

'No, it's fine. If you want to talk, it's fine.' I roll onto my back and look at the ceiling. 'But you'll have to tell me what you want too, OK? You're not getting away with the journalist routine. Don't be disappointed if I'm not deep — what you see is what you get. All right, let me think. I suppose I want to take it easy for a while, have enough money not to have to do things that I don't want to do. Rugby is pretty sweet but it isn't going to last forever, and I don't want to be forced into anything afterwards. I want to see the world and have the time to do what's right for me, you know? To do things that interest me. And to fall in love and, ah, have a family — though not right now.' The last bit comes out in a tumble.

Rachel laughs. 'It's OK. I wasn't suggesting that we settle down.'

'Right, your turn.'

'Wait, we haven't finished with you. So you're saying you want money?'

'I think I said I wanted freedom. And, you know, family and stuff.'

'Money will get you freedom.'

'True enough.' I've promised myself a six-month tour around the world when I stop playing, and I'm looking forward to doing it right. With rugby, I've never had a chance to do the touristing that so many mates of mine get under their belt by the time they're my age. You might get to tick off the place on a map, but all you see is the hotel, the changing room and a bar if you're lucky. And it'll give me time to think about what it is that I'm going to do next. For the last couple of years the prospect has been slithering around the back of my brain. When I was with Wellington the player development programme was still optional, and I took the easy option. ('Better people make better players' was the slogan. I'm not sure if the reverse is true.) To coach in France I have to do a course which, by all accounts, is quite tough, and I don't seem to have got round to it yet. Anyway, no rush: while the sun shines, I am making good hay. Some of it seems to drift away

— Ali, a few bad investments, some dumb toys — but I should have a reasonable stack by the time I've finished here in France. I'm negotiating with the club for another couple of seasons at the moment.

My phone rings. Rich's name blinks up on the screen. I let it ring through. 'Do we want to go out? It's just after nine.'

'Let's stick to us. I haven't finished with you yet.'

The phone rings again. Rich again. I feel obliged to pick up. 'Bruce Wayne's office.'

'You low-breed, you screened me!' The noise of a bar in the background.

'Nah, I was doing something.' I walk over to the window and look out at the lights of passing cars.

'Something Brazilian, was it?'

'I don't know what you're talking about.'

'Yeah, right. So where are you? We're moving on in about ten minutes.'

'I'm not sure that we're going to make it. My ankle's playing up.' Not entirely true — I remembered the anti-inflams this time.

'You'll get over it. Come on, all the boys are out tonight.'

'It's not happening, mate.'

'All right, just give Miss Brazil the address and pop her in a cab. I'll take it from there.'

'Rachel's pretty busy nursing me back to health.'

'I fucking bet she is. You're a very sick individual. Tell her to watch out for herself.'

'Count on it.'

The champagne bottle still has dew on it. It's more than half-full.

* * *

I wake just before the alarm goes off, hitting the button a second after it beeps. Rachel sleeps through it, lying with her back to me, her tattoo completely exposed. From the cleft at the base of her spine an Asian dragon coils up her back, a surprisingly bright blue with a red belly, whiskers and a flaming pearl beneath its chin. It doesn't look evil; mind you, it doesn't look all that friendly either. I reach out and lightly trace the lines of ink across her flesh. The vibrant colours, her warm olive skin and mane of dark hair spread across the pillow are a welcome invasion in the bright hospital-white of my bedroom. She half-turns her head to look at me, smiles sleepily and then rolls her head back. 'Mmmh. Keep doing that.' A few minutes later she purrs and, arching up towards me as I push myself inside her, reaches for a pillow to wedge it under herself. Looking into those soft grey eyes, connecting them with this delicious, melting friction, I feel positively blessed.

Later, my Sunday-morning routine brilliantly shattered, I am late for the recovery session. I promise to bring Rachel back a couple of croissants. She needs to use my computer — apparently her BlackBerry isn't working for emails. I lock the door from habit, then realise that this will lock her in, so I unlock it again. For a second I wonder about the wisdom of leaving her inside — it's not as if I know her that well — then shake it off. I can't think of anyone I'd rather have waiting for me at home. I have a fleeting vision of coupledom: 'Hi, honey . . .'

The doc and Christophe play out their roles in the medical room with the same result as the week before, and I'm not complaining. The ankle is manageable, and I can stand taking a couple of days off if Rachel is around. In the hallway I bail Christophe up about my contract. I signed for two years initially, but at the end of the first year they gave me a raise and signed me for two plus one which means the plus one will come into effect next season. I'm keen to sign for another two years for another raise — knowing that I'll need an op in the off-season, it's not the moment to be tarting myself around — and my agent reckons it should be fine, but they still haven't come up with an offer. He says that I need to talk to the president. Something in his manner tells me that it isn't the done deal that it should be.

There are a few cracks from the boys at the pool, nothing too serious. Eric, who can never judge a moment quite right, tells everyone that 'Fucking is good recovery', but even though I scowl at him for overstepping I laugh along with the boys. In a funny sort of a way I think they're quite happy for me. Sarah's been gone for a long time now, and apart from one horrific one-night stand — I was so nervous about closing the deal that I overdid the booze and when the athletic part of the evening arrived it was like trying to push a marshmallow into a moneybox — I haven't had a lot of female company. There's plenty of it around, though: there's a swingers club in the centre of town where we can get in for free, and some of the boys make good use of it. I've been a couple of times for a laugh — guys getting looked after on the edge of the dancefloor, bodies piled on top of each other in booths, red velvet upholstery, dark wood and porn everywhere. Sixteen euros for a bottle of Heineken. Call me old-fashioned, but it's not my scene. One of the club sponsors has these legendary parties: six guys, six girls ('models'), invitation only. Everyone gets stuck into the booze and whatever else is on offer, then it slips into something more comfortable. The kicker is that, at the end of the night, you get invited through to the master bedroom where the man of the house — with hands-on assistance from the 'models' — is waiting to blow your mind. You don't have to go, but don't expect another invitation if you cry off. He has a rich friend, even more twisted, who puts on his own very exclusive soirées, complete with 'models' and extras. Apparently the guy likes to get smacked around. Titi brought in a mate from out of town who got a bit fired up at all this decadence and didn't quite understand the rules. Party host ended up with a broken jaw. Anyway, as I say, not really my scene. It's not so much that it's sifty — I don't have any problems with that — it just seems so needy.

After the pool, as I'm waiting in line for the croissants and enjoying a review of yesterday's events I remember Diesel's story about the Fibber and look up the Fibonacci bloke myself. The other thing he brought back from the east was this sequence of numbers. You start off with 0 and 1, you get 1. Then you take the last number and the new number: 1 and 1, so 2. 2 and 1, you get 3, 3 and 2 become 5 then 8, 13, 21, 34 . . . If you plot it on paper and join the dots it becomes a spiral, a shape that replicates itself permanently, widening out in an ever-growing swirl as the past and the present predict the future.

When I get home, Rachel is in good form. Some bloke she knows put a stack of cash on our game on the grounds that I told her we'd win easily and had himself a tidy payday. He's going to send us a little thank-you present. Better still, she's spoken to her boss, and been told she can take the week off in Paris if she does a couple of restaurant reviews. The one condition was that they wouldn't pay for a hotel all week; gentleman that I am, I offer to take her in.

Chapter 12

When I get home on Monday afternoon there is a note from the concierge in my letterbox: I have a parcel to pick up from her. I guess it will be the tapes from Ali. I knock at the concierge's door — she's been pretty frosty since we had a piss-up in the flat a month ago, and the neighbours whined about it. I guess it was quite late on a Tuesday night, and towards the end Josh had AC/DC going full bore on the stereo. She hands over the packet, not looking any friendlier. It's not the tapes — it's about the right size but it's a FedEx package from London. I rip it open in the lift. A white cardboard sleeve slides off to reveal a thick cream cardboard box with a gold embossed crown on it. I take the lid off the cardboard box to find another box, this one in green leather, again with the gold crown. I've seen the crown before, but I can't remember where. The box flips open to reveal a steel watch with a purple face set in plush cream material. A small silver version of the crown is at twelve o'clock. Underneath it, in capitals, ROLEX. This must be the thank-you from Rachel's friend. I wonder if it's real. I pick up the package; inside there's a note on expensive-looking blue paper. Handwritten, in black ink: 'With thanks and best wishes, Philip.'

I don't know what to think. Assuming the watch isn't a fake, it has to be the most expensive thing anyone has ever given me by a distance. I wouldn't know what a Rolex is worth, but it has to be north of a couple of grand. At the same time, I couldn't possibly wear it.

Rachel is curled up on the sofa with her laptop. I hold up the watch, which is surprisingly heavy. 'Is your mate called Philip?' She stretches out a hand to take it.

'Wow, Philip sent you a Rolex! He's very generous. He can afford it, of course.'

'Who the hell is this guy? When you said he was going to send a present, I was thinking more along the lines of a bottle of Jack Daniel's. This is a bit much, isn't it?'

'I told you, he made a lot of money thanks to you. He loves his rugby, you know. He was the one who suggested that I do a story on you. He said you were under-rated but he thinks you're brilliant.'

'Sounds like a man who knows what he's talking about. What's his deal, though? Where did he get all his money? He must have put a bloody big bet on to be dishing out goodies like this.'

'He's in finance. He works out of London, but he has concerns all over the world. He loves gambling, and I suppose that when you're worth as much as he is, it's only fun if you make it interesting. He would have liked being able to make an intelligent bet. You made it intelligent, he won and he's grateful. I wouldn't be too flattered by the watch — it's spare change for him.'

'Yeah, well, next time you can tell him not to bother with the fancy timepiece. I couldn't wear this. Can you imagine what the boys would say?'

'You care that much about what the boys say?'

'They know purple's not my colour. Anyway, I've got my Granddad's watch.' It's nothing special — it must be fifty years old, loses a couple of minutes every day, I have to wind it and it cost me ninety euros to get it fixed a year ago — but it is my

Granddad's. 'Honestly, I'd feel like an idiot. I'm just a country boy. I don't do bling.'

'So put it away for when you grow up. Or sell it.'

The thought had crossed my mind. It's a bit rough though, flogging a present. We got a whole lot of handouts last season of base-layer compression gear ('For free!' as Rich likes to say, not even half-joking) that we were to use mainly for training from one of the sponsors — there was far more than we needed, so Josh rounded up the excess, sold it over the internet and divvied up the proceeds. We made about three hundred euros each. Strictly speaking, they weren't really presents and anyway, you don't feel quite so bad when everyone else is doing it but I hope the sponsor didn't find out. No one said anything, but we didn't get as much stuff this year.

I try the watch on. There's a nice heft to it, a reassuring solidity. My arm feels more substantial. I take it off to look at it more closely. The second hand sweeps smoothly around under the thick crystal. I really don't do bling, but even I can see that it is a beautiful object.

'How much do you think it's worth? It is real, isn't it?'

'Of course it's real. Philip wouldn't send you a fake. I don't know — three thousand, maybe five thousand euros? Maybe more?'

I'll run my own little investigation on the internet later on. I don't want to look too cheap in front of Rachel. For the moment, I walk through to the bedroom and put the green leather box in the drawer where I keep my championship medals.

'So how do you know this Philip bloke?'

'We met through friends in London. A girlfriend of mine used to go out with him.'

'How old is he?'

'Forties. Late forties, I guess.'

'Dirty old man. What are you doing hanging around with people like that?'

'I have a lot of different friends.'

I want to ask her if she's slept with him. She isn't easy to read, but her eyes are sliding all over the place and I'm not sure I'm getting everything here. Her past isn't really my business though, is it.

'So who are you guys playing this weekend?'

We're away again. 'The Basques. At theirs.'

'Are they any good?'

'Not bad.'

'Will you win?'

'We'll struggle. There'll be some rotation and it's not a game that we really need. Their home crowd are nuts, so they always get up for home games and their pack is awesome. You need to go down there with a mission or get very lucky. We're not on a mission and they need it so I can't see us getting lucky. So no, I don't think we'll win.' With a bit of luck I won't even be on the team sheet.

'Is that a prediction?'

'You mean, would I put your rich friend's money on it?'

She giggles. 'Would you?'

'Well, yeah. It's not my money.'

'What if it was?'

'What do you mean? Buggered if I'm betting any of my money against Rolexman. His powers are greater than mine. As far as coin goes, anyway. I have other strengths.' I make a lunge for her, but she bats away my paws and sits up.

'No, dummy — why don't you start up a partnership with him?'

'How would that work? He gives me a present every time we

win? I can live with that.' I make another lunge. She allows me a little more success this time, then pushes me away, lights a cigarette and walks over to examine her make-up in the mirror over the fireplace. 'You could tell him what you think about a game, what the opposition are like, how your team feels — that kind of thing. If he can make an intelligent bet, I'm sure he'd pay you for it.'

She does have a dirty mind. I quite like it. 'More than a Rolex?' Our eyes meet in the mirror. She turns to face me. 'It would depend on what the information was like. I would say he could pay much more than a Rolex — if he trusted you.'

'What's in it for you? I mean, I know I'm a sweet ride, but why are you pimping for me?'

'Philip can afford to be generous. If it works, he won't forget me.'

A pause. 'Wouldn't it be a bit like insider trading?'

'How could it? You don't know what's going to happen, you're just making an educated guess. It's more like normal trading. I wouldn't tell everybody, if I were you, but you're not doing anything wrong.'

'I'm not sure the people he's betting against would agree.'

'Everyone's looking for an angle, Mark. I'm sure someone else is doing the same thing. I was just thinking it could help you out. If you don't think you can do it, let's forget about it.'

'You shameless bitch! Of course I *can* do it, I'm just wondering whether I would want to. Anyway, there's no guarantee your mate would be interested.'

'I'll call him.'

'Do it later. I've got something else you need to take care of first.'

* * *

Around five, Rachel leaves a message for Philip to call her back. In the evening we go to one of the restaurants she has to review for her paper. It's up the hill on Montmartre, in a building next to a windmill. The area is all cobbled streets, photo opportunities and tourist traps, but it's winter so we don't have to fight our way through the crowds that were here last time I came. It's early too, and Monday nights are quiet. After dinner we walk over to the basilica of Sacré Coeur, the white stone curves of arches and domes proudly picked out by floodlights. Inside, a handful of the faithful are bunched towards the front, where a priest is officiating while rubberneckers like us — who outnumber the congregation two to one — wander around whispering and pointing out mosaics and paintings and so on.

A woman reads the parable of the talents: the story about the master who goes away and entrusts his three servants with some of his gold. The first two invest it; the third bloke buries his for safekeeping. When the master returns, he wants to know what's happened with his loot. The investors have doubled their money, making their boss very happy. The poor digger, who must have been leery about anything offering such a high rate of return (I put eighty thousand Kiwi in a building society that promised only ten per cent net and lost the lot, so I know how he feels) hands back the original sum and gets sacked for being too cautious. You'd like to think there's a twist, that God will come down and smite the moneybags for wrongful dismissal or, at the very least, offer the unemployed man a job. Instead, he gets cast into the darkness, and everyone seems fine with it because he wasn't looking for an angle.

Despite the good acoustics and the best efforts of the priest who leads it, the hymn that follows rings tinny: there are too few of them singing, the sound falls away and is quickly lost, too weak to resonate in that vast space.

Outside, I put an arm around Rachel and pull her to me in the cold air. We cross the road to the top of the steps that rake steeply down back into the city and look out over Paris stretching away south into the horizon. Over the tips of the trees to our right, the beam of the searchlight at the top of the Eiffel Tower sweeps through the blackness.

Next to us, a group of young Americans have just been ripped off buying hash and are discussing — loudly — what to do about it.

Chapter 13

Rachel is out when I get home on Tuesday. There's another package. This time it's the tapes, along with a couple of pages of newsprint neatly folded over. On one side, details of a ram sale in Feilding and a by-election in Pahiatua. At the top of the other, a headline: 'A Trip to the Somme'. Underneath this, 'A Mastertonian's Experience'. The typesetting looks dated as you would expect, but the paper is in surprisingly good nick — it must be nearly a hundred years old.

* * *

Rifleman Benjamin Stevens, of Masterton, writes the following interesting letter to his father, Mr LJ Stevens of Masterton:

Signallers Dugout, 'Somewhere in France', October 1916.

It is just a year to the day since I left Wairere; a year tomorrow since we marched up Lineola road to the strains of Tipperary and later in the day made our first acquaintance with Trentham. Four months training and eight months since we left New Zealand to come fourteen thousand miles around the world. We feel quite like veterans.

I was talking to one of ours just back from hospital the other day who was wounded at the Somme. He said that when he got to hospital the nurse asked him how long it was since he had a shave. Said he, 'Three weeks and three days.' 'Oh,' she said, 'and how long is it since you had a wash?' A little reckoning computed it at three weeks to a day. 'How long is it since you had a bath?' That was a poser, but it was close on two mouths since we had left the place where we were some months. 'How long did it take you to reach the Somme?' 'Four or five weeks — we walked most of the way in easy stages.'

It was an English nurse in a Tommy hospital, and it gave her a different view of things, for she said her impression had always been that the New Zealand troops got the best of everything. Talking about this reminds me that when coming back from the Somme a draft of reinforcements joined us up; we travelled back in one of these luxurious railway cars labelled 'Hommes 40 Chevaux 8'. Our first job was to clean it up after the late tenants, the chevaux (fact), and then I for one spent a comfortable night with a roof overhead, but next morning there were plenty of groans and 'hadn't slept a wink'.

Jim Cran, a Scotch boy, who used to drive the Tupurupuru car, was killed here — a fine Scotch boy, and a great friend of Peter and Bob. It was Jim who took the photo of us bathing in the Suez Canal. Three good Scotch fellows, all from Tupurupuru, clean, straight men — they all lie within a mile of each other.

Stewart Menzies and I were together till now (he was lance-corporal of the Signallers), and as we went down a small slope just outside the town of Flers, he sat down under a willow tree for a spell, and Casey, Bob Gibson and I in a shell hole a chain away. Suddenly a big shell burst almost beside him, and a tiny splinter killed him, piercing him from temple to temple. We kept on moving, and Mr Harrison passed a message along that he would go back to the village and try and get reinforcements. We waited for half an hour, and not a man in sight.

We collected in a big shell hole, eight of us, and talked the matter over. We were on a tongue of land running out from the village on the same level. In front of us was a gully, say, forty feet deep which came up from the right of the village and wound away to our left. It did not have a commanding position, Flers being rather lower than the surrounding country. So we decided to make back round the village, for at least one machine gun had got into position opposite us. We made for the ruined hedge in ones and twos, and when we were all on our feet the machine gunner got to work. Bob Gibson was the last of us, and when the gun opened he coolly turned round and tried to locate it. A bullet hit him in the abdomen. I was next to him, and he just gave one shout to me — a shout of surprise it seemed to me, for he suffered no pain and was dead when I reached him. Casey and I did what little we could, then went on with the others, and made a half circle of the village. We joined up with the rest of our company. Reorganised, we went through the village again and dug in along the edge of the tongue I spoke of, passing by poor Bob as we went out again. It took us till dark to dig in, and snipers were a little troublesome during the afternoon.

Just at dark the battalion on our right which had come up and joined us when we had dug in received orders to retire. This must have been a mistake, for it left us unsupported on our right, and as the Londoners had been held up in High Wood that morning, and did not get up till late at night, we were unsupported to a certain extent on the left also; so that the New Zealanders deserve every credit for holding Flers. Lieutenant Mackay, who, with Lieutenant Harrison, were the only officers left to our company, asked the Tommy officer for a quarter of an hour; but he said he had orders to go — and went. It was a dismal sight to see them filing away down their trench into the dusk; it looked as if we would have to retire also, and Casey broke into very fluent speech, for we had been digging hard all the afternoon. When every shovelful promises perhaps a little more safety, a bit of extra sweat does not count, but it was apparently all for nothing, and Casey set his shovel up in front and scarcely repeated himself for a minute. Lieutenant Mackay went along to consult another officer. It certainly looked as if we must retire in conformity with the others, but presently he came back and said we would stick to it. So Casey and I took up our shovels again, and there was some more swearing, for it looked a bit of a forlorn hope; but a few machine guns came up and took up positions by us, so we went on digging. Fortunately the night was absolutely calm; Fritz was evidently shifting some of his guns into safer positions, and left us alone. High Wood is a battered and forlorn-looking place that reminded me somewhat of the bit of white pine bush at Robert Johnston's.

Our ration parties came up during the night and brought us food and water, the water in oblong two-gallon benzine tins that tasted strongly of benzine still. Next morning the word was passed along that one of the other New Zealand Brigades was going over at a certain time, and about nine o'clock we saw the Tommies on our right coming up in great numbers, advancing, a number of them coming up a rolling gully to the right of the village, like, say, the Waipoua river bed. They were not being fired upon, apparently being out of sight of Fritz. Just then four Fritz aeroplanes came over, and the nearest one dived straight down at them and opened a smart fire with a machine gun and then came on over us and dropped a smoke bomb for the artillery over our corner. Casey and I were within two chains of the corner, and knew pretty well what would happen. Fritz opened up with his guns and the peaceful night promised to be succeeded by a very busy morning. Waves of advancing Tommies came through the village behind us in line with those farther out on our right, for the previous afternoon we had dug in on their sector, for that seemed to be the best method of defending the village. Our job now was to sit tight, and they advanced over us and dug in some distance ahead. The afternoon was fairly restful compared to the morning, though Fritz had the range of our trench with his 5.9s. By this time Casey and I (I write as if we were the only ones there, but I merely wish to give you our impressions) were beginning to look forward to being relieved, but ration parties came round again at dusk, and it looked as though we would not be relieved that night. We (Casey and I) went over and buried Bob Gibson, who was lying between us and the village. He was looking quite peaceful, and we put his name on a piece of cardboard and a stick at the head of the grave — all we had to mark the grave with: and I said what little of the burial service I could remember. Later on we went out with others and got the pay-books of some of those who fell the first day in front of our present line, and we got four and took little mementoes, note books, etc. They were buried a couple of days later by our chaplain.

About midnight we were relieved by one of our other brigades, and when we got back to the dressing station found there were still some of our wounded to be carried back, and all hands set to carry them back. We and two others carried Sid Fearon back, and a long carry it seemed, for we had but little sleep in the previous forty-eight hours, and not too much to eat. When we got to the dressing station we were told that a shell had killed Dr Bogle about five or ten minutes previously: and we had not got far with Fearon in the pitch darkness when a shell landed alongside the track about a chain to the right. A clod of dirt hit me on the puttee, and a man beside me said he was hit on the mouth, but it turned out to be with dirt, too. Fearon had a rough trip for the next couple of hundred yards, for Fritz dropped half a dozen in search before we got clear of that small zone — evidently he knew that track would be in steady use all night. Presently the road led us past Delville Wood, and we found the Second Battalion field cookers serving out hot stew and rum; so I gave the old familiar whistle, and, sure enough, Hubert was there and answered. He got me some hot soup for Fearon, and then we pushed on again and landed him at the green dump; from there we had to find our own travelling cookers, and when we did found plenty to eat and drink, for our numbers were now so small — food had been drawn for double our number.

Monday morning was still wet, and there was a discomfiting rumour that we might have to go into it again. We thought that having been into it once we were finished; little did we think we were there for another fortnight. Orders came out that we were to relieve one of our other brigades that evening and we cruised about in the wet getting our various gears together. We were told we were to get our overcoats, and they arrived about tea-time. A bird in the hand is usually worth two elsewhere, so we finished our tea and then went for our coats. I had some clothing rolled in mine, and arrived in time to see a jersey going in one direction, a coat in another, and underpants in a third. A rescue was effected, and presently we fell in to march away. We marched about a hundred yards and then found we had reached our position. The dug-outs we had just come out of were part of a long line captured from Fritz, and not uncomfortable, but now—! We were marched on a road three or four inches deep in mud and told, 'Make yourselves as comfortable as you can; we sleep here tonight.' Imagine the Northern Approach after a two days' flood and a big stock sale — three inches deep in mud wherever one tried to stand, and picture one's feelings on being told to sleep there for the night. Transport wagons were going and coming all night, splashing mud everywhere. A tot (not a lot) of rum was served out, and the army had washed its hands of us for the night, except we might be called upon any hour or minute.

Casey and I did some hard thinking. The dug-outs behind us had been filled by men relieved by our other companies, so they were no good to us. A few odd places there were and artillery dug-outs, and in ten minutes Casey and I had been round the lot: had alternately poked our heads in and asked, 'Any room, cobber?' and trying in vain to recognise some of the faces of those who were fortunate enough to be by the firelight. A grand circle brought us back to where we started; most of our company had by this time started digging holes in the ground to get out of the wind; already they were wet through, so did not trouble about the rain. The idea of nowhere to lay our heads did not appeal to Casey and your third son. This time I made for a built-up place that had a good fire in it, and courteously asked permission for a dry spot to change my clothes, holding out as evidence the rescued jersey, etc. I have noticed often that the best-hearted people are those who have had the best luck in collecting the wherewithal to burn, or shown the most energy in gathering (I am not moralising); so I got a place by the fire from them, and presently was told that they were Second Brigade men assisting the transport. They smoked nearly all my cigarettes before they asked me if I had a place to sleep in but once they did that I was safe, and a few minutes afterwards I was able to go outside and find Casey. We slept well that night, for did we not have overcoats and a roof that only dripped here and there?

About one o'clock they called for a fatigue party, and, glad to be doing something, away we went. The job was to carry string 8 by 4 planks from the dump right up to a place behind Flers, nearly two miles, if not more. Presently we got to where Fritz could see us plainly, so we had to get into a trench called 'Fish Alley', and a suitable name, too. There were no duck-boards in the bottom. We did not have to swim, but plough through the mud knee-deep. Fortunately I had wound sandbags over my puttees but the mud and slush was pretty bad. Fritz did not get a single shell on to us, though some artillery observation officers indulged in some prophecies as we passed — so for that matter did Casey and I prophesy, but we got home again to our good fire and slept another good night's sleep.

Next day we had to go up into support lines, and about four o'clock we started off to relieve one of our other brigades. We took the same line as we had done on fatigue the previous day; but the long lines of us were too tempting for Fritz, and a burst of shrapnel on our right sent the word along to get into the trench (up till now we had been walking along the top), so once more we jumped down into the knee-deep mud, and just as we did the first salvo burst over us — four shrapnels, for the first one had given the range. Peter Clark was in front of me, Casey behind me. Peter had a hole in his overcoat and a stinging arm, but he was carrying so much gear I could not see what damage was done, so he decided to go on. We went on a bit and then missed Casey. It seems he had got a shrapnel in the arm, and as soon as he was sure it was bleeding made off for the dressing station. 'Backsheesh!' he told Sergeant Blackman as he passed, and laughed outright.

As I write this it is 11.15 p.m., and now quite a few days since I started this. It is freezing outside and foggy, and I can hear an aeroplane steadily circling overhead, the whirr of the propeller alternately becoming louder and then fading away. On looking at Peter Clark's arm it showed that a shrapnel bullet had grazed it, making a black bruise which bled slightly; the sergeant sent him back to the dressing station, for blood poisoning is not to be trifled with, but the doctor sent him back to us, saying every man was wanted. Next day I may say Peter's arm was black and blue for a space I could just cover with my hand, but the doctor still could not send him out. Casey's bit of shrapnel had just penetrated the skin, making a small furrow its own size; and just think what luck he had, for he has not yet returned from the convalescent camp, and Peter lies buried near Eaucourt l'Abbaye.

From now on Peter Clark and I slept and worked together. He was a sniper and I was a signaller, but as there was no specialist work to be done, we carried a short-handled shovel apiece in addition to our rifles. Next day we went down to the big dump for rations, etc., and when we got back found a gas shell had affected our last two officers on hand — there are usually some kept in reserve — so our CO came up in charge, and that night we moved up into Flers village again not long after dark, and Peter and I occupied an old German dug-out in what they called the sunken road in Flers. It was late in the evening when we got settled down; almost to the knees in mud and slush as we had been, this dugout about five or six feet underground was dry: but hardly had we got settled when, about 11 p.m., all hands were ordered out to work. We were the reserve company of our battalion, and the other companies were holding the front line. A communication trench was wanted; the previous night it had been dug to within 150 yards of the front line, so we went up to finish it. Each man had 1½ yards to dig four feet down, and —

the usual bait held out to a fatigue party — when it was done we could go home again. But Fritz had not been blind during the day. We dug down a bit, but Peter's arm was sore, and I was very tired, so after going down about a spit, we sat down, in the fond hope, I suppose, that some fairy would finish it. But no; others were getting almost knee-deep when bang, crack, went a shrapnel shell beside us, just as we stepped in to resume work. I have never been averse to taking hints, and I wondered what that shrapnel was if it was not a hint.

Before Peter and I had time to exchange views on it the storm burst. We had been discussing matters in true navvy style, head to head and shovel at ease, and on the instant down we went, head to head, and strangely enough our boots both encountered obstacles — other steel helmets which had been about as quick as we had in getting down. Each man had only four feet six to dig, and I am six feet in my boots, and Peter not far short of it. The minute before, we had decided four feet six was far too much for any man to dig, but in that moment we had decided it was far too little. We had dug in a bare foot, and here was the Hun firing salvos of whizz-bangs four at a time. It was pitch dark, of course, but he had the range to a nicety, and at the bottom end of my four feet six was a steel helmet, so that I could not get my feet down the narrow trench. As the second salvo burst and my posterior was still projecting, I put in a mighty heave that put my feet beneath the steel helmet, and it seemed as if the whole German army was gunning for the seat of my trousers; but the next man neatly burrowed his head beneath my feet, and so, packed like sandwiches, we lay. No man who was in that little trench that night will have forgotten it yet, nor will he ever forget it. Salvo after salvo burst, all whizz-bang explosives — had he sent shrapnel he must have caught some. There were three flashes in particular that seemed very close, and covered Peter and I with dirt. There must have been about fifteen or twenty salvos in, say, five or ten minutes, and then quiet reigned again. The word was passed, 'Any casualties?' and, strange to relate, there was not one, and we resumed work. Gone was that tired feeling that oppressed me, and Peter's sore arm did not get a hearing. It was dig, dig, dig, and we sweated and raced to get to safety. When we got down to two feet six sure enough Fritz put on an encore but by this time the loose earth we had thrown out was a foot high, so we had nearly four feet of cover, and felt more at ease. We finished the job in record time, and strung off back to the village.

Peter and I put up a couple of oilsheets in the trench for our little bivouac, and made ourselves as comfortable as possible, and the parcel mail and the tot of rum supplied the inner man. We only had the clothes we stood up in, except an oil sheet, and it is often a job to know on a wet night whether to put the one oil sheet above or below you. Experience, however, sides with putting it over one in the rain, provided you can get a bit of board or such like to keep yourself out of the mud. That night the rain came down harder still, and the cold wakened me. Having a spare bit of candle I read all my letters through and through and by that time was tired enough to sleep off again.

The next night we were awakened by heavy shells landing near us. Fritz was trying for a battery with one gun, say a 5.9 by the hole it made. We were between two batteries. He fortunately was missing both, but was coming unpleasantly near us. We went to sleep again, but towards morning Fritz woke us again; a bit nearer this time, a bit farther off the battery. It is not the nicest thing in the world to be awakened by a man pulling a lanyard four or five miles away, with the intention of murdering you in your sleep. I do not know much about artillery, but when only one gun is firing he usually has a certain area or arc of fire which he traverses and re-traverses. We were certainly in that gentleman's arc. He was putting in a shell about every two or three minutes; so we decided to go to someone else's arc for a constitutional, and went, not unaccompanied, either, though when day broke shortly after and we returned all had a few souvenirs. Where we slept had been the scene of deadly fighting, and many a tartan kilt or pair of Hun jackboots were littered about — this was in a line between High Wood and Delville Wood. I had a sandbag full of various Hun odds and ends, but, though they got as far as Abbeville, coming back they got into other hands.

And then, on the night of October 1st, we moved forward once again, for the last time. We slept in front of Flers, and next morning moved up and relieved the Second Brigade, who the previous day had gone forward again and won more territory.

Altogether our division had gone 'over the top' about six or seven times, achieving their objective each time, though the first rush on the 15th had gained the most ground.

This day, October 2nd, it was raining, and the trench we went into was in a crumbling state from heavy shelling, and we were not allowed to dig because of giving away our position. As we went into the trench some behind us were drafted into a strong post behind the line. Peter and I just missed that. On such small things does fate hang. He and I could not get a hole to hold us both and took separate holes side by side. About 1.30 p.m. a shell from the right came down the trench. Peter got a small piece in the throat. We did our best, but he was gone in a couple of minutes. I soon got bound up and went back to the dressing station — bled pretty freely, but no depth of wound.

* * *

A thick black line marks the end of the final column.

He finished that letter just a few hours after the shell came down their trench. It was carried away from the front line, made it all the way back home, was read by my great-grandfather, passed on to the local paper as being 'interesting', cut out and kept safe by some unseen hand, nearly binned by Ali and has now come all the way back around the world into my possession, an hour or two's drive from where the words were originally set down a century ago. All those friends, dead in the space of a month. I read the last paragraph again. I want to be able to pull some kind of deeper meaning out of this tiny episode in the life of a man whose blood runs through me. 'On such small things does fate hang.' If this is one of those things, I don't want to miss it. I've never seen the photograph, but I can imagine a couple of mates splashing about in Egyptian water, then posing for a souvenir for the folks at home while thinking what a bloody great adventure it all was. I can see him scrounging a decent place to sleep for the night away from the mud and the rain, exchanging a happy grin with his mate at their good management even though any illusions about the great adventure must have been long gone by then. I want to picture what it must have been like to try to hold your mate's throat together as he dies in front of your eyes while your own body has a hole in it thanks to shrapnel from the same shell, but I can't get a hold on it, it's too much.

I try it with different faces: Rich, JT, my own; each time the image slips away, refuses to form in my mind. Instead I get only splashes of half-remembered war movies or horror flicks that won't do it justice. I should be grateful that my imagination can't stretch to this, but what I really feel is closer to jealousy. I know that thirty seconds in the trenches would have been enough for a lifetime, and yet I can't help thinking that my grandfather was lucky to have gone through this. He was twenty at the time — I think of the fresh-faced kids in our junior team — and had already confronted the void that lurks unsaid in front of us all, reduced it to a clipped phrase: 'We did our best but he was gone in a couple of minutes.' I guess he had to clip it just to survive. He didn't know it then but there were another two years at the front ahead, during which he must have lived the same thing over and over again, inflicted it on others, feared it for himself — perhaps he even hoped for it secretly.

Rugby players are held up as real men, but when we talk of sacrifice and death in hushed, urgent whispers it concerns nothing more than keeping the ball alive or defending a goal-line, the wilful illusion of deep seriousness that make-believe can produce in a changing room. You might get a bit battered, sure, but the end of everything is unlikely to hurtle in from stage right. I read the letter for a third time, still hoping that it will give me some deeper insight. Is there a right way of looking at this, an angle that will let me see a hidden pattern in a certain light? A kind of X-ray, or a hologram visible to the initiated? If there is a message, I can't see it. It's just something that happened.

I look at the tapes in my hand, three C60s with 'Oral History Archive: Benjamin Stevens, April 2, 1980' handwritten in black ink along the spines, numbered 1, 2 and 3. Maybe they have something for me. All three of them together are roughly the same size and weight as yesterday's Rolex when it was in its chunky pass-the-parcel box. I want to ring Ali to see if she read the clipping, but by now it's well after midnight at home.

I call Rachel to see where she is. I'd like to listen to the tapes in private, but I only have the stereo. It goes through to her answerphone, but she calls me back immediately. She's just a few minutes away. For the first time since I met her, I wish she wasn't going to be around quite so soon. I make myself a coffee and sit down with Granddad's letter again. He was a tough old bastard by all accounts, and randy with it — eight kids — although I guess there probably wasn't that much else to do once you got in off the farm of an evening before TV arrived, and no one had got around to inventing the pill yet. My grandmother was his second wife — the first one died delivering their fifth child — and Dad was number two of the second brood, born when the old man was already fifty. He ended up managing someone else's farm. Dad always said that was a waste of time, working fourteen-hour days to make a rich man even richer, but the life must have agreed with him — he made it to ninety-five. Dad was only sixty-one when he carked it. I was too young to remember much about Granddad, but he was pretty lively up until the end. He got rid of the stammer that had prevented him from making officer by quoting long screeds of Shakespeare to the sheep, who weren't going to laugh at him if he couldn't get something out. When I was about seven he took me out eeling one night at a bend in the creek at the back of his house; with his bald head that poked out over his chest, wrinkled skin and slow, precise shuffle he made me think of an ancient tortoise. I carried the plastic bag of sheep guts that we used to throw into the water to draw the fat, slippery creatures out of the mud towards our hook. As we walked, he pointed the torch at the ground and drew it in a line alongside him, behind him and in front, never holding it still. 'This is the way we used to walk in the trenches at night.'

Like most seven-year-old boys I used to think war was a great invention. Camping out, firearms, endless opportunities for bravery. I knew there was a downside, but the war comics that were the bedrock of my knowledge tended to gloss over it. I was slightly in awe of the old man and his war, but since he'd brought it up I asked the question that I'd been bursting with ever since I'd discovered he'd fought in one. 'Did you kill many Germans?'

We walked on in silence for a bit. Mum had told me that I wasn't supposed to ask about the war, but I knew this was ridiculous, the kind of thing mothers say because they are more concerned about good manners than the free exchange of information. Anyone who'd been in something like that must have some great stories that they would want to tell — you'd have had trouble shutting me up if I'd killed any Germans. The silence dragged on. I started to wonder if he'd heard the question.

Finally there was a grunt. 'Some. I killed some Germans.'

I had planned a follow-up question, 'So what was that like?', but I decided not to push my luck.

Chapter 14

'I spoke to Philip. He likes the idea. Let me know when the team gets announced how you think they'll go.' Rachel isn't letting go of her little brainwave. I don't suppose there's anything wrong with it, but I can't help feeling I'm being manipulated. I'd like to unsettle her, see how she reacts off balance.

'How I think *we'll* go.'

'I thought you said you didn't think you'd be playing. Anyway, he puts up the capital and he'll give you thirty per cent of any winnings.'

'It might not work, you know.'

'We won't know until we try, will we, baby?' Baby? Jesus. She moves closer to me, puts her hand on my arm and I tense the muscle reflexively. All those weight-training programmes have to be good for something. She opens her eyes wide, mocking. 'So strong!'

I feel like a dick. 'Hold on, how am I to know what thirty per cent is worth? He might be creaming it. I'm the one doing the work.'

'Do you want to take a share of any losses as well? If you were prepared to be a full partner with your own money . . .'

'All right, point taken. I don't suppose there's any point in arguing about percentage. Your Philip'll give me what he wants to keep me sweet.' Another hard-fought negotiation where I end up getting screwed. I always seem to get outmanoeuvred by anyone who knows what they're doing. Which leads me to wonder . . .

'So what's your cut?'

Hesitation. She looks away. Finally, the dragon lady who doubles as the ice-cream girl is off balance. 'We haven't decided that yet.'

'Oh, come *on*. Don't expect me to believe that you've got this whole thing sewn up without getting a slice for yourself. Twenty per cent sounds about right, doesn't it?'

'We'll just have to see if it works. If it does, then we all win.'

'So what sort of money is he putting up? Thirty per cent of fuck all isn't worth much.'

'It's a spread bet. The bookmakers work out what the margin between two teams is likely to be, to within three points. Last Saturday you were picked to win by between fourteen and sixteen points. Because of what you told me, he backed you to win by more than that. He laid out a thousand pounds a point — anything under a sixteen-point win, and he would have had to pay out a thousand pounds for every point less than the cut-off. Because you won with twenty-six points to spare, he made ten thousand pounds — a thousand for each point.'

I'm nodding. It does look like easy money.

'If the system works, he can put down quite a lot more, but placing bets like this is complicated, particularly if he wins. He needs to lay it off in a lot of different places so people don't get suspicious. There aren't as many people betting, and they don't bet as much on rugby as they do on football, so big money gets noticed. He might have to lose once or twice to make it look good.'

'So, brushing over the fact that we obviously shouldn't be doing this, because otherwise he wouldn't need to hide—.'

Rachel interrupts. 'Bookies don't like people who win all the time, that's all. If they pick him as someone who always wins, they'll just refuse his bet. It's like counting cards if you're playing blackjack. The house doesn't like it, so they'll turn you away if you're too good. It's not actually illegal.'

'OK. So what sort of end result are we looking at?' I can't help it — the scent of free money has this effect on me.

'It's hard to say. You won't find it easy to pick every game, and you need to be honest with me about that. We'll just have to see how it goes.' A pause. 'But there's no reason why you shouldn't make a hundred thousand euros over the next few months.'

I make around two hundred and fifty thousand a year, but after tax and rent and Ali and the girls and what I live on, I end up with round about a hundred grand in the bank, tops. This is a pretty good scheme.

'I'm going to go to the Picasso exhibition. I might write a piece on it. Do you want to come along? It would be good for you, a workout for your brain now you have all those nice muscles.'

I rise to the bait.

* * *

One of the reasons I came to Paris was that Sarah was so keen to live here — she was a huge fan of the museums and their art. She used to say that what separates us from the animals is this ability to communicate across time and space, using symbols that we understand outside language to take us out of ourselves and see what others have seen and lived and felt. I must have seen every work of art in the Louvre twice with her and, believe me, I felt it. I don't do a lot of museum time on my own. In fact, my visits to museums have always been initiated by girlfriends, actual or prospective. Which means that I spend most of my time trying to find something intelligent to say so that I look like I get it.

Ultimately, the whole performance is about my getting laid. On the basis of what I see here, it wouldn't surprise me if Picasso's motivation for his art ran along similar lines. A big chunk of the exhibition is given over to what is politely referred to as 'erotica'; if he'd made more of an effort — and even I can tell that the man could paint when he wanted to — it would have qualified as porn. Early on I spot a young woman closely examining some etchings of orgy scenes with a furiously straight face; behind her, an older woman, well dressed with a delighted smile as she drinks it all in.

If it's not sex there's a good chance it's death. A sheep skull takes me back to the home kills that we used to do on my uncle's farm. We had had a couple of pet lambs growing up and there were a few tears to start with when I was finally told about what happened to Barry and Barbara, but I got to enjoy watching Uncle Phil wield his knife. Behind the knife, the knowledge of all the weighty decisions and acts that gave him godlike status on his farm: what ram covers which ewes, who gets born, where they go, what they eat and when they die, and all through their lives they're working for him without even really knowing it. The death sentence was commuted to life, or at least suspended for a while, if their instincts were good enough. Each ram would be rigged up with a harness holding a crayon under its belly before they were put to the ewes so the ewes that had been tupped had a coloured mark on their backs — blue for the first cycle, yellow for the second, red for the third. The rams that didn't get through enough ewes would be pensioned off with a blade. The stakes were the same for the ladies: the rams weren't picky but any ewe that was still 'dry' after three cycles was taken out of the mob and ended up as dog tucker. It pays to be romantic if you're a sheep.

When I was eleven I got to do my first kill. The yards were next to a T junction in the lee of a steep hill whose grass was burnt yellow by the middle of summer. The killing shed stood a little off from the woolshed, two small windows covered with thin mesh high up on the sides; in front a spring-loaded door. A few metres away, its own pen where a couple of scraggly-looking flyblown ewes stood warily, trying to avoid my eye as I was sent in to choose a victim while Dad and my uncle leaned on the railings watching. We had sprayed water across the floor to ensure that the blood wouldn't penetrate the unvarnished concrete. Late morning on a hot January day, bright hard light bouncing off the packed earth of the stockyard and the white corrugated iron of the woolshed, the smell of sheepshit, the drone of fat black flies and further away the sound of hooves skittering over wooden slats and dogs barking. I felt nervous and elated.

Eeny-meeny-miny-mo made my choice for me: I preferred to leave the responsibility for which sheep I was going to kill with a higher power. It hadn't been very many years since I used the same technique to decide which of my soft toys would accompany me to bed. I chased the beast around for a couple of minutes unsuccessfully until Uncle Phil leant over and grabbed it with his hairy brown arms. I was slightly out of breath. 'Now wrap your arm around its neck and drag it in on its bum like I showed you.' As I pulled on its neck, the sheep reared up and toppled backwards into me, nearly knocking me over. We shuffled through the gate together, over towards the killing shed. Legs kicked but there was no bleating. Dad held the door open.

'Now lie it on its side. Don't leave it on its tailbone — they hate that. Put your knee in the flank. That's right. Now pull the head back.' I skinned my knuckles on the rough concrete floor as the sheep thrashed, the visible eye rolling, its dirty yellow iris almost wholly obscured by the swollen black pupil.

With a sharp knife and a strong hand, the first blow takes

you through the skin and flesh and sinew and windpipe into the spinal cord. My knife was sharp but I wasn't as steady as I might have been, and the blade scraped along the throat and up towards the jaw. It went home on the second attempt, slicing through the neck from left to right; I hit the carotid and kept going all the way through to the vertebrae and cut the whiteness of the spinal cord despite getting a red squirt in my face. Uncle Phil came over and helped me pull the neck back to break it. I kept my knee in the sheep's flank as the bright arterial blood spurted out across the wet concrete, its head tilted up at a ridiculous angle like one of those front-loading cargo planes, and the nerves made its back feet jangle for a few minutes. I was mesmerised; Dad and Uncle Phil talked about the price of sheepdogs. When it was still, we cut along the legs until the hamstrings were exposed and we could use them to hang it from the rusting hooks, Dad helping me to lift the dead weight. Flies landed and took off.

As we peeled off the pelt, the flat smell of blood and wool and shit was overcome by the high, recognisable scent of sheep meat. Electrical impulses continued to flicker disconcertingly across muscles. The flesh was surprisingly warm. Using the fingers of my left hand to ensure the knife didn't penetrate the guts, I carefully slit down the front of the belly to the brisket, then ripped the grass bag, intestines, liver, lungs, heart, kidneys and whatever else out of the chest cavity and allowed it to slop onto the floor. Uncle Phil separated the grass bag and the intestines out and chucked them in a bucket. 'There's a job for you, Sparky. Push the grass out of the guts and we'll boil the lot up. The dogs love it.' I sat outside on a tree stump forcing undigested grass through the intestines, rinsed them and the grass bag down with the hose while the men cut the carcass into joints and cleaned up.

The choicer pieces of offal and the head went into a foul-smelling cauldron equipped with a timer; the rest, along with the ruby-smeared off-white pelt, went into the even more foul-smelling offal pit. The dozen or so hunks of meat were left to cool before going into the freezer. An hour earlier they had been functioning parts of a living thing. The blood on my hands had felt warm and clean, but now it had dried and my hands and clothes were spattered with red and green and brown, colours that represented things that I didn't really want to think about. I washed my hands under the hose. Uncle Phil pointed at my face — 'Sort that out, mate. We don't want you scaring the ladies' — and I remembered the first spurt that had hit me. I splashed myself and dried off with my shirt, leaving a pinkish stain on the front.

As we drove back into town for lunch, I stared out the window. Dad noticed. 'You OK, Sparky?'

'I was thinking about the sheep.' I had actually been thinking about vegetarianism. I had decided it wouldn't be practical.

'You did bloody well, son. There's no point getting sentimental about it. That's just the way it is.'

* * *

I don't manage to come up with anything clever to say about Picasso — I don't think it's worth bothering Rachel with Barry and Barbara and the killing shed — so I throw out my backup line: 'I'm never quite sure what to think about modern art.' This way the company gets to decide whether they want to pick it up and run with it or drop the whole question and move on to, hopefully, food or sex.

'Mmmh. Let's get some ice cream and go home.' She's good like that. I don't think we'll make it out for drinks with the boys tonight.

Chapter 15

Today is my birthday. Thirty-three years old. I've decided not to mention it to anyone. When I woke up a text message was waiting for me from Ali and the girls, but otherwise it should fly under the radar. You get to a point where birthdays aren't really causes for celebration. I'll buy myself a present.

My ankle doesn't seem to be recovering as well as it has up until now, and this morning the heel is sore as well. I take three anti-inflams instead of the usual two.

Rachel is still in bed. The girl can sleep, no question. The phone rings while I'm having breakfast. It's Tony Stein, also known as the Bamboozler. He's another Aussie who played in France for years and now he's become an agent. Not my agent, but one of the good guys. One of us, anyway.

'The Bamboozler! Whaddya got?' Through a mouthful of muesli and banana.

'Don't be like that, mate. I'm the one who's supposed to ask you what you've got for *me*.'

'I'm happy to have another free lunch with your business mates for the usual.' He dropped five hundred euros, cash, on me a couple of times as an appearance fee for lunch and going to the French games during the Six Nations last year.

'That could be a goer. I'll have to talk to my man about it. But listen, mate, have you got a minute? I've got some, um, good news and bad news for you.'

I stop the spoon halfway to my mouth. 'Bad news first. Always.'

'There might be nothing in it but I was at a do the other night, quietly minding my own business.' Ordinarily, this would raise a laugh from me — you almost have to make an appointment to see the man; he has two mobile phones just to make sure he can keep up with the flow of information that runs through him. The idea of him minding his own business in a roomful of people is absurd. 'Your president was there. Now, I probably should have mentioned this before, but I happen to know that he's in the market for a gun five-eight, but I hadn't really given it a thought. You've got another year on contract, haven't you?'

'Next year's my plus one. I'm trying to get a raise out of them and sign for another two.'

'What's the fine print on that plus one?'

'If I'm on the team sheet for seventy-five per cent of the games it kicks in automatically, unless I want out.' Normally I would be wary of giving out this kind of information, but I trust him and it sounds serious. Given the oily behaviour of Christophe lately it's worth knowing how things might go down.

'How many games have you missed so far?'

'A couple. No, three.'

'Out of what? Fifteen, sixteen games?'

'Fifteen, I think.'

'So you're on about eighty per cent at the moment. If you miss the next one, you're on seventy five per cent.'

Shit. I hadn't even thought about it. 'That sounds right.'

'Yeah, well, like I say there might be nothing in it, but your president took himself off to a corner table and started having a chat with one of my competitors, who happens to be the agent for the French five-eight from Toulouse. I thought it would be worth finding out what it was all about, so I went and sat down at the table next to them and made like I was taking a call.'

'I like your moves.' My voice comes out slightly strangled, but credit where it's due.

'All part of the service. Anyway, long story short, it looks like they've sewn up a deal for next year. Big coin, too.'

'How much?'

'Thirty-five plus extras.'

This stings. He's not bad, but I don't see him being worth nearly twice what I am. My mind whirs around trying to find an intelligent thought to get some purchase on.

'Maybe they're replacing François.' I already know this is unlikely.

'Yeah, well, no, actually. He's with me and he's got another year with no out. He won't be all that happy about this either. I can't see him leaving, though.'

'You're sure about this?'

'As sure as I can be.'

Stephane Tisserand. Known among the English speakers as the Fibber. Mr President. Treacherous prick. He had us both out to his house, a huge modern place with an indoor swimming pool in the west of Paris, when we first arrived. All smiles and welcome and attention. He flirted with Sarah. His wife flirted with me.

'You said you had some good news as well?'

'Did I? Oh, yeah. Facebook tells me it's your birthday. Happy birthday, mate! Don't go changing.'

'Cheers. Yeah, thanks for that.'

'Don't worry, Sparky, just say the word and I'll dig something up for you. A couple of clubs are looking, and there's a gig in

Wales that'll pay top dollar. How's your ankle?'

'How do you know about that?' Given that he's just done me a favour — of sorts — my voice is a little sharper than it should be.

His reply sounds wounded. 'You've been carrying that for ages. Every idiot knows. I'd get it sorted out.'

Better and better.

Theoretically there's room for three guys who play in the same position in the squad, particularly given that it's a key role — even if good finishers are useful, you can more or less shove anyone on the wing, loose forwards are a dime a dozen, even a prop has to be very good or very bad to have much of an impact. The difference between a good ten and an average one is probably eight to twelve points a game. The problem is that they won't want to pay me good money — I'd be one of the top five earners in the team — to sit on the bench most of the year in a bit-part role. François is plenty good enough for that, and they'll scrape someone else up as cover for him. The kid in the second team would probably be ready by next season. 'There might be nothing in it.' I bet there is, though. An old mate of mine from New Zealand who used to play in France once told me, 'You're taking the place of someone they've just fucked over. They'll say and do all sorts of nice things for you, give you the money and then, in time, they'll fuck you over too. Just remember that you're keeping the seat warm. Enjoy the ride and when your turn comes, don't take it to heart.' Easier said than done. In any case, the Bamboozler doesn't need to spell it out for me — coming with the general shiftiness about my contract renewal, my future at the club looks like not much future at all. The fact that the whole world knows about my crocked ankle won't help me in the look for a new job, and I hadn't been planning a move.

I need to talk to my agent.

Rachel wanders out of the bedroom, wearing a black silk kimono that stops halfway down her thighs. Maybe things aren't so bad. She musses her hair and kisses me. 'Happy birthday.'

* * *

Crawling through traffic on the way to our gym. Violent Femmes playing 'Add it Up' loud on the stereo. I punch the steering wheel, hard. Once I hit the horn by accident, startling a motorcyclist weaving through the cars alongside. He shakes his fist at me. I flip him the bird. Not the sort of thing you'd expect from your typical Volvo driver but I didn't choose the sponsors.

After my initial fury at the president wears off I might get around to the idea that he's only doing what he thinks is best for the club, but that isn't going to happen anytime soon. For now, I allow violent fantasies of beating his grinning face to a bloody pulp to run through my head unchecked, imagining a satisfying pain in my knuckles as a rain of just blows levels the score. The steering wheel isn't enough. I need to set up a meeting with him.

My French-based agent isn't really my agent at all, just the proxy for an agency run out of London and Auckland. Apart from the initial start-up, with organisation running from boot sponsors to cable TV, I've never needed him to do anything. Which, I suspect, is just as well — I get the impression he isn't up to much, although at least he's straight with me. I hope. Perhaps I'd be better to talk to London. Fuck it, I'll sort it out myself. I'm probably not going to barge into his office and exact vengeance on the spot, but I'll enjoy thinking about the possibility a while longer.

I can bail up Christophe straight away. We've got weight

training this morning — my group is on the final rotation, at 10.30 — and he might be there. Otherwise I'll catch him this afternoon.

* * *

To begin with I contemplate shaving some of the session; instead I end up doing extra sets of everything just to prove something to no one in particular. Grunting and sweating to exhaustion in the weights room takes the edge off my anger, even if it's only a limited respite — we recover quickly because it's part of the job description — and the rage settles, cools, solidifying into something that sits inside my guts and becomes patient hatred. Still, the usual gossip is a welcome distraction. I sit on the sideline, ears flapping. Nothing. And so it goes. In a year's time they'll be talking about the same crap. At some point in the future it will become clear to everyone else how futile the whole deal is. The fans cheer you one minute, but if the powers that be decide you're not the right man for the job, pretty soon the same people are screeching at you because your jersey's the wrong colour. You're doing the same thing, maybe even on the same field, but because you're wearing a different shirt, you're no longer the good guy.

Christophe is a no-show. Probably best that way. The doc arrives just as we are all getting ready to leave. As usual, he looks stressed. 'Sorry, I can't be everywhere at once. One of my patients has cancer, and it got complicated.'

I've already spoken to the physio on duty. He pointed me at the doc. A queue forms and I can't be fucked asking him for a new scan. He'll be around this afternoon.

Rich comes bouncing down the stairs as I leave the changing room. 'Sparky, wait up!' He lands in front of me and I turn expectantly. He squats into a sitting position, points his finger at me as if it were a gun, lifting his thumb in the place of a hammer. A loud report cracks off the white tiles. 'Aah.' An eleven-year-old boy trapped in the body of a twenty-seven-year-old man. He snickers off.

For a second, I am speechless. 'Don't go changing,' is all I can muster as he bustles out the door, still smiling. He is beautiful, somehow, and I have a sudden feeling of tenderness. Just don't ask me to try to explain it.

Chapter 16

Most of the team are having lunch together at the clubhouse. I decide to go along as well. After parking up nearby I give Bertrand, my agent, a call, just in case he knows something I don't.

'*Salut*, Mark! How are you?'

'I'm fine, how are you?' Form requires the exchange of pleasantries.

'I'm good but you know, I'm pretty cold, actually. I'm from the south. I don't like the winter in Paris. I was in Perpignan three days ago and it was twenty degrees.' I had hoped we might avoid starting up verbal ping-pong about the weather.

'Yes, they're talking about the grounds freezing over the next few days.'

'That's right, it could really mess things up for training and the next games in the championship. But you Kiwis, you don't care about the weather, do you? You are hard, *non*?' Oh, for fuck's sake. He blew smoke up my arse for going to university as well: 'You're the kind of player I like to work with.'

'I was really ringing to find out if you'd heard anything from the club.'

'Sure, sure. No, I asked for a meeting like you said and I told them it was to talk about signing for another two years but they said they haven't really thought about next year yet. You know, it's only November, so the clubs—.'

'That's not what I've heard. I understand the club have been looking for a ten. And that they might have found one. And so maybe there won't be room for me here next year.'

A moment of silence. 'I knew that maybe they were looking for a ten, but I thought it would be as cover for you. OK, I'll make some phone calls and see what I can find out.' His tone, at least, is serious. He gets it. 'In any case, don't worry — we will be able to find you a club. Maybe you can go to the south and not have to live with the freezing cold for five months every year.'

'Just get back to me with some news. And please, make sure you get an appointment sorted out with Tisserand. If I get the chance I'll talk to him myself.'

The clubhouse is a small stone building that serves as an occasional bar for supporters, and dining room for us on Wednesdays during the week. High up on the walls, light pink paint is peeling and the heaters are going full bore. Salad is on the table and the boys are tucking in as I walk round the room to shake hands with those I haven't already seen.

The white plastic seat at the head of one of the three long wooden tables has been saved for me by my gang; at the table next to us Coquine, Thomas, Pierre and Titi have the usual card school going, even as they eat.

Moose and Rich have been playing a rugby video game. They have to manage a team, coach it, buy in players and so on. All our names (except for some reason Rich's, much to everyone else's amusement) are actually in the game. They are, quite literally, playing with themselves. Moose is grumpy because 'he' is overpriced and gets yellow cards all the time, yet — obviously — loyalty to himself dictates that he needs him on his own team. 'That has to be some sort of infringement of my image rights. Can we sue these guys?'

Rich, having had time to regroup, speculates that he might

have been left out because he was too famous. Most of the current French team are missed out as well, presumably for exactly that reason. The speculation is dismissed as groundless. Fofo, the friendly fat bloke who runs the clubhouse, plonks down plates of crumbed chicken and pasta alongside bowls of tomato sauce and grated cheese, then scoops away the empty salad bowls. There follows a long, poorly informed discussion of how the law works in image-rights cases.

We go up and get our own coffee, and when I get back to the table Josh pulls out a little package and they all sing 'Happy Birthday', joined by everyone else — same tune for the Frenchies, just different words. The wrapping is actually yesterday's newspaper, presumably scrounged up just before I arrived. Inside, a pair of brown tartan slippers and a pair of Batman pyjamas. 'You guys. You shouldn't have. Really.'

'Now you're getting old and you like to stay at home all the time, we wanted to make sure you were comfortable.'

'And that you would look good.'

I count myself lucky. Pierre, who has a house in the suburbs with a bit of a garden, got a couple of piglets for his birthday.

* * *

The team will be leaving on Friday morning. I had been hoping that I wouldn't go, but now I want to be on the teamsheet — it would mean that they weren't trying to stitch me up over the seventy-five per cent clause. Christophe announces the line-up before we start training. François is playing first five, Xavier is on the bench as cover — I am travelling but non-playing reserve, the worst of all possible worlds. No weekend off, no credit towards the contract, not even the satisfaction of a run-out. Normally it's a spot reserved for a junior player. I am seething. As the changing room empties out Christophe is still there and he makes his way over to me. He can see I'm not happy.

'Mark, I wanted to give you the weekend off but François has a little problem with his hamstring. Xavier is not a specialist and if there is any trouble with François before the game then you will start. The second team have an important game this weekend and they didn't want me to take their guy.'

What can I say to that? Starting an open war with Christophe isn't a great idea, at least not yet; probably not ever. And, for the moment, they're paying me good money to go and sit around and do nothing for a weekend. Maybe this is all some stupid misunderstanding, a collection of misinterpreted signals. Perhaps in a few weeks I'll be laughing about it with the others, how I got wound up for no reason. The Bamboozler's party trick of a half-overheard conversation, and the ensuing chaos.

I look him in the eye. 'OK.'

'You'll get a weekend off soon.'

What would have sounded like a promise yesterday now sounds like a threat.

'When are we going to be able to talk about my contract?'

'I don't deal with the contracts. I am an employee, just like you. I don't even know if I will be here in six months. You have to talk to the president.' There's some truth in what he says, but the change in tune — last time he didn't hesitate in saying that we would talk about it 'soon', even if this was on behalf of the president — suggests that he's avoiding telling me everything he knows, which is enough for me. At least the Fibber will be at the game with us, and there will be no more stalling.

* * *

I go through the motions at training for about twenty minutes then walk off to see the doc. This way I get out of the cold and first in line. The ankle is a dull ache, probably no more than what most of the rest of the team harbour somewhere in their traumatised bodies: bad fingers, bad knees, bad shoulders, bad backs; rheumatic joints in waiting. The kind of lingering pain that you factor into a daily routine, that might feel crippling if you weren't used to it. Christophe is just about to wind us up into full contact so it's a good moment to get out.

The physios and the doc are lounging on the massage tables discussing the mistress of one of our officials. One of them should really be out following training in case something nasty happens. They look up as I arrive. 'First customer of the day,' says Jean Claude, the eldest of the physios. 'What can we do for you, young man?'

I address myself to the doc. 'The ankle's not recovering properly. Now my heel doesn't feel right.' He pats the padded table and I jump up and undo my boots and take off a sock. He cuts up into the strapping with scissors, then tears it off and starts moving my foot up and down, then side to side.

'It's perfectly normal for it to hurt, Mark. The question is, is it getting any worse? If the answer is yes, then we have to stop. We can do another scan if you like. I have no problem with asking for another scan. But I am not going to inject you with local anaesthetic for every training. If the pain is so much that you can't train, and the anti-inflammatories aren't enough, you won't be able to play.' The whole room stares at me, waiting to gauge my reaction.

'It'll be all right. But I would like another scan, just in case.' The doc and Jean Claude exchange a meaningful look. I like to think they believe that the arse would fall out of the side if I was out for the rest of the season, and I like to think they'd be right.

'OK. Nico will organise it. He'll tell you when the appointment is. We'll try for Monday.'

Good enough.

* * *

I rummage around a couple of electrical stores for an old-fashioned Walkman that will allow me to listen to Granddad's tapes in private — if I'm going on this bloody trip south I might as well use the vast amount of dead time to do something. (The doc, who is a busy bloke with a shared practice, real patients to treat and a family of four, once confided in me that the thought of what he could be doing with the time spent on these away trips made him want to throw up whenever he assembled.) At least we will get back on Saturday night on the last flight out of Toulouse. After the second fruitless search, a salesman points me in the direction of the nearby hypermarket, and a sustained trawl of the labyrinth throws up a cheap tape player that looks like it was made in the late eighties. There's a jack for headphones that looks standard.

Rachel arrives home shortly after me, having been shopping. I become the proud new owner of two expensive-looking shirts and a new wallet 'because the old one is falling apart'.

Instead of going out for a meal she is preparing her speciality in honour of my birthday: black beans and pork, with caipirinhas as an aperitif.

'So how was your day?'

'OK. I'm writing a piece on the bars here where you can smoke even though it's illegal. The spirit of the resistance.'

'A journo I know's trying to do a story on how the little guys get screwed. You know Josh?'

'The huge Samoan? I hadn't thought of him as a little guy.'

'The club bought him off so that he wouldn't go to the last World Cup.'

'Why?'

'So he would stay here and play. We had half a dozen games while the World Cup was on.'

'His choice, I guess.'

'Not exactly. They told him they wouldn't pay him if he went. They don't do that to the guys who play for France.'

'Is it against the law?'

'You'd hope so, wouldn't you. Josh reckons he's not the only one, that there were a couple of other guys here who got the same deal, a pay-out if they stayed, nothing if they went — and it's the same sort of thing at a few other clubs.'

'People know about this?'

'So I'm told. The French, World Rugby — they're all in on it.'

'But it doesn't happen everywhere, otherwise the little guys wouldn't even have a team, right?'

'Or they're prepared to take the hit.'

'If it's against the laws, your team is effectively match-fixing.'

'That's a bit strong.'

'They're rigging the competition in their favour with money. How is that not match-fixing?'

'You thinking of doing a story?'

'Your friend sounds like he's a long way ahead of me. In any case, I don't think I can sell that to Brazil. No one cares really, and assholes like your president always win.'

'Isn't that the kind of thing newspapers are supposed to want to get their teeth into? The little guy getting screwed?'

'You're so sweet sometimes. Really. And yes, you're right, that is the kind of thing that people like to read about. As long as it sells, and some big shot doesn't bring a defamation case that could ruin the newspaper. In the case of your story, there are big question marks over each of those premises, so they wouldn't touch it. In the end it's just a business.'

As she goes to pick up her drink the little brown ringbinder notebook that holds her recipes falls to the ground and a loose postcard skids across the floor. The picture face is of a Barbie leaning against a wall with a fifties look, sharp white sunglasses, a red headscarf and long red and white striped jacket over a blouse with same colour stripes, this time horizontal, over those classic jutting tits. It's quite a good likeness. 'Ciao' is the headline. On the back, 'Receita para o amor'.

'What's this?'

Giggles. 'It is a recipe for love. A girlfriend gave it to me before I went to Madrid.'

'So? Pass it on.'

'Take one Spaniard. Small and hardworking is best. Catch his eye and hold it. Wait for Donna Summer's "I Feel Love" to come on. Ask him to dance. Let him buy you a drink. Drop casually into conversation that you have mastered the art of the tortilla. Prepare to meet his mother in the coming weeks.'

* * *

Over dinner I decree — spitefully? — that it's a second-string side that we are sending down, and that they will lose by twenty points. This prediction is duly noted. I'm starting to enjoy the idea that it might be worth something.

Chapter 17

Sitting in the bus for the hour or so drive from the airport to our hotel, I pull out the tape player. 'Ouf! Old school! Yes!' This from Xavier, who, at twenty-three, has probably never even seen a cassette or player before. It does look slightly antique. I press play and close my eyes.

'So we're recording now.' The voice of a woman, whom I've identified as Sarah Palmer from the jacket, comes over the headset, along with a low hiss off the tape. 'How did you find New Zealand after you came back from the war, Mr Stevens?'

'"A land fit for heroes" was what Bill Massey called it. I'm not sure that that was the case, really. The bit I got wasn't much good for man nor beast. I'll tell you one thing, though, before I forget, because it's annoyed me for years. You tell the people who keep talking about how the soldiers "gave their lives" that that's a load of old rubbish. No one I knew gave his life — they had it taken from them. It's not the same thing. Simple as that. I know one or two blokes who organised to get themselves shot in the leg, but that was a different story. They just couldn't take the trenches any more. And it didn't mean they were cowards, either.'

He must have had a microphone on his chest, close enough that I can hear him swallow a couple of times, breathing heavily, then settling back after this burst of emotion.

Sarah Palmer asks gently, 'Do you go to the Anzac Day parades?'

'I never did, no. They said it was a good way of catching up with your mates, but I couldn't see the point. I used to see my mates anyway. I wasn't going to put a load of tin on my chest and strut up and down the street. No, I could never see the point in it. You wonder what the point of the whole thing was, really. In 1939 it was a different story. We just signed up because it was the thing to do in those days, you see. "England expects" and all that. We felt that we were on the right side, at any rate, and I suppose I still feel that. And no one wanted to look like they were shirking. Then fifty years later the blighters stopped taking our sheep because they went into cahoots with the Germans! We thought that was a bit rich. And the French and the Belgians, well, some of them were all right but most of them weren't very grateful. When we were marching and would be desperate for water or somewhere to rest, sometimes they wouldn't even look at us. I suppose if a bunch of foreigners turned up on my farm and started blowing it to bits and taking off with the chickens and what have you I wouldn't have been best pleased either. I don't think it would have made much difference to them who was running the show, they just wanted to get on.'

There is a pause as the old man stops for a drink. Probably rum, the old bugger: he always had a bottle of navy rum nearby the big leather chair that I imagine him sitting in for the interview.

'When you're there you do wonder about things, but of course you can't get much of an idea from the trenches, so you just get on with the job. I have heard a theory that if, for example, the Anzacs had managed to hold on to that ridge at Gallipoli and were properly reinforced, then we might have pushed all the way through to Constantinople, opened up the Black Sea and linked up with Russia. I'm not sure whether it holds up or not, but if they'd managed that before Lenin and his mob got their ball rolling, well, they might have saved everyone a lot of trouble. So maybe there was a point to it all. Maybe things could have turned out very differently if we hadn't done what we did.'

'When did you join up?'

'It was October 1915. I had my twentieth birthday on the troop ship. We had a Japanese escort, which is funny when you think about what happened later on. The voyage was terrible, just terrible. We were sea-sick a lot of the time; there was no fresh water. Miserable. So we got to Egypt through Suez more or less in one piece, by which time Gallipoli was over, and we trained there. Egypt was an eye-opener for me, I can tell you, but I don't really want to get into that, it's not very interesting — and went on across the Med through France to England for more training, then back to France.'

'Where were you stationed?'

'Oh, golly, all over the place. We were on Salisbury Plain in England, then on the Somme. We walked in, it took us a few weeks. We were around Flers, you know, northern France and Belgium.'

'So you took part in the battle of the Somme.'

'That's right, yes.'

A long silence. I can hear him swallowing, shuffling around. Another pull on the drink.

'Well, you will have heard what that was like from other fellows, I suppose. I will say this, though: the organisation was wonderful, just wonderful. All those men, all that machinery in all that bloody mud. It wasn't perfect by any stretch of the imagination, and the tactics were no good, of course — the High Command weren't great for tactics — but the sheer feat of keeping the whole show on the road was all right, considering the shambles that war is when you get right down into it. The troop movements, the *matériel* that got shifted from here to there, telephone wires rigged up between every dugout. Mind you, there were breakdowns. When our time came for a push, we got ahead of the main line of the advance and found ourselves in a German trench getting bombarded from behind as well as from in front, and of course we'd gone too fast to have a phone line rigged up. Well, there was some pretty fluent speech about that, I can tell you. But when you had to dig, by Christ you dug! Every shovelful was a little more safety. We just dug in and retired as soon as we could. But there were some pretty amazing sights. The aeroplanes, for one thing. D'you know, I had never laid eyes on one in New Zealand, and suddenly there they were, flying low enough over our lines that you could make out the red, white and blue roundels on the wings. I got a crick in my neck just from watching them some days. They would manoeuvre for position, you see, going up and up and up. The man who got the highest dominated, and when they had got as high as they could the top dog turned to pounce and the fellow on the bottom would dart away as quick as he could. They must have been travelling nigh on a hundred miles an hour which wouldn't sound much these days but back then it was quite something. And our lot seemed to be a bit better than theirs, or there were more of us at any rate, so that was a comfort.'

'What was your experience of the trenches?'

'Well, it wasn't much fun, was it. The artillery bombardments were the worst. Being woken by a man three or four miles away trying to kill you by pulling on a lanyard. Gas. And the Minenwerfers, the famous Minnies, a great big drum full of explosives. They made a noise like the pop of a rifle, then you could hear them coming, going whoofle-whoofle-whoofle, like the wings of a wood pigeon in flight, arriving slow enough that you can see them. You can imagine the stampede along the duck boards. They never came on their own, so once the first one arrived you knew you were in for some exercise. Most of the time we kept our heads down, did what we were told and tried to stay alive. The real world that we'd come from was just a dream that you hoped you would be able to go back to one day. We did have one fellow in the outfit, a Jock — good fighters, the Jocks. You know that line from Robbie Burns, "The rank is but the guinea stamp, The man's the gowd for a' that"? Well, when I think of the distinction made between the officers and the soldiers, there was nothing truer than that. At any rate, this Jock — Alan was his name, he came out to Wellington just before the war — was a very good man with a knife, and he would go off sometimes into no-man's-land by night with his trench knife. But the rest of us, we went on patrols into no-man's-land only if the brass had decided we had to look for prisoners, and of course if we had a stunt then we went over the top and all hell would break loose. We weren't in any hurry, though. People did do some brave things, some very brave things, but most of the time it was because they were half-mad from grief or out for revenge, which was much the same thing, really. And because no one wanted to be thought of as a coward, well, you did what you had to do. You just did it.'

The first side of the tape fizzes to a halt and the 'play' button kicks up automatically. 'A very good man with a knife' reminds me of the spatter of blood from the sheep, the jerking of its limbs. What would it take to do that to another human being? What kind of a man was Alan to take off into no-man's-land with a knife on a night when he could have been brewing tea, just trying to stay warm and alive? Does that make him a hero or a psychopath?

Either way, I suppose you'd be pleased to have him on your side.

I put the tape player and headphones back in my bag. I'll have time to listen to more tonight.

* * *

Before the training run we have a quick meet to outline the programme for the next twenty-four hours. Titi, who has been named captain in Coquine's absence while he has a rest along with half a dozen of our best players, is evidently taking his duties seriously and starts trying to wind us up for tomorrow. There is more talk of the war that we will wage on our opponents. Particularly in the rucks, apparently. I find it surprisingly easy to imagine Titi stealing off into the darkness with a blade, but when it comes to the act itself I struggle. I put the president in a German uniform, hoping that this will liven things up. 'This time, it's personal.' Yep, now it works for me.

The man himself won't make an appearance until tomorrow, so I don't have much to do. After a particularly dull training — the doc tells Christophe that it's best to avoid me running if at all possible, so I have a bit of a stretch and boot a few balls back to François, then park up to watch the captain's run — followed by dinner, I sidestep movie night with the boys and settle in for some more long-distance family reminiscences.

Michel, the young reserve halfback who I'm rooming with (Jacques is rooming with François: I'd love to be a fly on the wall for that little party) spends the evening watching reality TV while he talks to his girlfriend. What with dislocated images of people eating grilled spiders, weeping would-be pop stars who don't appear to have made the cut and housemates arguing — none of them hold Michel's attention for more than a few minutes, so we get all of them — I find it hard to concentrate on what I'm listening to, so I turn it off after another half an hour. I smiled at a story about one of Granddad's mates who kept getting sent cheese from home: it was the one thing that wasn't in short supply in France, and by the time it arrived from the uttermost ends of the earth it was in a right state, but the poor bloke couldn't bear to upset his mum by telling her to send something different. He would just thank her politely and tell her it was delicious.

Chapter 18

'Nothing has been signed.'

I have finally managed to corner the Fibber at the after-match. He arrived late in the morning at our hotel and spent most of his time on the phone. When he spied me lurking around, he walked the other way; when I caught up he told me he could see me perhaps during the week, or maybe it would be better the week after, no, that will be Christmas, he's away, perhaps after Christmas? I asked him why we couldn't talk right now and his phone went off again. '*Excuse-moi, hein.*'

I sat through the game, waiting, boiling. François did end up having problems with his hamstring, and it looked touch and go even before kick-off. I was ready to strip but, under orders from Christophe, the doc told him to have a go and see if it warmed up. It clearly wasn't right and he came off after twenty minutes, leaving Xavier to marshal the backline. His kicking game wasn't as bad as I thought it would be but he lacked the extra room he's used to at centre — where he receives the ball on a plate from me — and got caught a few times, and then he got rattled, calling the wrong moves and shovelling passes on without the necessary precision until he got so desperate that he started crashing it up himself and someone else had to deal with the recycling. To start with, the forwards did hit the rucks hard and there were an uncomfortable few minutes when it looked as though we might actually dominate them up front, and anything could have happened. Before François came off it was 6–6; after Xavier moved in the spark went out and they ran away with it, 28–9, just one point short of my prediction.

Eric wants me to do fitness afterwards along with the other reserves. I play my get-out-of-jail-free card by pointing him at the doc, which gains me a head start on everyone else dribbling through the post-match routine of showers and wound-licking and press. I intercept the president as he makes his way back from the buffet. So he stands there with a plate in his hand, having told me there's a number of different things to take into account, they're not sure of the budget for next year and so on. Having built up to this for the last couple of days, I'm not quite sure how to handle it now that he is so obviously stalling me. I feel like a dog that's spent an afternoon chasing cars and now, having finally caught one, doesn't know quite what to do with it. I mean, I can't actually bite him, can I?

So I blurt out, 'You've signed the guy from Toulouse. You're sure enough of next year's budget to do that. And from what I hear you're spending plenty.'

A weary sigh, then a wary look from hooded eyes, presumably wondering where I've got my information from.

Which brings us up to where we are. 'Nothing's been signed.' He looks me in the eye: 'Listen, if I remember correctly, you have another year on your contract. It's very simple: we will honour our side of the contract, providing you honour yours. More than that, I can't say for the moment. We can talk again in a few weeks. It really is complicated. OK?'

I am quite seriously out of my depth now. If I ask for more information I am going to look desperate, which even I know isn't a great negotiating strategy. On the other hand, after all my build-up he's just brushed me off and I don't want to let him get away with that. Deflated, I hesitate, and he is already walking away. Nice moves. By tomorrow I will have thought of half a dozen things I could have, should have, said. I can imagine Rich's reaction. 'Silk, Sparky, that is fucking silk. You've got the skills all right.' I turn to go and look for a beer, and a couple of kids come over and ask me for an autograph and a photo.

* * *

Because I can bear only so much reality I bump Michel from a card game down the back of the bus — age has its privileges — for the ride back to the airport, lose €50 in just under an hour and laugh more in that time than I have in the last week.

* * *

It's nearly midnight when I get home to an apartment that feels depressingly empty now that Rachel is in London. We agreed that it would be silly for her to come over for weekends if I was playing away. I call Ali — it must be nearly noon at home. It rings through to the answerphone first time, so I try again and this time Darrin picks up. He passes me over like a hot potato to Ali, who is just waking up. I wonder what they say about me. Does he respect me so much that he finds it hard to speak to me, or am I the rich prick who's dumb enough to send money and they laugh every time they think about it? I stopped being able to connect with Ali about ten years ago.

'Hi, Spark. You're up late.'

'Not really. Sounds like you were, though.'

'Oh yeah, Darrin had some of his mates round. It was a good

night. Ow, shit. Jesus, where are those Panadol, hun?' She yawns.

'Have those kids had breakfast?'

'They're fine. Sasha knows where the cereal is, and she looks after Steph. Sasha's quite independent. She's nearly eight.'

'How do you know they're all right?'

'I can hear the TV from the bedroom. Thanks, hun.' Sarah would have seen the irony in this exchange: the man who didn't want to have kids because he wanted to keep being a boy getting wound up about his sister's loose interpretation of parental duties.

'Well, that's all right, then. Listen, I'll let you get over that hangover, but call me some time this week.'

'That's OK, I can talk now. Busy week coming up.' I bet. Another yawn, then a stifled giggle. Darrin will be feeling horny. I know I always do when I wake up with a hangover. He's probably pawing her under the sheets. I shake my head to get rid of the image. It's bad enough that they're in our parents' bedroom.

'No, honestly, let's do this another time. I wanted to talk about Granddad's tapes. Did you read the clipping?'

'Ah, nah, I just sent it all off to you.'

'You weren't even the teensiest bit interested in what he might have been up to?'

'You were always the golden grandchild. He was never that interested in me. As far as I remember, the old bastard reeked of booze and mothballs, or something nasty. And he said I was chubby, which I didn't think was that cool. Anyway, you know I've never been interested in war and all that stuff.'

'All right, forget it. See ya, wouldn't wanna be ya.' We used to say this when we were kids. I'm trying to be friendly but I haven't used it for a while now, and after it slips out I realise it might be a bit close to the bone.

'Yep. Bye.'

I decide to go out for a drink myself. Rich and Moose can't have pulled yet.

* * *

Rachel calls Sunday afternoon. I haven't said anything to her yet about the contract problem. It would make me look weak. I met her because I was supposed to be some sort of star. Now I'm getting junked by my own team — or the guy who calls the shots on the team, which amounts to the same thing.

'Philip made thirty thousand pounds on the game.'

'Sweet. So I pick up ten grand.' It's nice to have good news in a phone call for once.

'Nine. He's going to set up an account for you in Jersey, in the Channel Islands. I've emailed you some forms to fill out.' I already have an account in the Caymans for my bonuses, set up by the agency. The fewer people who know about that the better.

'And you're getting a little slice of the action?'

'You know I have expensive tastes. It's lucky that someone is looking out for me. Oh, the article I wrote on you will be online today. You can check it out if you want.'

'I might need some help with my Brazilian.'

'There's translation software online. Find a search engine and translate it from Portuguese to English.' Damn, I knew it was Portuguese.

'Or you could tell me.'

'It says you're a big star, with big muscles, and that you're very good in bed.'

'That's all I needed to know. Come back soon, will you?'

'You can come over here sometime. Why don't you come over for Christmas?'

'London is always a downer. I've got a better idea. We've just come into some money — let's go somewhere sunny for Christmas. Your choice, but Brazil is too far. I've got eight days off and I'm not spending two of them in a plane.'

A squeal of delight. That's something to look forward to, at least.

Chapter 19

The second tape has a surprising start to it.

Sarah Palmer asks, 'Did you ever meet Ettie Rout?'

'You know about Ettie, do you? I didn't think I'd ever hear a woman in New Zealand bring that name up in polite conversation. Perhaps the conversation isn't all that polite.' A sort of grunt, then a pull on the drink, and the splash of a refill being poured. 'If you know something about her, perhaps you can tell me how she died?'

'She took an overdose of quinine and died in Rarotonga.'

A long silence, then another grunt. 'Isn't it incredible? She seemed like an unstoppable force. I suppose I only met her for a few minutes. We had a whip round for her at the RSA after the war. Then I didn't hear anything for a long time, until I heard she was dead. In a way, she was killed by the war as much as any of the fellows who died over there. Or rather, she was killed by the people at home for what she'd done in France. No one had a good word to say about her after that. The women wanted her hide, and the men didn't have the gumption to stick up for her, you see. It would have looked like they had got a leg over with her help. I told you no one wanted to look like a coward — no one wanted to look like they had loose morals either, not when you were back home with your own woman. Well, it's all a long time ago now. I don't think there's much chance of my wife listening to this, God rest her soul. Fire away then, Miss.'

'When did you meet her?'

'I met her in Paris. It must have been July 1918 or thereabouts. She came and picked us up off the train. Leave in Paris was pretty special, and they gave it out according to alphabetical order, so I was a way down the list, and I'd already heard a few things about her. There were a few jokes, you know, not all of them savoury. But my word, what it meant to me to get away from those god-awful trenches to that place with all the rush around you — soldiers and civilians, men and women leading normal lives! — but even then not knowing what you were about, not really speaking the lingo and so on, and out of all the confusion have this woman call out "New Zealand!" and come over and give you a kiss on the cheek and ask you how you were. And she listened, and she understood, and she didn't judge.' He blows his nose into the microphone and the sound of thirty-year-old snot explodes in my ears.

'What happened then?'

'Well, she took us over to a hotel room that she had set up as a little office just over the road. I remember the name because it was in English, the New Hotel. There was a group of us, about twenty, and she took us up and gave us these little kits and told us how to avoid getting ourselves in trouble, you see? She gave us the name of one of these licensed houses.' His voice drops to a stage whisper: 'Bordellos, they were. I always thought a licensed house was a pub — at any rate, she told us the girls here were clean, she'd inspected them herself, but if we were to go elsewhere then she wouldn't answer for it, but for God's sake use the kit. And she told us to come back for a cup of tea any time, and that she would appreciate our dropping some coins into a box on the way out because of course no one would give her any money for what she was doing. Which was ridiculous really, when you saw the mess some of the men got themselves in — even the priests!

VD was a terrible problem. There was no penicillin or anything like that, syphilis would just eat away at you until you went mad. Each platoon got checked out on dangle parade, and anyone with a dose was sent off to a special hospital. It was considered a self-inflicted injury, so you had your pay docked. No, a lot of us had good reason to be very grateful to Ettie Rout, the army included. They tried all sorts of things — none of them worked, least of all the long speeches we had about the women at home and how we shouldn't let them down. It made you feel guilty all right. I wasn't married, mind, but even so. You have to understand, it wasn't like normal life. When you've seen so much suffering and death and you know that in a few days you're back on that train and it might be your number that comes up next, well, you don't want to die wondering, I'll say that.'

'What else do you remember about Paris?'

'We ate very well, and drank well too. Us New Zealanders were on five shillings a week, so we had money to spend and we spent it. We did the sights. The Eiffel Tower. The metro was something else, this churning, heaving mass of people surging in and out of a bare oblong box. You had to look lively about yourself, because there were pickpockets — we saw one of them caught by some French soldiers, and didn't they give him a hiding? But the prostitution was unbelievable, worse than Egypt even, and some pretty low things went on there. You'd walk past these women in the street, in the middle of the day, and they'd say "*Voulez vous couchez avec moi, ce soir?*" You understand? It was hard times for the women as well. We were billeted with a family at one point, the husband had been killed at the front, and the mother was as white and pinched as a skeleton. She had these two little girls, and the elder one who must have been about twelve, she told us that we should come back in a couple of years when she would be ready to make money for the family.'

'As a prostitute?'

'As a prostitute, yes.'

Jesus. The good old days. A text comes through on my phone. Nico — I have an appointment tomorrow for an MRI scan and an arthrogram at 10.30. Normal people have to wait a month for one. We always get special treatment. Just as I'm putting it down again, the phone rings. Bertrand.

'Bertrand. What's new?' This sounds seventies or worse in English, but it's what the French say. When in Rome.

'Hi, Mark. OK, I've spoken to some people and you're right, it looks like the ten from Toulouse will sign. This will make things complicated for you. Stephane tells me he has already spoken to you. What did he say?'

'That I would have to wait and see what happens. That it was complicated. It doesn't sound like it's all that complicated — they're trying to shaft me.'

'I'm not sure. OK, it does look like that. What would you like to do next year?'

'I hadn't thought about it. I was planning on staying here.'

'You can still do that. You know your contract runs for another year if you play enough games. Even if they don't keep you they will have to pay you out.'

'Things are starting to smell pretty bad. What else can you get for me?'

'The market is only just starting to open up, it's really only the top players who are being contacted at the moment.'

'So I'm not a top player?'

'No, no, that wasn't what I meant, just that no one thought you would be on the market is all.'

'I am now. Who's looking?'

'I'll find out.'

'Who's running London these days? Is it still Charlie?'

'Yes, Charlie is still there. Do you want to talk to him? I can set up a meeting — he's going to be in Paris in January.'

'That would be good. You must have some idea what's out there?'

'There will be plenty of opportunities for a player as good as you. I'll come back with something soon, I promise.'

* * *

Sitting waiting among the white tiles of the radiology department. The team has training and I'm now considered big enough to look after myself so no one from the medical staff is here to hold my hand. I would have preferred to have had someone to keep me from my own dark thoughts. The ankle has calmed down slightly, which might be a good sign — for some reason, little niggles often go away when you take them to the doctor. Perhaps it's just a flare-up. The joint has been vulnerable since the medial and lateral ligaments were first distended eight years ago, when I got bashed in a gang tackle against the meat-eaters in Pretoria. By now it must have been twisted and sprained half a dozen times, each time a little slower to recover, each time the damage to the cartilage a little worse. The bone spurs are the result. I've had a couple of arthroscopies. I had some cortisone a couple of years ago which I suspect wasn't the best idea. Then some gel, which worked for a bit. Then some more. Most recently local anaesthetic before games, which probably isn't all that clever either.

To distract myself I pick up the sports paper that someone has left behind and flick through to the rugby pages. Among the chitchat and a look forward to this weekend's game I notice that I get a small headline and a little paragraph to myself: now the whole world knows that I'm having tests on the ankle. And they quote my age as thirty-five. That fucking reeks of the Fibber — he'll want to discourage anyone else just in case the bloke from Toulouse falls through, and telling the world I'm thirty-five is a good way of doing it. No team with any sense is going to sign a thirty-five-year-old with a crocked ankle. Who knows whether anyone will believe it or not, but it's the kind of detail that might just stick in the minds of potential recruiters. I want to ring Bertrand to tell him to get the paper to print a correction, but when I pull out my mobile phone the receptionist tut-tuts and points at a sign with a mobile phone in the middle of a red circle with a line through it. I move seats so she can't see me and text him instead. It's not as if the bloody machines are going to crash into the side of a mountain.

After a twenty-minute wait I get on to the cream plastic platform that slides in and out of the MRI machine. The interlocking circles at the mouth of the contraption click and whirr and bang metallically while I try to think happy thoughts and ignore the desire to scratch myself. Then another half-hour wait before a jab of a milky liquid, more waiting for it to diffuse and the arthroscanner itself. Another wait for the results. I'm starving now. Finally I am called through to discuss the results with the radiologist, a tired-looking woman in her mid-forties wearing a white coat in a small room with backlit boards, on which there are a series of cuts of my ankle showing white images on black plastic sheets and numbers that mean nothing to me. We shake hands. No smiles.

'We can see here and here that you have very little cartilage left in the ankle. You are a high-level sportsman?' I nod. 'It looks as if you have had a number of sprains. The joint lacks stability — here we can see the medial ligament has been torn, though it's not recent. It's a question of stress. There is significant swelling here — you can see the black outline? That shouldn't be there. There are several bone spurs, three of which directly affect the joint and must be causing you some pain.' I nod again, grunt. 'There are some small elements of cartilage that have broken off and can be removed by arthroscopy, but they may simply be ground down by the bone. They aren't big enough to justify surgery on their own.'

'So what does all that mean?'

'It's not for me to say. You will have to see your club doctor.'

'What does it look like to you?'

'Your ankle hasn't been treated well over the years, and now it's starting to tell you that. If you want to be able to lead a normal life after you stop playing sport, the sooner you stop the better. But it is not for me to make that decision. OK?'

Not really, no.

* * *

The doc's verdict is a little more upbeat. Initially, anyway. 'It's a question of how much you can take. Some people have higher pain thresholds than others.'

'But the ankle itself is gone.'

'Not gone, exactly.' He slips a cigarette out of his top pocket — I've seen him do it before; he won't show anyone the name of the bad habit — and beckons me outside. We walk onto the flat spread of concrete that leads away from the changing-room door in every direction. He lights up without offering me one.

The doc is a good man. He is there to look after us, which he takes to mean much more than what the club would consider his remit: he is there to protect us from ourselves as well as healing the damage that others do to us. I saw him take aside our young reserve lock after he came back from summer break looking way too muscular for two months in the gym and give him nothing more than a quiet talking to. He's ten years older than me, but then I am ten years older than some of my teammates, and he seems like a man among boys. Christophe is as much of an overgrown adolescent as any of us; the doc operates on a dry sense of humour and a distance from the daily grind that we all enjoy blowing out of proportion.

'Listen, Mark, your ankle isn't great. There are several things we can do: we can say it's done, finished, kaput, or we can say you can grit your teeth and maybe you can play through the pain. Maybe you can. Or we can try to find a solution. The best-case scenario is that your ankle will allow you to play for another year, two years at the most. No doubt I should have done something about it earlier, but you need an intelligent coach to listen, and that isn't always the case. Perhaps the coach is intelligent but he doesn't trust François. Whatever the case, we've already injected you with gel and that hasn't made much difference. We can do more cortisone but chances are that is really going to rip it to bits. The last chance we have is to try growth factors.'

'Growth factors?'

'We take some of your blood, put it into a centrifuge, and take out the growth factors that are naturally present in the blood, then we re-inject them into your ankle. It can help. You might even be able to play tennis in ten years. Do you want me to give you all the science?'

'No. I trust you. What else am I going to do?'

'You could become an ankle surgeon. You already know more about it than most people.'

'Really?'

'No. But you do need to start thinking about a new career, dumb-ass.'

Chapter 20

I can feel myself slipping out of the bubble. After talking to the doc I go into the changing room, where the rest of the team have arrived after training. Coquine calls us all in and gives us his big speech, or at least what qualifies as a big speech for him: 'This game is so important for us. For the club, and for us as a team. If we win, the door is open. If that door shuts, we've pissed a big part of the season away. I want you all to take a moment to think about that. Just think about what that means, this early in the season, to be out of the European Cup. Because that's the reality if we screw this up. It's one of the goals we set out for ourselves five months ago. Either we're a big team, or we're a little team. We find out on Saturday. Just make sure that you're not the one that makes us a little team. We've done too much work, we've got too much talent to be a little team. This club has a big history. A lot of very talented guys have worn the jersey before you, have worked for it, have loved it. Don't let them down.'

I can remember what it was like when I believed this shit, when my whole existence turned on the outcome of a game — on what I do to make sure my team is on the right side of the scoresheet. Measuring yourself and your colleagues against fifteen others, or twenty-three others, or (in reality) those players plus the staff, the front office, the back office, the sponsors, the goodwill of the fans, if necessary the referee; the everything combined to make that team what it is: lesser than us. Measured in clean-cut points, tallied on the scoreboard, marked cards dealt openly and played honestly in the arena in front of everyone who cares to look. Believing in it doesn't make you an idiot, it just makes you normal.

Not believing in it is the problem.

And yet, and yet . . . I look around at the faces. Sylvain, our loose-head prop, who isn't a great player but always gives it death, starts to speak. 'Where I come from, you have to leave your guts on the field. It doesn't matter if you lose, you have to leave your guts out there. Last Saturday, we didn't do that. This weekend we have the opportunity to make up for it.' Thousand-yard stares all round, or nearly. A few seconds of silence, then Josh — who hasn't been listening to a word because he wouldn't understand anyway, having resolutely declined to learn the lingo but feels he's waited the requisite amount of time between the end of an obviously heavy speech and the getting on with everyday necessities — starts banging the dirt off his boots on the floor, breaking the magic circle. The boys start getting undressed. Moose catches my eye and makes a face. I take a couple of steps off to the side away from the entrance to the showers so that no one can see my suppressed laughter.

Freddie the Argentinian, who played well at the weekend, comes up to me and says in English: '"Where I come from, you have to leave your guts on the field." What does that mean? Everyone comes from somewhere. Where I come from you have to leave your guts on the field as well. Is there anywhere in the world where they say, "It's OK. Hold onto your guts. It's just for fun."? It's bullshit, no?'

He's bright enough not to say it too loudly. I don't know why he's asking me. Then I click on: he played at the weekend, I didn't — he's second-string, I'm a senior player, and he wants some reassurance that he isn't as rubbish as the collective guilt-trip that is being foisted on him and the others would seem to suggest. He'll get it from Christophe if he asks, but like so many things that come out of Christophe it will be relatively meaningless PR. He respects me enough to come to me for back-up. Freddie is a tidy player — no, better than tidy even if he's short for a flanker: his profile passes him off as six foot though he's at least a couple of inches shy of that, probably more — but densely packed with explosive strength, and his low centre of gravity is useful for jackalling the ball at the breakdown. He's worth a few turnovers every game, which is valuable ball, and he tends to pick up a few knocks while he's there, always coming away with head wounds that need stitching. God knows I wouldn't want that job. I think he's quality, but he does tend to get lumbered with playing in second-string teams, so he doesn't get much glory, and he's locked in a vicious circle. People don't tend to notice that you've played well if the team has shipped thirty points, on the grounds that no one is innocent, but he's the kind of player I like — having the talent to turn a vital game with a stroke of genius is great for results and makes you a hero; holding onto a sense of urgency when the score is way beyond reach and the guys around you are packing up is more of a test of character. You can't do anything about talent, but having a pair of balls is what makes you a man.

'You could have won at the weekend. I thought you played well. It's not your fault.'

'I know. But why does this always happen to me?'

* * *

Christophe has spoken to the doc, and calls me into his little den that serves as his changing room and office. 'How does your ankle feel?'

'Not so bad. All right for the weekend, anyway.'

'Good. The doc tells me he wants to inject you with something again. Apparently it will take a couple of weeks for you to get over it. We can do it at Christmas or during the Six Nations. In between I'll try to rest you as much as possible but you have to play this weekend, and I would like you to play next weekend as well.'

I have some leverage here, and I should work out how to use it. 'We'll see how it goes on Saturday. Have you got some tape I should look at? I missed the session this morning.'

He flicks through a stack of discs in his bag and pulls out a couple. 'They run a very tight rush defence with the halfback sweeping but there will always be a hole for a chip out wider. If you can hold up a pass long enough to get one in behind them that might work, and the double switch with the blindside winger will work, if the timing is right, which it wasn't last time you ran it — Thomas over-anticipated. I've talked to him about that. It wouldn't hurt for you to remind him. They have a big winger who usually plays on the left — he's slow to turn and isn't much of a kicker, and the fullback hardly ever runs but he's got a good boot and likes to stick it up. The flankers play open and blind and the openside is quick so give yourself another metre whenever you can. Jacques will be playing and he can help with that. The number eight isn't that fast but he is strong — a couple of times they have played him at halfback and the halfback at number eight off the scrum so that he can get wide enough to attack the ten, so if that happens make sure you come up quickly and don't give him any room. The centres like to cut back, and they're big boys so make sure you don't come across too quickly. I'm not sure which ten they'll be using. One kicks, the other runs, so that will tell us a lot about what they're planning. Other than that they're methodical, patient, meticulous and a bit static — British. For me the danger is the eight and the centres. Eric will give you some bike work tomorrow morning to go with the weights and you'll run with the backs tomorrow night — very light, I promise.'

* * *

In deference to the importance of Saturday's game, Josh, Rich and Moose decide to go out for a few beers on Monday rather than Tuesday. I join them (as Rich points out, 'Yoko isn't around') and call Freddie who comes along. By the end of the night he has got himself into trouble by telling a couple of girls he has been chatting up that the reason he is wearing a wedding band and still trying it on is that his wife — whom he left at home for the evening, along with their two-year-old daughter — is dead.

When he realises what he has done, he is inconsolable.

* * *

Tuesday morning, sitting on the exercise bike going nowhere in the gym, I have a bright idea. I call Rachel and ask her to find out what the odds are on my scoring first points in the game with a drop goal. Half an hour later she calls back.

Thirty to one.

'Can I get Philip to put three grand of the last payday on my dropping a goal for first points this Saturday?'

'That shouldn't be a problem. It won't have gone through yet because you haven't sent me the paperwork for the bank.'

'I'll get onto it. Do you know what the spread is supposed to be for this weekend?'

'It doesn't come out until closer to the time, once the bookies have looked at the teams and so on. Probably not until Friday.'

'All right. I think we should be good for a ten to fifteen-point win though. We'll talk about it later. Where are we going for Christmas?'

'The Seychelles, the Maldives or South Africa — your choice. Or there's a little island just off Zanzibar. It's quite expensive.'

'How much?'

'About two thousand pounds a night. But everything is included. It looks very cool.'

'Two thousand pounds a night! I should hope everything was included. You do have expensive tastes. Let's wait and see if I can pull this thing off.'

That afternoon at training, I get Jacques to stay behind to sling balls to me while our reserves try to charge me down. It's never been a speciality, but after the best part of an hour, I feel quite comfortable off either left or right foot.

When we come off, Christophe nods his approval. 'That's a good idea.'

I'll do some more tomorrow.

Chapter 21

I concentrate on getting the ball as high as possible. Kick-off can be a great weapon. It comes down right where I want it to, five yards in from the touchline and with enough air for Thomas to have gone round the back. Pierre, wound up like a six-year-old at a lolly scramble, gets high for a challenge and clatters into their man who spills the ball backward into touch. Lineout for us. I call a crash ball on Xavier. We win our ball cleanly and it comes fizzing out from Jacques. Running on a slight diagonal, I hold on for long enough to draw their flanker onto me, then pop it to Xavier cutting back, who straightens up when he takes it, making good yards with their ten and the number eight holding onto him. I pick myself up from the marginally late tackle, and drop back into the pocket cleared for me behind the ruck. The ball is slow and our forwards have time to get into a screen, shielding me from their chasers. I'm thirty-five metres out, slightly to the left of the posts. I take another couple of steps back, just in case. The distance is still comfortable. I nod to Jacques. He fires a bullet back to me, slightly off to my right. I have time to roll the ball round in my hands unconsciously, then drop it on its tip. I keep my head down, adjusting the weight onto my left leg as my right foot describes an arc, striking the ball sweetly up and over the outstretched arms of two defenders. I watch its end-over-end trajectory towards the posts, but as soon as I hit it I know that it is headed in the right direction. The referee, neck craned round behind him so he can follow the flight, raises his arm and blows the whistle. It is a perfect moment. Planning and preparation bring their reward. I will remember this as long as I live.

As we turn and jog back to halfway I collect a couple of claps on the back, nothing more — there's still a long way to go — and the tension that I have been feeling over the last few days dissipates. Barely a minute gone and I'm the best part of a hundred grand to the good. I almost don't care about the result now, but last night I had to take two sleeping pills, having told Rachel I didn't want her coming over Friday. A small sacrifice, given the week that now stretches out lazily in front of us on some island whose name I can't pronounce.

Their kick-off comes long and lazily flat down the right side. Rich gathers the ball, jinks twice off his right foot to beat first their wing then their fatties before offloading to Coquine, who busts a tackle before going to ground ten metres inside our territory. I look up the field and see the number eight hanging back deep on the right, the fullback in the middle and their big right wing lurking just on their side of halfway in no-man's-land. They're worried about our running game. Beautiful. I yell for a chase from Thomas, just in case, call for the ball and rifle it diagonally across the field from right to left, rolling it into touch just outside their twenty-two. They win the lineout, drive a couple of metres then their halfback kicks high along the line. Thomas jumps to take it and gets hit in the air, legs cartwheeling over his head as he crashes into the ground on his back. A hush across the ground as he lies spread-eagled on the turf. The ref blows, calls their hot-headed right wing over and presents him with a yellow card. The doc arrives with physio and stretcher-bearers follow close behind.

Coquine checks on Thomas, who is at least moving his legs, then tells me to kick to the corner. It's the right decision — they're a man down and the penalty is on the outer edge of my range. We can't talk about killing the game this early but we can get a good head start in the next ten minutes. We mill around aimlessly, everyone waiting to see if Thomas is going to get up. The obligatory, ineffectual cold spray is applied to his back. One of our reserves is running up and down on the sideline, bursting to get on. Eventually Thomas is hauled to his feet, swearing. Clapping from the crowd, after they've finished booing the winger into the Plexiglas hutch for reserves and staff on the sideline. The angle for the kick to touch is acute, so I settle for a safe twenty-five metres. Greed can get you into trouble.

Jacques calls for a lineout drive. Their pack is one short now as the openside has dropped off to cover for the winger. Xavier wants me to run a move out wide; instead I decide on a grubber kick through behind their rush defence — the fullback will defend in the line and my guess is the flanker will hesitate to come across in cover. They don't contest the ball in the lineout, waiting to spike the movement on the ground. They force our pack into reverse for a couple of metres; we take a few seconds to consolidate, then rumble toward the tryline. The maul is held up once, then Moose breaks off the side, goes to ground and a pile-up ensues. Their defensive line closes up, centres crouched as though they are in the starting blocks. Pierre and Josh stand off the ruck, Jacques flicks Josh the ball, and there's another pile-up. Then Coquine and Moose go with the same result. We are crabbing sideways now, starting to run out of room for the play I want. I am yelling at Jacques but there is so much noise from the crowd I'm not sure that he can hear me. Now Pierre is waiting for his turn at the line. Finally Jacques puts his foot on the ball and looks up, assessing the situation. With the palm of my hand I show him that I want it in front of me. He waves Pierre out of the way and, diving to avoid any traffic, sends me a spiralled pass. I edge another couple of steps right to get outside the flanker before even touching the ball, dummy to Xavier who holds up two defenders on a feint, and slip a kick off the inside of my foot into the space that has opened up behind their defensive line. It wobbles and curls, then sits up just enough for Rich who bursts onto the pick-up, runs around behind the posts and splashes down for five points. Grins, high fives. This feels good.

As I line up the conversion, I can hear the lilting voice of their captain trying to regather the threads as his team huddle around. No one is even interested on putting pressure on my kick. 'Let's just keep our heads, all right boys? There's only five minutes gone. No panic, now. There's plenty of time to get back into this game. Slow it down. We're missing Bert for the next few minutes, so for now keep it tight or go to the corners. Work the short side, plenty of pick and go. Let's just settle down.' I bang it over and trot back, passing the tee to Nico and squirting water into my mouth as I go. I would have preferred to hear them shouting at each other. It doesn't sound like they're going to roll over. That would have been too easy. They made such a racket warming up before the game I started to think they were afraid, but someone is holding them together.

Moose takes the kick-off cleanly and is flattened almost immediately — they put it higher this time. A mess of bodies forms on the floor, and the referee gives them a scrum, eliciting hoots and whistles and insults from the crowd. The scrum goes down, resets, goes down again. The ref talks to the two front rows. This is wasting time when we should be taking advantage of their being a man down. The scrum sets again, then goes down again. Penalty to them. More hoots and whistles from the sideline. It's kickable, so their fullback lines it up, taking his time. He throws a bit of grass in the air to check out the wind, more superstition than real information-gathering — the ball flies a lot higher than that. Coquine rallies the troops: 'We must score in the next three minutes.' Statistically, all things being equal, teams are most vulnerable in the three minutes after scoring. 'And no more bloody penalties. Don't let them back in.' The fullback hits it well, confirming what I'd seen of him on the tapes: 10–3 after only ten minutes.

From the kick-off they drive, then, rather than kicking back to us, send a series of two-man pods to carry the ball, interspersed with individual pick-ups from the base of the ruck. They're not making any ground, just soaking up time and hoping for a misstep from us to gift them a penalty. Their centres come in to help with the grunt work. Our pack have fanned out across the line, making the tackles without being able to wrestle the ball away. Seconds tick away, a minute, more. Dull thuds as bone and muscle impact on bone and muscle. Their halfback yaps busily: 'Tiger ball. Get over it. Plus one, plus one!' He lines up runners who shout their readiness: 'Yes, Jonesey!' The ref shares his thoughts: 'Ruck formed. Hands off, blue. Hands off!' Our defensive line bends and straightens, reforming as the actors swap roles. 'I've got the inside,' 'I've got first man,' 'Push out, push out.' You couldn't call it balletic, but the chaos is carefully choreographed, drills and instincts and communication combined to make a muddy pattern that ebbs and flows according to a greater design. They start to make headway, a couple of passes take the ball wider and I have a tackle to make on their big number eight. I grab his shoulders and throw him over my leg, judo style. No, it's not orthodox, but I'm not putting my head near those slabby thighs and their pumping knees. Besides, the rule book doesn't have anything against it as long as I'm holding onto him. They recycle again. As I'm getting up to return to the defensive line, their number eight is still untangling himself from a couple of other sets of limbs on the ground, and he grabs onto my jersey, looking to delay me. They have made a half-break: I have to get back in line. 'Oi, piss off.' Our eyes lock for a second. He grins, and I can see a black mouthguard. He doesn't let go. His nose is bleeding already. I stand on the inviting pinkness of his other hand, not hard enough to make it obvious to a touch judge, but turning the studs all the same. A yelp, a curse, and I am free. 'Oh, shit. Sorry, mate.' I imagine I get a dirty look but I'm not hanging around to find out. A light rain starts to fall, and at the next breakdown the ref whistles for a scrum.

* * *

Fifteen minutes later we've swapped penalties. The ball is now as greasy as a butcher's handshake and the game has settled into attritional kicking. Long periods of aerial ping-pong as each side looks for position, waiting for the other to make a move, or a mistake. Typically, we lose patience first. Moose runs back a ball from deep in our half, gets turned over, and their centres combine cleverly to create an overlap for the left wing who steps inside Denis and runs under the posts: 13-all.

Chapter 22

Half-time. Still 13-all. As we file back into the changing room, Christophe is flailing away with a combination of pidgin English and hand gestures to the referee about the scrum: 'The left prop, he is like this . . .' The ref makes a few noncommittal noises and heads to his own room. Christophe rolls his eyes and mutters.

We traipse in, sprigs chattering, take a seat on the benches. Different units hold their own low-voiced conversations. Xavier wants me to try more chips over the top: 'They're on fucking horseback in the centre. I'm sure they're a yard offside every time.'

Recovery drinks are consumed, bananas peeled and eaten; a couple of icepacks are distributed; the doc hustles Thomas into the treatment room.

Titi, to no one in particular: 'We're not losing to these bastards.'

Christophe: 'OK, sit down, take a moment. No injuries? Good. In ten minutes we'll start making a few subs. At the moment we're letting them dictate the rhythm. They've slowed it down so now we're playing how they want us to. We have to speed it up. Try to stay on your feet in contact, wait for support, then get some momentum and a quick release while we're going forward.' The Fibber comes in, lurks in the corner chewing a nail. 'Mark, the inside ball on an angle for the blindside wing. It's worked once. Do it again. Maybe channel two this time. And the drop goal is still a good option. If they're slowing our ball down, don't hesitate to have a go from wherever.'

Coquine gets to his feet. 'Bring it in. Come on!' Our huddle smells of sweat and liniment and freshly cut grass. His voice is raised almost to a full-blooded shout. Adrenalin and the urgency of the situation has all of us operating in a hyper-reality. Off-field worries slip back into insignificance; my big win of the first minute has been filed away and is now irrelevant. Almost. Arms lock around bodies. Inside, away from the open sky of the field, heat from our assembled bodies forms droplets of moisture on the cold concrete of the changing room roof; the intensity is distilled, refined, regenerative. 'Forty minutes, boys, just forty minutes. Home game. We have to physically fucking smash them. We have to. Play the next forty minutes like a final, because that's what it is now.'

Christophe gives us his final words: 'The next ten minutes are crucial. We have to work harder to clear out those rucks and get quick ball. I don't care what you do to make it happen, just get it done.'

The Fibber stands at the door, claps each of us on the back as we file past him. 'Come on, boys. Come on. Let's go. Come on, boys. Come on, Mark.'

An afterthought from Christophe reaches us in the tunnel. 'And discipline!'

I'm not sure that everyone can hear. Or if they do, that they're listening.

* * *

Five minutes into the second half, it kicks off. A scuffle at a ruck develops into a roiling mess of enthusiastic malevolence.

The ref blows his whistle to no effect. The ball rolls towards the touchline, suddenly unimportant. Without the unifying centre of attention there are simultaneous flare-ups, and for a moment the ref doesn't know quite where to put himself. Along with the other backs I wander in slowly, pulled by a sense of obligation to bear witness at least. In the few seconds it takes to cover the ground, everyone calms down into stares and mouthing off. One of theirs is on the floor. The ref orders the two teams into neutral corners and along with the video ref and the big-screen replay begins unravelling the knot of blame. Coquine is quietly doing his nut: 'Fuck, boys, discipline.' Crouched over the prostrate figure that now lies in no-man's-land, their physio bleats at the referee, who, having finished his consultation, wanders over to see the patient who stumbles to his feet, seemingly embarrassed by the attention.

Every eye is fixed on the big screen. For all the pushing and shoving, no one appears to have thrown a punch until a new angle shows Moose pushing their lock in the face and he tries to milk it with a dive. Played back at real speed it becomes clear the dumb bastard has had an absolute shocker. The crowd jeers. The ref calls the captains over, and their number five. Moose, charged with translation duties, rolls up as well. I can't hear what is said, but the ref shows a yellow card to their lock. Booing from the stands switches to clapping and shouts of encouragement. No one needs to tell me to take a shot. Nico is there with the tee already. I place the ball carefully, already visualising the imaginary vertical line a couple of metres inside the left-hand upright that I will aim for. Kicking right to left, with a slight breeze coming from my left. A touch under forty metres with the angle. Bread and butter for me. I expect to kick every one of these, everyone expects me to kick it. I measure out four steps back on a straight line away from the posts, then two to my left. Breathe. Look towards the posts, seeing my imaginary line again, readjusting it slightly to the right. At the bottom of my field of concentration, one of their props is standing just ten metres from the ball, leaning to his right, hoping that the lines on his striped jersey will skew my vision as I run in. A stupid distraction, lame, ordinarily futile — but now it is in my head. The referee is looking at me. Everyone is looking at me. I look at him, enquiring, then at the prop. The ref follows my look, catches on, tells the prop to stand up straight. I don't have time to worry about whether this means I have won or lost this tiny battle of wills, I have to kick the bloody ball. Sixty seconds between the whistle and the kick. Don't feel rushed. My niece, Sasha, pops into my head, presenting me with her drawing of me and an oval ball and an arced trajectory through the posts. I am good. I am fucking good. I know where this is going. I take another couple of seconds, because now I know that I have won and I am relaxed. Head down, follow through. A sweet strike. I pick the tee up and frisbee it to Nico. Cheering, pats on the back as we retreat. 'The team that scores first after half-time wins the game.' My coach at school used to tell us that. I hope theirs did the same.

* * *

Less than five minutes to go. We still lead by three points. I told Rachel we would win by ten. Logically we should play it safe, slow it down, kill the game and take the win. That logic means a loss of face for me. It also means a bonus point for them. Coquine goes off reluctantly, replaced for the last five minutes. I can hear him tell Titi to ride it out, get hold of the ball and do the windscreen wipers: one pass, from side to side of the ruck with no intention of going anywhere, the carrier just holding onto the ball, flopping into the tackle and denying them possession. They can't do anything without the ball. Unless, of course, we cock it up somehow and get penalised.

A scrum for us, just outside our twenty-two-metre line. Titi picks it up from the base, is tackled after gaining a couple of metres. Jacques waits, sets his forwards then pops to Moose, who goes down on the advantage line. Another pile-up. Their defensive line tightens in, seeing the way this is going. Four or five of their forwards are now piling into each ruck to try to turn over the ball, leaving more room elsewhere. Behind the back of my hand, I call a chip kick. Their ten can see the communication, guesses I want to spread it, orders his line to fan out again. More one-off runners, more sterile rucks. Six phases of play and we haven't moved. Eight phases. Shuffling sideways. On the tenth, Josh makes a couple of metres and at last we are on the front foot. I call to Jacques, who looks at me, hesitates, then pops it to Moose who is hit hard and driven back.

Square one. Slow ball. Titi picks and goes. I look up at the clock. Less than three minutes to go. Xavier goes in to carry some of the load. He is wrapped up on his first carry, running too high, dumped into the turf by two tacklers. With no chance of the ball coming out, the ref blows for a scrum. Our put-in. Lucky. That will make it less than two minutes to go. We're barely out of our quarter. A penalty to them will be a gift, and they will take the draw — it will be as good as a win for them. As the scrum sets, ten metres in from the right-hand touchline, I can hear Christophe shouting instructions at me. He wants me to play it safe. I am standing on the left-hand side of the scrum, inside the twenty-two-metre line with the centres lined out to my left, Thomas on his wing, Denis at the back in the middle,

Rich on the right behind the scrum. I give myself another couple of steps diagonally away from the scrum, turn my back to the opposition and make the call. 'Curveball.' Denis's eyes widen. Xavier splutters. 'Curveball? Are you nuts?' I glance over towards Rich, too far away to hear and show him my hand bending out towards his wing on the right. He smiles, nods. I turn back towards the scrum, and call to Jacques who is looking towards me as he waits to put the ball in. I point to myself and, with a flat hand, show him that I plan to kick it deep into leftfield. He nods. Their right wing takes a few steps back, and their centres spread a little wider to take up the space.

The scrum is set and almost immediately the two front rows buckle, but the ball is available and the ref waves Jacques on to play it. He whips it out to me, and I shuffle left, conscious of their flanker rapidly closing on me, shoulders facing towards the left-hand corner at their end, and make the kick a split second before his dive to block it. The ball comes ballooning off the outside of my foot in a banana shape over the outstretched hands, over the top of the scrum, touching down just on our side of halfway, ten metres in on the right-hand side. Their wing, anticipating the kick left, is already twenty metres out of position, wrongfooted, stranded.

Rich reaches with one hand and plucks the ball out of its high bounce. Their cover, momentarily stunned, is now coming across though, and he still has the fullback to beat. He breaks infield, towards the fullback, and their chasers switch direction as well, Xavier and me converging on him in support, their fullback slowing as he lines Rich up, not wanting to be beaten on the inside. Rich shortens his strides as he approaches contact, feet stabbing the ground like the needle on a sewing machine, making his next change of direction impossible to read. He is almost within reach when he pushes hard off his left foot, away from the grasping arms, and hares towards the corner flag. Their right winger dives despairingly at his legs as he crosses the line, forcing Rich down on one knee; he pushes off the grass and trots behind the posts to dot the ball down as we arrive and he is swamped in congratulations. A couple of supporters jump the fence and Moose grabs one of their flags, waving it to the crowd.

Part Two

Chapter 23

The noise is barely enough to wake her. She's hungover — again — and over the years she has become accustomed to screening out all but the most urgent-sounding cries of the kids. This is something else. Not inside the house. Blue light bleeds through the curtains: 5.58 on the bedside clock. Not the wind. Maybe a dog. That bloody fence needs fixing. She gives the lump beside her a kick with the back of her heel but doesn't bother with the reasoning behind it. It wouldn't make any difference. Her mouth is tacky with booze and cigarettes and a persistent vegetable taste. She won't be getting any more sleep but she can stay there, wrapped in her cocoon, for a while. She snakes out a hand toward the glass of water that she had the foresight to leave beside the bed.

A shadow moves past the window, on the outskirts of her field of vision. Did she really see that? Then a second. Man-sized. Footsteps move briskly onto the deck, then across it. Cops? She quickly rewinds what she can remember of last night. No reason for them to be here. Ah, shit. She gives the lump another kick, harder this time. No response. A shake, then a whisper that comes out in a hiss. 'Wake up, you dozy bastard. Cops.'

The lump rolls onto his back, starts to snore. She cocks her hand, looking to get a decent angle on his face. Half-playful.

The sound of glass shattering down the hallway.

Cops would have knocked first.

She rolls out of bed, hoisting an escaped tit back inside her singlet and sweeping the duvet around her. Knocks over the glass of water, swears, ignores it. She fumbles for her glasses, can't find them, throws back the flimsy door harder than she needs to. Now she can hear some kind of liquid being poured onto the floor. It comes quickly, in glugs. An instantly recognisable smell cuts through what remains of her hangover. She drops the duvet, starts to run down the hallway.

Her elder daughter comes to the door of her bedroom, all tangled blonde hair and miraculously unsmudged eyes. 'Stay in your room, Sasha.'

Short footsteps patter close behind her as she crosses the few remaining feet to the living room. She doesn't scream. Later, on her own, she will be proud of this.

A man wearing a dark sweatshirt and a black balaclava is standing at the space left by a smashed window pane in the top half of a sliding door — her front door — and emptying an orange plastic can into her living room. His arms move in a wide semi-circle, making an effort to throw the liquid as far away as possible. He looks up. 'Probably not a good idea to turn on the lights, eh, lady?'

She picks up the closest thing she can lay her hands on — a cordless telephone — and hurls it at the figure in black. It bounces off the metal window frame. 'Get out of my fucking house!' The second dark figure steps forward, next to the first man now, clearly visible through the broken window. She is close enough that, even without her glasses, she can see he is holding some kind of gun. He sits it on his forearm, pointing it at her. Steady. Two barrels. A sawn-off shotgun. No, definitely not the cops. He shifts his aim to just behind her. She turns and, seeing

Sasha, puts herself in between.

The first man finishes emptying the orange plastic can. The room smells like the forecourt of a service station with the volume turned up to eleven. He puts the can between his feet, extracts a sheet of paper from his back pocket and holds it up against the neighbouring, unbroken window pane.

Something is written on the paper, but she can't make it out. 'What the fuck does that say?'

The men look at each other. Neither of them move.

Sasha, peering round from behind her mother, reads out the three words on the sheet of paper.

What the fuck does that mean?

Sparky.

Part Three

'Pity the country that needs heroes.'
Galileo to Andrea
The Life of Galileo, Bertolt Brecht

Chapter 24

'The world isn't the nice place you like to think it is.'

Rachel's money-making scheme has developed a twist. The greedy cow wants me to fix a game. Maybe the fancy Christmas holiday has gone to her head.

'I don't care. I'm one of the good guys, and I'm not fucking over my mates just to make some money. Things are going all right as it is — why get greedy?'

'We're running out of time. You're running out of time to do this. Mark, you and your friends don't really care what happens, and if we pick the right game it won't make all that much difference to you anyway. From what you tell me your president has already been arranging games to suit himself. He made sure your friend Josh and the others, they played here instead of for their country while other teams were disadvantaged because their players went to the World Cup. Everyone rigs the game in their favour if they can, it's just business. Only suckers still play by the rules. And it's not as if the club care about you — you said so yourself. You got knocked out last week and they want you to play again this week.'

There is something in that. I am feeling more and more like a piece of meat. Coquine clocked me with his knee piling into a ruck. I had to come off. I knew what I was supposed to be doing but I couldn't remember any of the calls or how we had got to the second half. I only know what happened because I watched it yesterday at the video session; everyone had a laugh. The doc seemed to think I was all right, and I trust him. We missed the spread, though only by a point. There is a mandatory three-week stand-down for head injuries but there are loopholes if the club wants to work them. They generally do. 'It was only a concussion; it's not as if I was throwing up or anything.'

'You told me you still had a headache on Monday.'

'Is this what you've been lining me up for all this time? Did you plan this right from the start? You open your legs and I fall in, that's how this is supposed to work? Fuck me, I am an idiot. You even talked about it the first time we met.'

'It's an opportunity for you to make some cash before you get thrown away because you're past your sell-by date. It's an opportunity for you and for me. For us.'

'For us? Except that I do the dirty work. Great opportunity for you. The very best kind. Jesus, I really am an idiot.'

'Explain to me why you think this is such a bad idea.'

'It's just plain wrong.' I am walking away now, into the bedroom. She follows.

'Why? Someone has to lose. What difference does it make who it is? It's only theatre, entertainment, another kind of business. People are still going to come and see the show, and it's going to look just the same as any other day. You just miss a few kicks and make some mistakes. And to make up for that, you get enough money to do what you want for a year or two. Or five, depending on how fast you spend it.'

'How much money?' If you're thinking about selling your soul, you might as well find out how much it's worth.

'It all depends on you. A couple of hundred thousand pounds. Maybe more.'

I can't run the drop-goal trick any more. After the first one they dropped the odds from thirty to one to twelve to one. I had another go in the next game and missed. Since then I'm at six to one to score first points with a drop. Barely worth my while.

'It's not enough.'

'How much do you want?'

'I'm not doing it, end of story.'

'You have this idea that the rest of the world plays by the rules, that everyone is honourable. If you work hard it will all turn out OK.'

'Turned out all right so far.'

'You're such a little boy. It doesn't work like that. Life isn't fair. You must know that by now. And if you don't, you'll find out when you get into the real world — and that is coming very fast. I've seen you on Sundays, you can barely walk. You're ruining yourself for people who don't care about you now, and they'll care about you even less in ten years. In a few months you're on your own. When you're just the guy in the street, you won't have any leverage. And you'll regret passing up on this. Do you know what the average wage is? Here in France it's less than two thousand euros a month. What do you call it, "chump change"? Your apartment costs more than two thousand euros a month. *Average* wage — lots of people make a lot less. And what are you planning on doing? How's that coaching course coming on?'

'I'll go home. I can live on what I've got in New Zealand. I'll do some coaching there, pick up a trade, maybe do some commentating. I'm not playing bloody Judas.'

'It's not a question of playing Judas, it's about taking advantage of a situation. Just think about it. It will make no difference to anyone else, and all the difference in the world to you. Think about the freedom you can have if you just have the balls to grab an opportunity.'

All my life I wanted to play pro. When I was twelve I met this guy who was playing in Italy and I asked him what he did, and he said 'I'm a professional rugby player'. And I thought, 'That is a great job. That's what I want to do.' Even more than playing for my country. Fixing a game, even now . . . I don't know, maybe if I was broke.

'It just feels good to be part of something like this. I like how that makes me feel.'

'You sound like a boy scout. I can't believe it. They've chewed you up and now they're going to spit you out. Look at how your president has treated you. You're nothing to him, so why should you be loyal? You're either weak and you lose, or you're strong and you win. I didn't think you'd want to line up on the side of the losers. We're not responsible for everything. You're not fifteen any more. It's just the way the world works. No one needs to know, and no one is going to get hurt.'

'This conversation is over.'

'Just think about it. I'm going out for while.' The door to the apartment clicks shut.

I suppose I can't complain about home life being boring. An hour ago I was thinking we might settle down, get married, the whole deal. We stopped using condoms at Christmas. She's on the pill, though. I'm not that much of an idiot.

I probably should have thrown her out as soon as this started. I didn't, though. The truth is that somewhere, a long way back in my brain, a little voice is saying, 'Well? Why not?'

Put aside the fact that I'd be crossing over to the dark side. I wouldn't be the first to do that. A guy I used to play with showed me the ampoules of steroids he used to inject himself with. He got them from the trainer, who had the right contacts. The guy was coming back from a shoulder injury and he asked if he could get a little boost. The trainer told him he didn't really approve, but the guy was a pro, it was his livelihood, and he'd sort him out with a short course.

The problem isn't breaking the rules; the problem is getting pinged. Even the old man, who was a ref, said that a team should always be penalised at least once a game for offside just so they know where the ref draws the line. 'Cheats never prosper' is all right for children but a guy I was at school with used to write crib notes on his thighs. He wore long shorts to the exam. He made his first million before he was thirty.

I know why Rachel is pushing so hard on this. She got laid off from her newspaper at Christmas. Cost-cutting. Her visa runs out in June. She says there's not much out there at the moment for her and that isn't likely to change. She'll probably have to retrain. A friend of hers who got laid off from a paper six months ago is working as a drone in a white-collar factory in La Défense, writing news wrap-ups for client corporations on minimum wage. She's happy to have it. Another one of their friends is stripping. She was going to be an actress. Rachel has virtually moved in with me, subletting her room in London to another girlfriend.

When she was growing up, her old man was a butcher in a suburb of São Paulo and her mother worked the till. They got squeezed out when a supermarket opened up next door. They moved a couple of times, tried to set up again in the same neighbourhood. He poured all his savings into the first one, which went under quickly. The second time round he went in with a partner. That ended messily. The old man found himself, mid-fifties, no job, no money, no prospects. They couldn't pay the second mortgage on the house, so that went. Rachel's mother started working as a cashier in the supermarket that squeezed them out. The old man just curled up and died. Rachel had left home by then but wasn't working yet. Her mother still lives in a unit opposite the supermarket.

* * *

I am in awe of a woman who could go to Afghanistan, put on a burqa and wander round interviewing Taliban commanders. It's just one of her many faces: difficult to line up the apparently bulletproof side with the moments of fragility. She started getting snarly much earlier than I would have imagined. I thought we were still in that honeymoon period where minor irritations slid off. I was having a moan about not having continued to study.

'No regrets — there's no point in having them. If you had really wanted to you would have done it.'

'I'm not saying it's not my fault. Just that if I knew then what I do now—.'

'So make up your mind to do it now. Or don't do it. But stop acting like a little boy. You don't know what you want, you feel sorry for yourself, it could have all been different. Pathetic.'

She has a scar on her face just above her left cheekbone. It is invisible when she wears make-up, but she doesn't usually — and she doesn't need to — although she always has eyeliner on. Along with her olive skin and dark hair it gives her a vaguely Middle Eastern look.

'How did you get the scar?'

'I ran through a sliding door at my cousin's house. I was ten.'

'Did you regret it?'

'It isn't the same. That was an accident. You're a grown-up, you make choices.'

I found her later that night weeping silently in the spare bedroom. She had just received an email. I didn't ask who from.

'I fuck everything up.' It wouldn't have been the right moment to make a point. I just held her, and tried to decide whether I was pleased or disappointed at the evidence of weakness. Then felt bad about being cold-blooded while I could feel the sobs make her gasp for breath. I hate women crying: they look terrible and they make you feel guilty.

* * *

Charlie reckons he's got a couple of gigs for me. Not as much as I'm on now but still good coin. The sticking point is going to be the medical test. I'm basically walking wounded now, excused all training on Mondays and Tuesdays, given weeks off whenever possible — which suits the club as well: unless we make the finals in both competitions, I'll have to play pretty much every game from here on to be over the seventy-five per cent mark that gives me another year. There's a lot of talk about the ten from Toulouse in the press but Tisserand still assures me that nothing has been signed. We both know that for us to have any chance of making the finals I have to play, so he's not about to give me a reason to throw in the towel.

I'm nervous about where things are going. For the first time ever, I have trouble sleeping. That used to be one of the great things about the job — at home, I would watch Sarah, who hated her work in a data-processing company (I never really understood what that was, or why she hated it so much), get more and more wound up on Sunday nights, while I would be looking forward to weights at ten o'clock and an afternoon playing games to sweat out the bumps from the weekend. The worst thing that could happen was a bollocking at the video session. Now I can see the void. Another contract will put it off.

I did do a couple of days of work experience in Wellington in a real estate office. Jesus, it was dull. Lunchtime banter revolved around people asking each other what they were eating and what they watched on TV last night. No one talked money, which was what they were all there for. Perhaps they didn't want to do it in front of me. The boss was rapt to have me there. He sold me a property.

How would I go about rigging a game? I'm not saying I'll do it. Just out of interest, a sort of intellectual exercise. The kicks, obviously, but there's always a back-up kicker and I can only miss so many before he gets wheeled in. And there are only some kicks I can miss without arousing suspicion — the sitter in front of the posts might go wrong once, but not twice. If I call the wrong moves, throw passes on the hip instead of out in front, that'll slow things down. Can't be too obvious, though, or I'll get subbed. Same with missed tackles. One is already a lot, two is too many, three and I'm off. A misunderstanding would work once. A yellow card would help. Red for me would be a push, though it would be pretty much a guarantee. We've got an away game coming up in a couple of weeks against the bottom-ranked battlers that we really should win but it wouldn't be a disaster if we didn't. I'd need to be careful not to look so bad that I kill any chance of a contract somewhere else, but anyone can have an off day. It could work. I'm not saying I'll do it, but it could work.

Chapter 25

After eight days of rest the ankle feels less like a bucket of razorblades, though there are still some sharp edges. Eric wants me to run on it, which is a bloody stupid idea if you ask me but no one does, so I get ready to run. The justification is that I can do all the cycling I want, I'm still not likely to use a bike around the field. There's probably something in that. I prefer to think the worst of him.

François is coming back from his hamstring problem and he is to run as well. Light stuff for both of us, but lighter for him than me. Eric has a bright idea: 'Here, you can run with grandpa. He's taking it easy, as usual.' I get the stopwatch by dint of seniority. Something to go with the sneer. Sixteen 150s, the length of the pitch then almost the entire breadth of the pitch. Eric drops a cone ten metres short of the other side. François is to run a short course, starting on the inside, five metres ahead of me, then turning five metres before me. Thirty seconds on, thirty seconds off, then come back. Two sets of eight, with a five-minute break. Piece of piss.

We jog a couple of laps for a warm-up. Companionable silence for the first half-lap, then he asks how old I am. I tell him.

'How does that feel?'

'How does what feel?'

'You know, thirty-three.'

He's a good kid. 'The same as you, just ten years older.'

He can't take a hint. 'That's what I mean. This is the first time I've pulled a hamstring. Is it going to get worse?'

'That depends.' He likes his nightlife. Fair enough, so would I in his situation. He must be pulling in some serious cash, probably hasn't even thought about a mortgage. Ten years ahead of him and the way things are going he looks set to make a mint.

'On what?'

All right, he's not the sharpest. 'Luck, good management.'

I raise the pace for the second lap. We both start to breathe through our mouths. I can smell last night's booze on him. 'You all right?'

'Fine.'

'Good night?'

'Mmfh.'

Nothing more is said. We reach the finish of the warm-up, stretch. The doc pulls up to the side of the training ground on his scooter. 'Don't do too much, all right?' This isn't directed at me.

Eric: 'Don't be too hard on the old man.' This isn't directed at me either. François grins. He has green eyes that shine in the sunlight.

We do the first one easy. Thirty-one seconds. We start on the minute.

Thirty seconds each for the next three, as per instructions. I feel good: loping easily, the smell of the grass, the sun, a crisp late morning. My ankle has warmed up, no problems. It's a strange kind of sensual pleasure, pushing up towards the limits of your physical ability and still feeling comfortable. François is a few metres short when I finish the fourth. He's blowing a bit.

'You all right? Don't bust a gut for this.'

'Of course I'm all right.' Shit, mate, I'm just trying to be nice.

He takes off on the next one, I catch him at the corner flag then he pulls ahead with his short-course advantage. I have to change gear to arrive at the same time. We finish in twenty-eight seconds. We go on the minute.

He hares away again for number six. I have to pick up my pace, even though I'm the one giving the off. I ease off at the corner flag, he finishes ten metres ahead, I'm slowing down for the finish. I've got nothing to prove. Twenty-eight seconds for me, he must have gone through in twenty-six, twenty-seven.

'You all right?' He's asking *me* if I'm all right. I'm fucking fine.

I drop the recovery to twenty seconds.

I'm already running when I give him the 'Go!' for the next one, set slightly forward in a sprinter's style. Short stabbing steps to accelerate, flowing into a lean run just below flat out. I've overtaken him by the halfway line. Then we run into the forwards who are walking back to the water bottles from whatever they've been doing. '*Piste!*' I bang into the flag with my shoulder as I round the corner, and out of the corner of my eye I can see that he has cut across the right angle that he is supposed to respect. I wind up for the last forty and he still beats me by fifty centimetres. I look at the stopwatch as I cross the line. Twenty-five seconds. He has his hands on his head, sucking it in. I walk around with my hands on my hips, breathing in through my nose. No matter how much it hurts, never let the other guy see that you are vulnerable. We don't say anything.

I keep the recovery at twenty. This is getting childish.

'Five seconds. Three, two, one.' I can feel the moulded studs in the soles of my sponsor's product bite into the grass as I shave a couple of metres. 'Go!'

François has anticipated as well. Into it. We are both eating the ground, quickly. He cuts a great hunk off the corner this time, and I — running round the flag still — am a couple of metres behind when he finishes. Twenty-five seconds.

Even if I try not to show it, we are both sucking lungfuls when Eric walks up. 'Hey, the old man's got the bonnet up. The radiator looks like it's blown.'

Idiot.

'Good stuff guys. Good work. Take five minutes, then the next set.'

We walk around for a bit, grab our water bottles, then I sit down and stretch. I can't see what the other guy is up to, and I'm not looking. Concentrate on my breathing. Within a minute I feel good again. My quads feel a bit tight, but otherwise I'm operating at full capacity. I give it another minute or so, then call time and set up on the cone.

'Three, two, one.' François has already gone so I don't bother with formalities. A dead-set fucking sprint. I cut inside the corner flag on the same angle as my opponent. We hit the tape together. Twenty-two seconds. This is ridiculous.

Twenty seconds to recover. The first one of the set is always easy, but he doesn't have enough in the tank to do another seven at this speed with that recovery. Shit, *I* don't have enough in the tank to do another seven at this speed with that recovery. He should walk away. Perhaps *I* should walk away — I'm supposed to be the grown-up. Pride is at stake, though, and perhaps more than pride.

We go again, both anticipating. Same result. Another one comes, quickly. Just before the off I sneak a look and he is hurting, eyes closed, whooshing air then spitting a long hoick of phlegm, half of which winds up on his T-shirt. He doesn't wipe it off. Going, going . . . My legs are burning now, my lungs are burning, working hard to hold my form. Just as we hit halfway, neck and neck, he fades out of my field of vision. I slow, grateful for the respite, and look over my shoulder once I've turned the corner, back to where he is hobbling on one leg. Hit by the hamstring sniper. Another few weeks.

I wander back towards him. Somehow the physios have got wind of what's happened and are already piling out onto the field. When I get up close the thrill of the chase evaporates. But I didn't pull the trigger and I refuse to feel the melancholy of the hunter after his kill.

François' eyes are filled with tears of rage or pain. Or maybe it's just sweat.

I feel pretty good.

* * *

'What is honour?'

A fat, bearded, ginger bloke is lecturing us on teambuilding. We have signs up in the changing room and the weights room. You know the drill: 'Honour', 'Excellence', 'Teamwork', 'Humility' and so on. It makes the place feel like a Japanese car factory.

'If the words don't mean the same thing to each of you — and many of you don't even speak the same language — then the foundations of your group and the goals to which you aspire are going to be confused. If the words are empty, how can you believe in them? If you envisage one thing but your friend envisages another when you are talking about a concept, how can you agree on what is important? So I'm going to repeat the question: what is honour? You, *monsieur*, what does honour mean to you?'

The poor bastard has picked on Josh, who has been studying something on his shoe and hasn't even heard the question let alone got an answer ready. Coquine, seeing where this is going, speaks up. 'This isn't an intellectual exercise. We're not at school. We all know what honour means, even if we might have problems defining it.'

'This is what I'm trying to explain. What I think of as honour, or an honourable action, is probably different from your definition. We live in different worlds, and the world that I inhabit has different standards from yours. But you need to agree on your set of standards if you are all to adhere to those standards. Otherwise you might as well have pictures of naked women on the walls.' Snickering at the idea of nudie photos. The flecks of grey in the consultant's beard look more pronounced. Everyone has broadband.

Josh, having been nudged by Moose and had a translation, now has an answer. 'Where I come from, when you are made chief of the tribe, the tribe gets a pig and they give it to you. So it's your pig, right?' The teambuilding consultant looks a bit puzzled but appears to speak English and be following the Pacific Islands version. 'Now, you can eat the pig on your own, or you can share it around the tribe. Sharing it around is the *honourable* thing to do. And plus you get free feeds from everyone else afterwards, 'cos they owe you. And eating a whole pig on your own is a bit of a struggle.' Josh sits back looking pleased. He is nicknamed 'Obelix'. He is a Kiwi but still in touch with his Samoan roots, though not as much as one of his cousins playing over here who, after a couple of years of sending a good chunk of his French salary home to the family, his church and having bought everything he needed — basically a car and a house — said, 'I don't know what to do with all this money.' How we laughed.

Once the room settles down, the consultant picks up again and tries to tie pigs and honour together. 'This is a very interesting way of looking at honour. What you are saying is that you perform a good action with the pig in order to receive something from those who have observed your action and benefited in some way from it. Society, or your entourage, gain from your actions and you in turn gain from them. You are respected as an honourable man *and* you put some more pork in the bank for later. But is that what you really think of as honour? Is it about self-interest?'

Silence. He looks around the room, hoping for some feedback. Nothing. Christophe is sitting a couple of metres away from me at the front of the room, and when the consultant's hopeful gaze reaches him he points to his watch with his finger running round the dial.

The consultant nods. 'Perhaps honour is not the easiest concept to agree on? We don't have much time. I think it may be too philosophical. Should we turn our attention to excellence?'

I stare at Christophe's wrist.

* * *

By the time Christophe thanks the consultant everyone is half-asleep but I am curious enough to want to push it. If I'm right to be suspicious, I don't want to draw attention to myself so I throw out a line for some help. 'Jesus, Coquine, did you see that? Christophe has a Rolex.'

'A what?'

'A Rolex. You know, the most expensive watch you can get.'

'Really? Showy bastard. Hey, Jacques did you see this?'

A small gang of us clusters round, demanding to know what the time is. Christophe looks sheepish but not too unhappy.

'Is it real?'

'Of course it is.'

'Why would you get one of those?'

'It's my wife. She works in advertising. This guy she used to work for said that any man who doesn't have one at fifty is a loser.'

'You're fucking with us. So she bought you one?'

Christophe smiles, raises his eyebrows.

'How old are you?'

'Forty-seven.'

'So you're ahead of the pack.'

'How much is it worth?'

Chapter 26

Tuesday-night drinks. Rachel is in London. The talk has turned to women.

'I think of it as a game of blackjack. You look at the cards you've got in your hand, you weigh them up and you decide if you want to stick or twist.' Rich is holding forth on his unifying theory of women to Josh, Moose and me.

Josh is sceptical. 'That is the shittest theory I have ever heard. And I have heard a lot of shit theories. Mainly from you. For a start, who are you playing against?'

'You're always playing the bank.' Rich spreads his arms. 'Because the bank is life itself, my friend.'

You can't help feeling intrigued. 'All right, I'll bite. What happens if you go bust?'

'That's the beauty of it. You just deal yourself a new hand. There's always a new hand. You can't ever really go bust.'

'So how do you know if you've got twenty-one?'

'What do you mean? You just know. It's obvious. There's not a lot of twenty-ones out there. True quality stands up and smacks you in the face. Myself, I'd settle for two picture cards. I'm not greedy.'

'But you do nothing but twist. You twist every weekend. You'd have to get to know them, wouldn't you?'

'Mate, I have the well-trained eye of a connoisseur. Anyway, statistically speaking, the more cards I turn over, the more chance I have of getting it right.'

Josh is a bit sceptical. 'I cannot believe anyone is taking this tit seriously.'

'Have you ever thought about what girls think you're worth? I mean, if I were a girl, I'd look at you and think you have to be going for a five-card under.'

'Come on, mate, I've got a full house. Looks, brains, money, a giver in the sack — and I'm a good guy. It doesn't get much better.'

Moose: 'A full house is poker.'

'Yeah, whatever.'

'So in concrete terms, let's talk examples. What's the best hand you've ever held?'

'Well, now, there's been a lot of good hands.'

Moose takes his cards seriously: 'You know that you're supposed to stick on anything higher than sixteen?'

'Look, this is bloody ridiculous. Let's say you're holding seven. How do you twist?'

'Mate, if you're holding seven to start with you're playing some very bad blackjack. I mean, you get to look at the cards before you pick them up.'

'Come on, how do you know what your hand's worth? You can't just take it on face value.'

'Fair point. It is true that, for example, the best lookers are often a bit lazy at bedtime. They've been spoilt by all the attention. Whereas your run-of-the-mill worker bee knows she's got to do a little bit extra — and that can count for a lot. Mutton has its advantages too: a bit gamey, sure, but tasty. Your older woman is grateful, experienced and cunning — and in general there are no strings attached. That's why you need to look at a large sample.

You build up better understanding of the market by looking at a big cross-section.'

Josh, always practical: 'Moose, your round.' Moose can go a bit T Rex, forearms apparently not long enough to reach his pockets.

'Examples.'

'I could tell you some stories but you wouldn't know the characters. In terms of someone we all know, Mrs Josh is a good sort but you're married so that doesn't count — and I don't know all the ins and outs of the situation, of course, which is a shame — but I would have to say that Mark seems to be holding a couple of picture cards at the very least.'

All eyes turn to me. 'Rachel?'

'Mate, Miss Brazil is getting double ice-cream cones from me.' Rich puts out his hands, thumbs up. 'She is a queen.'

Moose, getting up to go to the bar, claps me on the shoulder: 'You're milking a good cow, buddy.'

* * *

After I left school and went to the academy in Wellington I did a few courses at varsity, which is where I met Sarah. A girl I knew was taking a paper in sociology, doing some kind of field study on how men rank themselves in a pecking order. She had a set list of questions, asking what factors made a difference when assessing the success of anyone. I hardly remember most of them, and they didn't apply to guys I knew. Basically how much they earned, what kind of house they had, car they drove, how funny their jokes were. No one was making any money except me and I knew how precarious that was, flats were all shared, if we had cars they were only for getting around. Jokes were just jokes. But there was one question that stuck: 'How attractive is their girlfriend?'

I told her straight off that would never come into my calculations. Which, at the time, was true. I wasn't blind, but I'd never even thought about it — or never consciously thought about it. Some guys got lucky, the others managed to convince themselves they were lucky. I suppose anyone not getting laid wasn't doing so well, but who was small enough to keep score? Anyway, I'd learned enough by then to know that it was clearly a bad move to admit to any woman at university that you were so superficial as to judge them on their looks.

Still, it made me think. And by then I'd seen enough to know that the hero is supposed to get the girl. Not just any girl, *the* girl. The right girl. You mightn't be raiding temples for treasure or killing bad guys or just muddling through a rite-of-passage movie on a daily basis, but if you wanted to cast yourself as the hero in your own life — and having other people see you that way helped you see yourself that way — you needed to get the girl sorted out. I thought I'd grown out of it, but the vote of confidence made me realise I hadn't.

I thought I had the right girl. You know, the one that makes you feel the way you think you were always supposed to, better than what you are on your own. Nothing to do with being clever or playing rugby or being able to do anything at all really, except just live. Proud to be who you are, just so fucking pleased that someone that good in so many ways wants to spend their life with you. Which makes it sound as though it revolved around me and the way I see myself through other eyes, and that is part of it — just not all of it. In fact, those were the extras. I'll struggle to tell you exactly what I mean — either you know, so you understand, or you don't, so you won't — but I would do things that she wouldn't even know about, and I would do them for her. I wasn't even grandstanding, which is something of a first. I felt good because she would have thought that was the right thing to do, and I didn't need to tell her. I could take risks and not worry about the consequences because I knew that it wouldn't make any difference to what was really important. I can remember having an op on my back and being advised to make a will beforehand and all I could think about was how unhappy she would be if it turned out bad. 'Cuntstruck' is how Josh describes this state of affairs, but I think it goes a bit deeper. True, the initial period of lust and the deep hole I felt in my guts when I was away from her wore off after a while, but there was still enough there that on mornings when I woke up before her — given that she had a real job, this was mainly weekends — I would drink all of her in and think to myself how good the world was to have let me into the same room, let alone the same bed, as Sarah.

We came to Paris looking to live it up, enjoy the place, put some money aside and be ready to get on with the next thing after a couple of years. I planned to stop when I was thirty-two, thirty-three tops — which is over the hill and on a (still gentle) downward slide at home — but I liked Paris, the club liked me and the money kept coming. But Sarah found it hard to fit in. She learnt French, went to the museums and enjoyed showing off the city to friends who came to stay. That lasted for about a year — probably less if I had been paying attention. She worked for a while at an English-language magazine, then took a couple of university papers. None of it really grabbed her. I had taken her out of her element. Then she started talking about kids. Most days. I told her to wait until we got home. The calls home went on for longer. An hour and a half to her sister, an hour to her mates — even two hours, once, towards the end. I didn't recognise the number. The spark burned down to a glow, then to a glimmer that I could only see when I looked closely, and then one day I couldn't see it at all.

* * *

A siren sounds across the city as I leave the weights room, jogging towards the car in the rain. Midday on the first Wednesday of the month. Just a test signal. The first time it gives you a bit of a fright: what does it mean? Ask a local and they shrug their shoulders and tell you that it's in case of emergency. Ask them what kind of emergency, and what you're supposed to do if you hear it at any other time, and you get another shrug of the shoulders. Paris has always managed to roll with the punches.

One of the old bufties at the club, Didier, told me that he started playing rugby in 1943, while Germans in grey uniforms marched up and down the boulevards. At the same time, shops opened to sell their wares because there were bills to pay and mouths to feed; French girls were lying back and probably not thinking of England. Some people were resisting; most weren't, which didn't stop them shaving the heads of the women who had been horizontal collaborators after the cavalry had arrived. When the moment came for the German army to cut and run, the staff officer commanding Paris was supposed to blow up the place, and particularly its monuments. Yet Notre Dame still stands, and the Eiffel Tower and the Arc de Triomphe and everything else. Apparently the commander refused, making him the hero of every Paris guidebook written since 1945. Someone on his team must have been pissed.

I got in after midnight last night, and Rachel was in bed. I did some drink and dial, called JT who's back at home now. He was on his lunch break at the construction firm he's working for.

He told me that Birdy, one of our mates who played in England and Wales for years, is back now and dying on it. He's coaching the second team at his club, gets a hundred bucks a week for expenses. His wife is looking after their two kids. He's got a load of monkey on his back thanks to an investment strategy based on playing Monopoly: get geared up to the hilt and hope everyone lands on you. The dice haven't been rolling his way lately. I know the feeling. In better news, JT's girlfriend is expecting. He's lining me up for godfather duties if I come home.

* * *

Coming out of the car-park building, I get jumped by a little girl. 'Monsieur, Monsieur!' She runs towards me, hand outstretched expectantly, skittering over the slick black tarmac. She's wearing a white puffa jacket designed to keep out the cold but not the rain, and she looks soaked through. Wisps of curly black hair poke out from under the hood. Beneath it I can see big, black, tearstained eyes above a snotty button nose. At first I think she's made a mistake, but my hand goes out to her almost without thinking and, confident in my own goodness, I push away the lurking suspicion that this might be some sort of trap. What am I supposed to do? She is crying, the small breathless sobs of a young bird that has fallen out of its nest, and she has turned to me in trust.

Once she has latched onto me, I feel the satisfaction of a man charged with an important mission: she can't be more than six but she is unmistakeably a damsel in distress. A man could wait all his life to prove his worth and never have a chance like this come along.

'Can you help me to cross the road? My father is over there.'

She points to the door of the school across the street. Shouldn't be too difficult. I pull her closer so that she is under my umbrella, and together we move to the kerb of the busy thoroughfare. As we wait for the lights to change, cars surge past hissing up jets of water. I can't see anyone near the door of the school.

She can see this too. A wail goes up. 'He's not there!' As soon as the man in the traffic light changes into his walking green, the little girl breaks into a run, dragging me twenty metres to the empty space, her outstretched arm taking her beyond the range of the umbrella's cover until I catch up with her when she stops. No father.

'Over there!' This time a group is indicated, and she sets off again, only to slow down almost immediately after a fruitless scan of the handful of faces. There is a fresh sound of despair, deeper and keener. The faces turn to look, then turn away. Each of us consider our options.

'Where was your father?'

'He was at the car with my sister's friend.'

'And where's the car?'

'I dunno.' A sort of gurgling sound escapes from her.

Just as I am regretting this simple mission turning into a quest, three figures come pounding down the pavement at a run.

'Is that them?'

'Yes, that's them.' No smile, but the tears have stopped flowing.

I let go of her hand as the first girl, perhaps ten years old, arrives, taking my charge in her arms. 'You scared the living daylights out of me.' A strangely adult phrase in the mouth of an older sister still so young. The other girl, presumably the sister's friend, stands off to the side.

The father rolls up, a North African man in his thirties, features tight with rage and fear. I suppose I had been expecting a rueful smile, some heartfelt thanks for his daughter's safety and the warm glow of a good deed. Now it occurs to me that my position is ambiguous. I stand aside, unable to move on for fear of looking like someone escaping from the scene of a crime that hasn't come off.

'I told you not to move. What did I tell you? Don't move! So why did you move?' In the face of all this shouting, the little girl starts crying again. 'Stop crying! Stop it. I'm warning you!' The father holds his daughter's sleeve with his left hand and raises the right. She flinches and tries to wheel away out of range.

I can't help myself. 'Hey, mister.' I don't know what to follow up with, but at least he's uncocked his hand as he turns to examine me. 'She was very sorry, and she was looking for you everywhere. She didn't know what to do.'

'And who the hell are you? What were you doing with my daughter?'

Why is it not so obvious that I'm the good guy? 'She asked me for help. I have a niece about the same age.' My adrenalin has started to flow. Fight or flight. I'm not running. I try to force a smile. He looks me in the eye.

'You should mind your own business.' He pulls the little girl to his side, holding her hand so hard that she gives a little yelp. Her sister has an arm around her. The small tribe departs the scene.

Chapter 27

Charlie, the London agent, calls mid-afternoon. 'The Welsh have dropped out of the running. They're signing a younger guy.'

'Who?'

'The ten from Auckland.' I mentored him in Wellington when he was an under-twenty. Good player. 'It's not that they think he's better, he's just cheaper. Budget cuts. You know the score.'

'So what does that leave us with?'

'You've still got the second-div club and it's still early days but I think the best thing to do now is for you to hold on until late in the piece. You're not going to get picked up by a big club as first string but there are usually one or two injuries or no-shows late in the day. And if nothing turns up, wait until the start of the next season — there's always an injury somewhere. All the top dogs are already under contract, you come in as the white knight and charge whatever you want because they're desperate. And it will give you time off your bung leg, so you can get that right. How is the body, by the way?'

'I'll live. I've been jabbed more times than a fucking pin-cushion but I'll live. The doc did some test on my eye to see if my brain was all right on Monday. It's still there. What are you hearing about our friend from the south?'

'Nothing more than last time. It sounds like it's a done deal.

I can't see him walking away from that kind of money.' That's the kicker — the Fibber has been seeing some of the guys to renegotiate contracts and he's offering them less than last time. He's got this speech about how people who come to Paris are prepared to take less than elsewhere because it's such a great place, and anyway there are money problems but this is their family and they should stick with the club that has given them so much — and yet everyone knows he's dropping the best part of half a million euros on the new boy.

* * *

Fuck it, I'll do it. Just a one-off. That away game is in a little over two weeks. We'll be missing a couple of internationals because the game is on the same weekend as a Six Nations game. We still ought to win — even allowing for home ground advantage, they just don't have the firepower — but it won't be such a drama if we lose. We might drop a place but there's plenty of time to make up for that. And what do I care, anyway? If I'm honest, I quite like the idea of a little payback on the Fibber. Rachel's right, he's a scumbag who's been rigging things to suit himself for years, throwing his weight around just because he can with no thought for anyone he might be squashing. Nobody's lifting a finger to stop him, or doing anything about it. I mentioned Josh's story to a mate from school who used to work for a bank in London — the one who wrote cheat notes on his thighs, made a million before he was thirty. Even he was shocked. 'It's the kind of thing you see all the time in business, but code? Jesus. The pricks'll ruin everything. The Manu as well. It's not as if anyone else is doing them any favours.'

So this will be kind of a Robin Hood thing, won't it? All right, that's a stretch. If I get pinged I'll look like the lowest of the low. But Samoa drew 15-all in Dublin then got slaughtered 55–0 against the Irish nine months later at the World Cup when it counted. Same team, different faces; some of them just couldn't afford to make it. Rachel is right. If everyone knew it was rigged but let it slide, that amounts to match-fixing in plain sight. Why should the rich guys be the only ones to get away with pulling that kind of shit? '*This* is business' says Rich, indicating his own dealings with the world. Then he points the finger outside his own patch: '*That* is a rort.'

OK, not Robin Hood. Bonnie and Clyde? We'll need to get out earlier than they did.

We haven't talked about it at all since she first brought it up.

'So, about this game.'

'I saw Philip. He can help you get a club for next year.'

'What?'

'You're having trouble with your contract, right?'

'How do you know that?'

'He told me. I wish you had. It looked like you were hiding things from me.'

'How does he know?'

'He didn't tell me. But he understands that this might be making it harder for you to make the right decision.'

'So how the hell would he get me a club?'

'He knows the right people.'

'That isn't how it works.'

'Isn't it? I guess you would know.'

'Anyway, I'll do it.'

'You're sure about this? Truly?'

'Yes.'

'Brilliant.' I get a lingering kiss. 'This is going to be fun. What made you change your mind?'

'I don't know. Lots of little things. Nothing in particular. I guess I have a sort of all-round feeling that I'm getting screwed. I don't like doing it but you're right, I may never get another chance like this and it won't do anyone any real harm. It'll be a nice surprise for the other lot.'

'Have you thought about how you'll do it?'

'A bit. Listen, it's just this once. We need to be clear about that. I don't need you coming back to me saying, "Just one more." We do it once, and walk away.'

'Mm-hm. Just once, no problem. I could see if we can get the referee on board.' She takes a swig of red wine, turns back to her cooking.

'What? Jesus, no. The fewer people involved the better. You, me and Philip is plenty. He'll keep his end up, won't he?'

'Of course. I'm just glad you've said yes. He always seemed very charming, very smooth, but when I told him you might not do it he was very annoyed. Furious, actually.'

'But we could have all walked away happily and still been well up. What's his problem?'

'It doesn't work like that.'

'So how does it work?'

'He talked about your family.'

'That's nuts. What does he know about my family?'

'They came up in conversation, weeks ago. Anyway, don't worry now, you're going to do it and that's great. And he can help you get a club for next year, something in London he said. And he's put three thousand pounds from the other weekend through to your account.'

The carrot to go with the stick I've just been shown. And how the hell does this guy know about my contract? A voice at the back of my head is shouting at me to get out, *now*. This is what getting engaged must feel like, if your beloved is a mobster's daughter. Straight after the proposal Daddy's holding a pre-nup in one hand and a blowtorch in the other.

'Why doesn't he tell me?'

'Strict instructions. I am to act as the go-between on everything.'

'He doesn't trust me?'

'It's not that. The less everyone knows about each other, the safer it is. Less chance of anything going wrong.'

'What could go wrong?'

'Nothing really, as long as no one gets sloppy. Philip takes care of everything and he knows what he's doing. No one pays attention to rugby, anyway. It's too small, there's not much money involved compared to football or horse racing. Philip likes it for exactly that reason. It looks clean, and there's a big spread. If you're going to lose anyway and you go out the back door, it will work well.'

'You've been studying this?'

'No, I'm just passing on what Philip told me. But you're right, I'm talking too much. The less you know the better.'

'You know an awful lot about me. He knows enough as well. Obviously you keep him well informed.'

'Only what he needs to know.'

If I think about this, I get scared. Best not to think about it. At all.

I have to be able to trust someone.

* * *

On one of my grandfather's tapes he talked about his 'tribe', who he owed his loyalty to and who he could rely on, and how that shrank down to almost nothing over time. When he started off he was all for England and Empire, and even the Frogs and all the Allies because they were all on the same side. Then when he saw the unwelcoming reception that they got from the French civilians he cut it down to guys dressed in khaki, because he felt he could trust them. But the High Command kept on with their idiotic tactics that had men dying when they shouldn't, so he revised it down to the New Zealand Division. There was a run-in with the Kiwi brass because of a riot over some MPs killing a drunken Scotsman who'd stepped out of line, so he cut it down again to the soldiers in his company. Then his position was almost overrun because the neighbouring platoon weren't where they were supposed to be. Another revision. His first platoon commander was a good man, he said, but after he was killed the new bloke wasn't trustworthy. So he brought it down to the seven or eight guys around him every minute of every day. Granddad ended up a corporal, head of his section, so he could hardly blame anyone else for running that badly. 'We all signed up for the big idea; but you actually fight for the bloke standing next to you' was how he put it. He said the only real reason that he used to get out of the trenches when they had to go over the top was because he didn't want to look like a coward to his mates.

One time he was commissioned in the field, from corporal to platoon commander for an afternoon. They had taken such heavy casualties on a first attempt that there wasn't anyone above him to run the show. He couldn't stay lieutenant — he had a stutter and had hardly been to school — but for a few hours he was in charge. The order came down to go over the top again. He knew it was idiotic, and he hesitated. He was supposed to blow a whistle as the signal. He could hear the other platoons on either side going, but his lot were waiting for him. He knew they were never going to make their objective. 'We hadn't got more than thirty yards an hour earlier — there was no reason why we would this time round. It all happened afterwards, of course, but just following orders didn't stand up for the Germans after the Second World War. Why should it have stood up for me? I thought we might wait for a bit, then they would sound the retreat along the line and no one would be any the wiser. So I just waited. After a while — it felt like quite a long time, but I don't suppose it was — Dougie Robertson came up to me and said quietly, "Listen, Ben, we have to go. We have to go. It's not your fault." So I blew the whistle and we went up the ladders. I don't think I was cut out for being an officer.'

The problem with the second lieutenant who commanded his platoon came about through Peter Duncan's death. He didn't get 'a small piece in the throat' at all. From what I can make out from the tape — Granddad doesn't say, it sounds like he points ('he was hit here') — he got his balls blown off. They'd already seen wounds like that, where guys might live for days before infection or loss of blood carried them off. Peter asked Granddad to finish it quickly, so he did. The platoon commander wanted to put him on a charge. His sergeant talked him out of it.

* * *

This weekend is our last pool round of the Heineken Cup. It should have been played in the middle of January but the ground was frozen and unplayable so they postponed. Both teams are unhappy that it is being played the same weekend as the Six Nations but there are no other holes in the calendar before the quarter finals, unless we play mid-week.

I told Rachel that I'm not going to call it. We're picked to lose by between five and eight points, and I don't think we'll win, but I'm playing and I'm not fixing this. If we win we'll have a quarter-final at home; even a bonus point will qualify us for the next round. Winning the European Cup would be good. There'd be a bonus, too.

The game is to be played on Friday evening so that it doesn't clash directly with the Six Nations. On Thursday morning we assemble at Gare du Nord to take the Eurostar across to London. I get Rachel to drop Josh and me in front of the station. Josh spots his favourite fast-food dump. 'How much time have we got?'

'You're not going to do that to me. We're meeting in five minutes. The train leaves in forty-five.'

'Sweet. Just enough time for a snack. Come on, my shout.'

'Get a takeaway. I'm going to grab a paper. I'll be here. Just the smell—.'

'Here, hold on to my bag. You're the man, Sparky.'

Stooging outside in the cold, I notice a sign for the New Hotel on the other side of the road. The New Hotel doesn't look very new. It must be the one that Granddad went to with that woman before going out to the whorehouses in 1918. He would have walked across this road here in front of me. He said the wagons they travelled in had a sign on the side: 'Hommes 40 Chevaux 8'. I suppose other wagons carrying human cargo must have left from here during the Second World War. At home we were so insulated from history, or perhaps just uninterested, that we used to call kids who were tight 'Jew' without even knowing what it meant. I thought it started with a 'd'. The old man gave me a clip on the head and corrected me when I told him about one of my mates who hadn't shared the chocolate cake in his lunchbox.

The station has been given an overhaul since I first came through here on the way to London. The great stone façade that I remember being ash-grey, heavy with history like an aged black-and-white photo, is now a light honey colour. Statues draped in togas line the roof, their clothing suggesting origins more ancient than the city itself. Underneath them, the names of the places you can reach from here: the great European capitals, strung out in a line like a long-winded hint of glamour on a perfume bottle. Some homeless people have set up camp on the concrete outside and, as I watch, a thickly bearded man in ragged clothes pulls a pink newspaper from a rubbish bin, flips to a specific page, scans the text then throws it away, cursing. One of a band of women in headscarves and long skirts approaches me holding a piece of paper. 'Do you speak English?' I can see gold in her mouth when she speaks. Her grandparents might have been on those trains too.

'Ah, no.' I look away.

Josh arrives, stuffing a plastic-looking muffin into his face. 'You don't know what you're missing.' Between mouthfuls: 'Breakfast of champions, Spark. Thought you were getting a paper?'

'I had to look after your bag, didn't I? If I'd looked away, your boots would have been on sale at the flea market within the hour. Don't let Eric see you with that.'

We cross the street, entering the main concourse. Most of the team are there already, dressed in blazers, drinking coffee. Handshakes. The younger players are wearing ties, as is Coquine. The manager has a clipboard. He ticks us off as we arrive and gives us our tickets. 'You've got your passports? Right, you can start going through.' In three hours we'll be in London. I look around the vast space. A lot must have changed, but the immense girders and columns must have been there for over a hundred years. For Granddad it would still be recognisable. The idea of taking a train under the Channel would be a surprise, though.

After clearing immigration, there's more milling around and coffee-drinking. We are travelling in business class. The late change in date means we don't have a whole carriage to ourselves as we usually do; instead we are scattered across three or four. I find myself in a pair facing a middle-aged man in a suit and tie. He has his laptop out already, and is talking to someone on his mobile about plans for the weekend.

The card school have taken up seats around a table and are dealing out. A woman arrives, checking her ticket. Pierre looks up, but stays seated: 'Excuse us, madame. I have a seat over there, number forty-one. Would it be all right if we swap? You don't mind?'

The woman looks frosty. 'As you wish.' As she stalks off, the other three try to hold their laughter in. They don't make a very good job of it. 'What?' says Pierre. 'I was polite.'

Through the window the sprawl of high-rise apartments in the suburbs gives way to low-rise villages then open fields. I decide to go and see the battlefields. Flers can't be far away. That was where Granddad's mates died. I could probably manage it on a day off.

As we pull into St Pancras, the card players settle up. Jacques is pleased with the result of the trip so far. 'As Coluche said, only two things matter: money and sex.'

Chapter 28

Potential is a treacherous idea, as much a curse that foretells eventual disappointment as a promise of future glory. Xavier, who was talked about as a potential great, has busted his knee. It looks very much like the anterior cruciate ligament, the worst of the lot. He's only twenty-three, so he might come back from it. That is, he will come back from it, but it will take him a while, and he might never make it back to where he is now. Confidence, speed, change of direction: everything will be affected. In six months he should be able to play again, but it will take him a year to feel good. In the meantime, someone else will take his place, and in three or four years he will probably be looking back on what might have been. I have won enough to know that victories are fleeting; disappointment on this scale can be crushing.

The game was a draw. A good result for us. In April we will travel back across the Channel for a quarter-final. By then, things should be clearer for me.

We're sitting, eating, at the after-match. The English-speakers are complaining about Christophe. At the next table, Jacques is holding up a piece of pink, boiled meat as evidence. 'Every culture in the world has a restaurant: Italian, Indian, Chinese, Thai, Lebanese — even the Americans have their hamburgers. But I've never seen an English restaurant. You wonder why.'

Josh, gnawing contentedly on a bone, has picked up the gist

of what Jacques is saying. 'Nothing wrong with this. Frenchies, they eat snails and frogs' legs and fuck knows what, but they complain about chicken. Weirdos.'

The Bamboozler slouches over. 'Gentlemen, congratulations.'

Moose: 'We didn't win.'

'No, rugby did. That's a good result. Anyway, stop your whining. You're through. What are you clowns up to?'

Rich pushes back his chair to open the circle. 'Few schooners, bagging a couple of blokes . . .'

'I'll have a slice of that.' He pulls up a chair.

'So, what, you were in the neighbourhood and you thought you'd drop in?'

'Business, business. Just organising a deal — signing up a leaguie. Bloke over there, talking to their captain.' Heads turn.

'Rugby league, more better.' Taking the piss out of leaguies for being dumb is one of Rich's preferred pastimes.

'You laugh my friend, but there is method in their madness. Get this, he was telling me how at his first club, his first run with the prems, the boys are playing this shithouse team — but they're good, right? — first half they let the other lot run riot. These dudes can't believe it, they're wooden-spooners, getting all pumped because they're whipping a team that looks like they're going to the grand final. They go into the changing room at half-time, losing twenty to zip, something like that. All the boys are straight onto their mobiles, call their bookies, place bets on themselves. Odds on their winning are through the bloody roof by now. They turn around, back out into the second half, they win it 34–30. Everyone collects, big-time. Genius. That is gold, right there. Put it in the bank, bronze yourself on the spot. Erect a statue to a winner. They won't teach you that at university, though, will they?'

'Did your man get a piece of the action?'

'Nah, it was his first game. They thought it wouldn't be cool to get him in on it. He was all fired up to do it again, but the bookies were filthy about it. They paid up, then they boycotted the club for the next year.'

'Which club?'

'That, sir, I cannot divulge.'

'How many clubs has he been at?'

'This'll be his seventh, I think he was saying.'

'Slut.'

'So, don't let me interrupt you — who are we bagging?'

'French coaches.'

'Oh, Jesus. Where do we start?'

'Hold on, isn't that illegal?' Moose, bless him. I've been wanting to know more about this myself. He has a long line of stitches through his split eyebrow, and the area around it is swollen in shades of purple and red. All in the line of duty.

The Bamboozler rolls his eyes. 'Sydney bookies are not well known for their formal observation of legal niceties. Nor are leaguies. Strictly speaking, though, I think you're right. You're not allowed to bet on a game that you're playing. I don't know about league rules, but in union you're not even allowed to bet on other games. I don't know if it's a criminal charge, but the IRB condemns it according to law 16, subsection 4.'

Rich finds it hard to believe. 'You know all the laws?'

'As it happens, I am shitting you about law 16, subsection whatever, but yeah, you're not allowed to bet on a competition you're involved with. Five months of study for the agent's exam.'

'What about through a third party?' I don't think this is going to arouse suspicion. An innocent question.

'Well, I don't know how anyone'd find out. I'd have to ask

my lawyer. They have some pretty sophisticated machinery for tracking these things. A guy I know was telling me about how they follow the betting on the horse races. IP addresses, everything.'

'You're doing horses now?'

'I'm always looking to expand.'

'Some of the boys are at it. Titi reckons he got fifty euros worth of free bet to start with, now he's up a hundred and fifty.'

'Well, I'd keep that quiet.' The Bamboozler drops his voice, sits forward. 'We are in England, Rich. They speak English here.' He sits back. 'I can't see anyone getting sticky about a hundred and fifty euros. Mind you, our friends at World Rugby do like to play it by the book.'

'They wouldn't be that up on rugby, these machines?' Yes, that's me speaking.

'I can't see it, no. But those horses, they turn over a lot of money. Soccer's huge too.' A yawn and a stretch. 'Ah, shit. Jetlag.'

'Where'd you come from?'

'Toulouse.'

* * *

On the train back to Paris, Christophe is more solicitous than ever about the ankle, ensuring that I have a spare seat opposite me on the train to keep it up, ordering Nico to get ice from the bar trolley. Now that I have decided to go through with Rachel's scheme — or Philip's scheme — I am equally concerned that it holds up. Sitting back as far as I can, looking out the window, I calculate my total net worth. Between the money in the Caymans from the club, the drop-goal bonus in Jersey and the houses at home, a bit more than three-fifty thousand euro. Various accounts another thirty odd, say three-eighty all up. Exchange rates from here to home are filthy at the moment and real estate is insane. Not as much as I'd like.

If I can make three hundred euro from the fix and the rest of the year, that will give me a bit of cushion. If I don't go through with the fix I'm going to struggle to do the schooling and buy the house. No point in bullshitting: chances of high-paying jobs in the future are slim at best. I don't know whether I should count Rachel into this or not. There's nothing wrong, but there's something not quite right, the warmth in her eyes seems to have chilled. At the risk of sounding overwrought, I love her and with that goes the secret dread that it might end. I'm not going to tell her because I'm not sure what the response will be. 'That's nice,' would kill me. She has told me not to expect anything from her, that she finds this a turn-off. So instead I daydream about ways of proving it to her and that is at least part of the reason for getting into this fix. There are unexpected consequences in going towards what you think people want of you. Sarah was unhappy when I brought her back a scarf from an away trip: the other girls had told her that it was the kind of thing we did when we wanted to ease a guilty conscience. I still don't know what Rachel wants, despite interrogations. She has an extra dimension to her, a worldliness that escapes me. I guess that's part of the attraction. In any case, she is right: I'm not likely to get a chance like this again.

* * *

Saturday night, we are curled around each other in bed. Skin on skin. I am drifting off to sleep.

'So what are you going to do with your money?'

'Mmh. Put it in the bank and get some more.' A pause. 'You?'

She sits up. I can make out the curve of her bare breasts in the half-light from the street below that filters through the shutters. 'I'm going to do something for you. What would you like me to do?'

'I can think of some things that don't require money.'

'Come on. You've been good to me. I'm not even paying rent here, you took me on holiday — I'm a big girl, I can pay my way.'

'Surprise me.'

'Do you want to talk about what you're going to do next weekend?'

'Not really.'

'You know what you're doing?'

'I think so. Don't worry about it. But you do realise that they could always substitute me. Or I might get injured.'

'I thought you said there was no chance they would substitute now that the other man is injured.'

'I still might get injured. I can't guarantee that I won't.'

'There's always risk involved. In everything. You have a lot of ideas about how things might be. You need to get rid of anything that distracts you, that slows you down.'

A long silence. 'Where is this going?'

'Us?' She rolls towards me, takes my head in her hands. 'It feels good, doesn't it? Just enjoy it. Lick up the honey. Don't waste your time with questions.'

Chapter 29

There is a rustling in the undergrowth. Close. Rich and I swing guns up to our shoulders. Over to our left, about fifty metres away, yells and the pok-pok-pok of small arms fire. 'Marco?'

'Polo.'

Moose. Rich sends a couple of shots toward the sound of the voice.

'I said "Marco fucking Polo", you low-breed.' Moose stumbles to his feet and charges into our little foxhole. 'I'm out of ammo or you'd have been toast.'

'Out of ammo? In that case . . .' Rich squeezes another round off at point-blank range, just missing his target.

'Ah! You bastard!' An orange stain splatters on the inside of Moose's thigh.

'I owed you.'

'Jesus, fuck. What for?'

'You know very well. Don't come the raw prawn with me.'

We've been out here on the paintball range all afternoon. 'Establish a perimeter!' was Rich's initial offering, but it fell on deaf ears. Flags have been captured, bunkers stormed, and my early enthusiasm has been dented by the fact that my gun is rubbish and I keep getting hit without hitting anyone else, although I did get Christophe a good one from behind. Small victories. I apologised, but I didn't have the French for 'friendly fire'. Everyone likes to think they'd be quite good at war, so it's annoying to discover that isn't the case. Below us, Thomas scuttles from one tree to another and we send off a couple of balls in his direction, looping harmlessly over his head. He dives to the ground, turns to identify the source of trouble, returns fire equally badly, then disappears into cover.

The game now is 20 ball, having to eliminate the other team with limited ammunition. Rich and I felt it wise to take up a sniper's position on the edge of proceedings. I have too many nasty coin-sized welts to want to go into the field again. Shit sniping is a bit of a drawback, but I maintain the fault is with the weapon. Moose is still enthusiastic enough to want more balls.

'I'm going to outflank them, then come up behind that bastard Eric and pepper the fucker.'

'Sounds like a good cause. Here's a couple. Actually no, have some more. Don't miss.'

'Go get 'im. What are his legs?'

'Springs. Steel springs.'

'What are they going to do?'

'Hurl him down the track.'

'How fast can he run?'

'Fast as a leopard.'

'How fast is he going to run?'

'Fast as a leopard.'

'Then let's see him do it!'

Moose sets himself on the edge of our dip, looks out for a second, then catapults himself forward. We do the theme tune from *Gallipoli* which turns mysteriously into *Mission Impossible* halfway through.

Someone takes a pop at us so we duck down then inch up to follow Moose's progress.

'We watched that the night before our game against the Poms with the Under Twenties.'

'You and every other Strine team that ever played England.'

Moose has disappeared.

'I'd be dead by now.'

'Eh?'

'If this was for real.'

'If this was for real we wouldn't have been running around. I'd be sitting well back taking a view.'

'I don't think you had a choice about where you got to sit.'

Silence.

'We'd have had some training, though, wouldn't we? And the fucking guns would work properly. You wouldn't get far with this piece of shit. Amateurs. I can't work with that.'

A few shots and a yell. Moose comes running back up the slope. Laughing. I am reminded of a couple of mates who laughed pretty much all the way through *Apocalypse Now* when we went to see it in the cinema. To the point where one guy nearby got up halfway through the film, gave them a dirty look and changed seats. The funny thing was that they would have been the first to sign up for any war.

A ball hits the tree behind me. Then another, lower, zinging into the dirt in front of me. It doesn't explode. 'It's that gung-ho prick of an instructor. What's his mission?'

The guy who runs the place is obviously something of a fanatic: he was wearing full camo gear when he showed us the deal and after watching us muppets bounce around ineffectually for a couple of hours appears not to have been able to help himself from joining in. Now he is zigzagging towards us through the trees and his camouflage is complemented with some kind of seaweed-like foliage hanging off him. And he is carrying a gun that looks more like the real thing than the ones we are holding. I duck down again.

'That cunt scares me. Seriously.'

'Whose side is he on?'

'Not fucking ours.'

'Nearer to thee, my God, nearer to thee.' Rich's expensive education has furnished him with a set of hymns for appropriate moments.

Giggling. 'The whites of his eyes, wait 'til you can see the whites of his eyes.'

'You'll never see the whites of his eyes — he's got a bloody mask on.'

A shout comes out of the bushes. 'You should be moving. The point of the game is not to stay still.'

'I thought the point of the game was to shoot everyone else without getting shot?' Rich says this quietly, just to us. Then, louder: 'We surrender!'

'Move!'

'I've only got one bullet left.'

I have already spotted the next bit of cover. A couple of balls pelt into the branches above me. Rich follows me in, then makes a run for the fence, taking himself out of the game. The psycho instructor hits him in the middle of the back with three shots, one above the other.

'Ow! You dirty—. Right, that's it.'

The instructor has already melted away.

* * *

'That was all good clean fun.' Rich swings into the seat next to me. 'I did get done in the eye by that black-hearted French bastard, though. Where was he in '44?' Louder: 'I don't believe the Australian people have been officially thanked yet for their effort in once again liberating French soil.' No one understands the reference or if they do they don't bother to pick it up. 'Still, a few pots tonight. Can you imagine what it must have been like?'

No, Rich, I really can't.

* * *

Sarah used to have a go at me from time to time about being too competitive, too wrapped up in what the rest of the world thought of me and needing to prove myself. 'Why can't you just enjoy life?'

Which was funny, because she had a dog of a character herself. Towards the end of our time together in Paris — there were already wobbles — we went out for a meal with Rich and Tom, a South African centre who went home at the end of last season. I preferred going out with company because meals with just the two of us held long silences when I thought I might end up blurting out something about getting married and having kids just to fill the void. Safety in numbers.

We'd had a big day training and the restaurant had been recommended for its tasting menu — quality and quantity. Three entrées, two mains, cheese platter, two desserts. The three of us didn't even look at the menu, we knew what we were getting. Sarah said she wasn't very hungry so she'd just have the fish. The waiter arrived, we respected the niceties enough to allow Sarah to place her order, then piled in. The waiter explained that if we were to have the tasting menu, Sarah had to have it as well. I don't know what the reasoning was. We had a go at changing his mind but he wouldn't budge. We all looked expectantly at

Sarah. There was a pause. In hindsight I should have jumped in here. Tom, who was one of those English South Africans with impeccable manners, took the temperature and started backing out. Rich would not be moved, and I couldn't see the harm in it. I was pretty hungry.

She looked me in the eye, handed the menu to the waiter, and accepted.

By the end of the entrées I didn't need any more. Whether this was because of the food or the slightly sick feeling of pending public embarrassment I'm not sure. To begin with Rich yabbered away and Tom held up his end. Sarah didn't say a word. She just ate, looked at me and raised her eyebrows in mock enthusiasm whenever a new dish appeared. 'Mmmm.' She even ate the bread, which she never normally touched at the evening meal. The fish in the tasting menu wasn't what she had wanted. The sauces were rich. I felt more and more queasy. Rack of lamb followed. She hates lamb but she put that away as well. By now even Rich understood what was happening, and offered to deal with the surplus. 'No, no, I'm enjoying it.' Conversation dropped off. The other two exchanged looks with me — Tom's rueful, guilty and sympathetic, Rich's appearing to indicate that my girlfriend was a whack job.

When the cheese arrived she had a taste of each. There were fourteen. Rich declared himself stuffed. The first dessert arrived and again she finished her plate; we were only nibbling. It got to the point where I was worried she might actually throw up on the table. The second dessert, the final act of her ordeal, was a citrus soup with little madeleines on the side. Three of them. I forced two down and that was overkill.

Sarah's face was white. I had already told her to stop a couple of times but she wasn't going to do that for anything. It must have taken her ten minutes to chew through them, a sheer effort of will. It felt like an hour. Rich and Tom were talking now — their shame couldn't go on for ever, and the wine helped them think of other things. I still have this image of her with her cheeks full, doggedly chewing.

She insisted on paying her share of the bill.

'You didn't have to do that.'

Silence.

'We all got it. I'm sorry. It wasn't very gentlemanly.'

'Shut up. I'm trying to concentrate.'

'On what?'

'Just shut up.'

Later, after she'd locked herself in the bog for twenty minutes: 'It's not even a question of being gentlemanly. It's just common bloody courtesy. You and your mates are so fucking wrapped up in your own little lives, you can't see what is happening around you and you don't even care. What you want comes first and too bad for the rest of us. Not everyone has to bow down to your will.'

When I think about her this is one of the memories that always comes up. I thought it was a shitty trick at the time but with distance I can see that was one of her strengths — she was always teaching me something about myself that I was too thick to see on my own.

Chapter 30

At home in Wellington Sarah's parents would have us round for meals, more and more frequently as the departure for France grew closer. It was a big house, with a covered pool in a suburb overlooking the harbour. On one of the last occasions, another couple were there — friends of her parents — and after I had smiled through the usual chat about rugby with the men (both season-ticket holders), talk turned to the children of various mutual acquaintances. I didn't know any of them except one, by reputation. I was asked what school I had been to, and when I replied there was a short silence, someone speculated incorrectly that so-and-so's son might have been there, and then conversation started again in another direction. Most of the subjects were a few years older than me, mid-thirties or more. More than one's marriage had 'collapsed'; several had 'done very well', meaning 'has made piles of cash'. There were no marks awarded for how it was made.

Then Sarah asked about one of the sons of the family friend who had been off overseas and recently come back. Mrs — Merriweather, I think it was — looked down at her napkin and across at Mr, who actively avoided flinching and said, 'The thing is, Sarah, he's mad.'

Oh, shit, thinks me. This is untidy. Turns out there are different kinds of mad. 'He's become one of those tree-huggers or I don't know what. Lives on an ashram or something. His brother says to me, "Don't worry Dad, Chris is just mad" — and he is. Maybe not stark, raving mad, but he doesn't get it. He just doesn't get it, Sarah.'

Mrs M: 'Ed's doing very well, though.'

Sarah's father: 'It's a different world from the one we grew up in.'

Sarah's mother: 'Would anyone like some more salad?'

'Thanks.' Apart from that I'm not saying a bloody thing. Murky waters.

Sarah: 'He's all right, though?'

'Chris? I suppose so. We hear from him once a month or so. When was the last time? He'd been beaten up for protesting some damn fool thing — banks or whatever.'

Sarah: 'But the banks—.'

'I know about the banks.' Mr M was a lawyer, like Sarah's father. 'I just wish he'd grow out of it. He'll be thirty in six months.'

Mrs M: 'His girlfriend is lovely. She's artistic.'

Sarah's mother coos. She collects art. And is thwarted by her daughter, again.

'I think it's brilliant that he has the guts to do something like that. Somebody needs to. As a society, we—.'

'Fair enough, I'm not saying you're wrong. But I didn't get up at six every morning bar weekends for forty years to send him to a good school and pay university fees so that my grandchildren would run around in grass skirts and smoke dope and whatever else they do.'

'I don't know about grass skirts—.'

'They've had a baby?' Sarah's mum. Bless.

'No, but with all the rooting they do — stop it, Sal, we're all grown-ups — I don't imagine that's far away. Then he'll have his mitt out. Just you wait and see.'

* * *

The taxi ride back from the airport was unsettling. I had imagined I would feel relieved when Sarah was gone — onwards, upwards — but some of the things she had said had got a hook in, and I couldn't shake it. To my line about this being better for everyone given 'the circumstances', she had replied that I was missing the point and was 'missing out on life' which I hadn't really felt was the case but since I'm easily suggestible . . .

'It was difficult for you, not knowing what to do with yourself,' I said. 'I'm sorry.'

'I watched over you. I watched over you.' The last twist of the knife. We were close enough for me to see my reflection in her eyes, warped, my big nose looking even bigger. Her eyes shone. Then she went through passport control earlier than she needed to, and didn't look back.

I was pretty sure this was the right thing. And I'd given her some money. No one would be saying that she'd 'done very well' but my conscience was clear, in that department at least. Still, someone would be saying that something had 'collapsed'. Not a marriage, but close enough.

By the time I got back to the flat my mind had been scratching at those fucking hooks long enough for the wound to become infected. I wished we had training but we didn't. TV. Always helps. Flicking through channels. A British series set in the sixties that Mum used to watch was on, dubbed, but the soundtrack was the same: 'The purpose of a man is to love a—.' I knew it just well enough to flick before it stings. Films: *In Bruges*. We went to

Bruges last Christmas, drank hot chocolate overlooking a canal. Go to a news channel. Actually, news channel and background noise is a better idea, so hook my phone up to the speakers and turn it up. A drink. That'll help. Think about ringing someone, scroll through the names, stop at one, can't think what I'd say, move on, same deal. Forget about it. Another drink.

A short time later, sitting on the couch where we first . . . did what? Made love? Had sex? Fucked? Sitting there I could see the knives on the otherwise nude kitchen wall and wonder what one of them would feel like in a warm bath. Roman-style. Just a couple of months since I told Sarah, 'Everything will be all right.'

'Missing out.' How much does anyone have the right to expect? It wasn't turning out for me the way I would have thought the movie version would.

For a while, all of my dreams were nightmares. I could feel the value of my life shrinking. I recalibrated expectations.

* * *

I listen to Granddad's last tape in the plane on the way down to the game.

'Well, now you've got me thinking about it all again. I suppose you have to ask yourself what you were fighting for. I don't think we did at the time — I didn't anyway, and we didn't talk about it, it was just assumed. God, King and Country was the line and that probably sounds faintly ridiculous to you.' Muffled protestations from the interviewer. 'Well, your generation, at any rate. And that's probably right. I have thought about it at various points. You see these programmes on the television or what have you and they get these upstanding characters saying they were protecting freedom, or protecting the next generation or what have you. I wonder if they really believe that. The Germans must have told themselves the same thing, I'd imagine. Our war, I mean — the other one was different, but there still would have been some good Germans in among the riff-raff. Really they're no different to you or me, except that they lost.

'I mean, Gallipoli. What were we doing there? Bloody Churchill, for a start. The Turks were just defending their homeland, weren't they. And their freedom and their future generations and all the rest of it. So what were we doing there? And what gives us the right to tell everyone we were doing it for future generations?

'France was a bit different, they didn't want the Germans there. If the Turks or the Japanese turned up down the road here at Castlepoint, I'd like to think we'd give them what for and it wouldn't matter what the hell their reasoning was for being here. And I wouldn't be inviting them back every year to weep for their dead, either. Pretty reasonable blokes those Turks, when you think about it. No, I've never really got to the bottom of it. Every explanation you hear is self-serving, it seems to me. Everyone has a barrow to push. That Franz Ferdinand was assassinated in Sarajevo by some Serbian revolutionary character and somehow it all kicked off — well, honestly, what did that have to do with me or Peter or Casey or the rest of us? For a while I thought it was the English ruling class who'd somehow managed to get us wound up. As I said, bloody Churchill, though I suppose he redeemed himself a bit later on — but really, we did it ourselves, got all wound up and ready to go.'

The chair creaks. 'Men were lying about their age to get in uniform! In a sense we thought it was a game, a great game, and you had to be in it. It sounded a lot more exciting than life on the farm but once you were there you just wanted to be back home. You tell yourself a story about it afterwards because that's the best way to make sense of all the dead men. Ask yourself too many questions and you can end up pretty confused. But when you came back you saw what a joke it all was. We were thin as rats and they gave us some land. That was all very well but without the capital to get it on track, you weren't going very far. I didn't have any of that, nor did the others I knew, and even then it would have taken time and times were hard anyway. The Depression hit and that was that. The only people who could weather it were the ones who had already got their capital and they didn't always strike me as the most deserving.

'I suppose we felt bound to some sort of code of honour, this sense of duty that we really did have. To us it was an extension of common decency. I'm not sure if we were somehow tricked into it or not, believing that it was the right thing to do. Once we were there, this idea got twisted — warped beyond recognition. Or perhaps we just didn't abide by it, threw it overboard by common agreement. After a friend of mine was killed on the Somme we took a German trench. They'd been throwing everything at us, grenades and what have you at us as we advanced but when we got in close they didn't want a bar of it, they wanted to surrender. That didn't suit me, not in the mood I was in. I got stuck into them. The rest of our blokes were the same. A few Germans started running away, over the field. So we set up a machine gun, quick smart. They never got to where they were going.'

Drink and a pause. 'Probably best if you don't put that in. It was an untidy bit of work, though I don't suppose anyone's bothered now. Funny thing was, one of our fellows got a gong out of it. We had done well, or so we were told. Didn't change the fact that it wasn't right. You can dress it up however you like, tell yourself the circumstances called for it, but if you understand common decency you know the difference between right and wrong. Betraying that is about the worst thing you can do to yourself because you build your world around that, and once it's gone . . . Well.' Another drink.

'Thank you very much, Mr Stevens, we have enough now. May I ask, have you enjoyed being interviewed?'

'I only hope I've shed some light for you on the whole palaver. I will wander off into the darkness at some point soon enough and I suppose it's made me think about everything. When you're eighteen you realise you were a fool at sixteen. Then when you turn twenty-one, you understand you were an idiot at eighteen. I'm eighty-five now and can say that I know myself. One thing that helped, because a good one makes all the difference, is that I was lucky with women. You always like to think you could have done better but all things considered I did all right. Betty was a good girl, and I brought some good ones out of her, but Connie, Christ, I was lucky with Connie. They say you make your own luck but it doesn't take much for things to go wrong. You've made me think about Peter Duncan and I haven't thought about him for years. You get into the wrong foxhole and suddenly it's over. But then I know fellows who got so excited about a roll in the hay they put a ring on the wrong finger and signed themselves up for a lifetime of misery. Connie . . . I wonder if we'll meet again. I don't suppose so. She threw a pan at me one night after I came home late with a skinful once too often — and she was quite right, too!' Pulls on his drink. 'I'm sorry, that wouldn't interest you . . .'

'Thank you very much.' A crackle, then just low hissing.

Chapter 31

The night before the game. I can't sleep. Maybe it's because I have had to stay off the ankle, and I'm not getting the exercise that I'm used to. Maybe. I held back the last side of the tape until now, hoping that it might help get me over this hump, reassure me that I am doing the right thing, taking one for the team, for my tribe — me, really. Now I have to negotiate with the living dead, or perhaps a ghost. Something haunting, definitely. With my eyes closed my brain jumps from one idea to the next, and after a while I realise that they are the things I am ashamed of. I used to drift off to images of glory, past or future; now the film that runs through my head is ugly. The darkness brings it all to the front.

After an hour or so, I look at my phone: 1.15. More than two hours since we turned out the lights. This is ridiculous. Breakfast is at 8.30, first meeting at ten. I can skip breakfast. I like to have at least eight hours before a game. I suppose even if I don't sleep it's not the end of the world — it's not as if I want to play well. I do want to sleep, though. Jacques is snuffling quietly a few feet away. I get up, pad to the bathroom, close the door before turning on the light. I've got some sleeping pills in my toilet bag. I take one, wash it down with some water. I turn out the light, then turn it on again and take another. Jacques rolls over as I sneak back to bed. I step on what must be a shoe, giving my ankle a twinge. Luckily it's the good one.

We are picked to win by between four and six points. Every point below that will be worth nine thousand pounds to me. I'd have preferred it if we had been picked to lose. Going out the back door would look better than losing a game we should win, but options are limited and the pressure is on. Rachel was a bit edgy seeing me off: 'You're sure you know what you're doing? You know there's a lot on this?' I think I managed to look cool about it. Inside, my guts were churning.

I can feel the drowsiness coming over me. The pills are working. Think about nothing. 'Write the bad thoughts down on a piece of paper, then scrunch them up and throw them in a bin' was what Mum used to tell me. She'd think I was doing the right thing. She was never all that fussed about rugby. I'm a man now, anyway. I make my own decisions. Any moment now I'll be waking up to a new day. Come on, blackness. Drifting . . .

Fuck it. This isn't working. The drugs have turned my brain to mush without sending me to sleep. It's like Alice in Wonderland in here. I was nearly gone, then that prick Tisserand's smiling face floated up in front of me. He's still avoiding me in the real world — what is he doing in my head? No, no, no and fuck: 2.23. Still time for seven hours, at least.

I rustle round in my pants pocket, find my headphones, listen to some music. I wish I had some classical. The slowest thing I've got on here is the Doors. 'Weird scenes inside the gold mine . . .' Bad choice. He died in Paris, didn't he? Neil Young. That'll have to do. Just the acoustic stuff, though. Can I do that? Apparently not. 'Out of the blue, and into the black . . .' Think of trees, a lake. Peaceful. Sarah and I used to talk about that — 'Summers by the lake.' Don't think about Sarah. 3.07. Fuck. I could rub one out. That's the logical thing to do. Not that cool with Jacques next to me, but the situation is getting desperate. Give it another ten minutes. Still time for six hours.

I think I slept there for a bit. 5.24. When my eyes are open, I can just make out the ceiling.

6.40. Getting light. It doesn't matter any more.

8 am. Phone rings. Wake-up call for breakfast. Jacques gets up, takes a shower. Now, it seems, I can sleep.

9.25. Jacques tries to wake me. Ten more minutes, then a shower.

9.35. Ten more minutes. I don't need a shower.

9.45. For a few seconds I can't remember where I am. Am I really supposed to fix the game today? Or is that a dream? Pull on yesterday's clothes and splash water on my face. The hair on one side of my head is standing up from where I slept on it. A splash of water doesn't change anything. I slap my unshaven cheeks.

9.55. Two coffees at the bar go into a single cup. Down in one. Walk to the meeting room. Rich makes a comment about my new look. 'Sort of werepig? Is that what you're going for?' Stephane, the young ten who's been called up from the junior team to replace François on the bench, comes and sits next to me. Everyone else is wearing team kit but because he isn't part of the professional squad he hasn't been given his yet. He is wearing a T-shirt that says: 'All that I know most surely about morality and the obligations of men, I owe to football.' I was enjoying mentoring him — now I make a mental note to tell him he should concentrate on breathing out as he kicks the ball. That'll fuck him.

* * *

I go back to bed after the meeting and manage an hour before lunch. If I'm going to do this right I need to be in control. I almost forget to take a towel from the hotel bathroom for after the game. Luckily, Jacques sneaks a couple of fresh ones, one for each of us, off the maids' trolley. You've probably done the same yourself.

By the time we get to the ground I'm feeling a little less light-headed. The jab from the doc, the strapping around my ankle, the routine building towards the moment of action all help clear the fog. Adrenalin will carry me through the first half at least.

We have an English referee today, part of a drive to push back the boundaries of cross-cultural misunderstanding. That might be useful. I've had him before in Europe. The props don't get his scrum calls. I think he's pretty good, but he does a lot of talking in play, which I can understand but the Frenchies can't. He spots me when he comes into the dressing room to check boots. 'Hello, Mark. I might call on you for some translation, if that's all right?'

I force a smile. 'Moose — Richard, the number four — can help out as well. Should be a little closer to the action.' Christ, if he isn't I haven't learned anything.

'Fine. How're things?'

'Yeah, good. How's your French?' He's happy to see a friendly face. Or at least one he can talk to. It's almost touching. Referees — poor bastards. Where's the fun in that? No mates to stand by you, at least half the people you're dealing with are going to be unhappy, the calls are often so marginal that they can't know themselves with any real certainty — they just have to bluff. The best they can realistically hope for is not to make any mistakes, or if they do, that no one notices. I could understand Dad, who was doing it without any pressure, but I don't get these guys. I suppose there's money in it now.

'I have "lachez" and "hors jeu". Does that sound right?'

'Very impressive. Have a good one.'

'You too.'

He is getting the front rows together to explain his set for the scrum as I leave to warm up. Josh should be able to deal with that, at least.

I run through the same warm-up as always. No point in arousing suspicion. We're using their balls — I'm not used to them, though we have a couple at the club and I did a little practice with them on Thursday. That will be a useful excuse. And I can always bullshit Christophe that they weren't pumped up to my liking. One of the disadvantages of away games. I kick four at the posts meaning to put them through. I miss one, hooking it. For my last one I shift the vertical line that is my target to the right of the posts. That works. I get Rich to kick it back to me and have another go at the posts, so I don't look lazy. It's not just vanity. With luck I might still squeeze another season in here. And you never know who else might be watching.

Chapter 32

I send the kick-off straight out on the full. A good start. They take this to mean that we have come for a fight, and the first scrum breaks up in a flurry of punches. Coquine pushes our guys back quickly, and for one horrible moment I think the ref is going to assert his authority by sending one of them off. A penalty for us. Coquine looks enquiringly, and I call for a shot. This one is completely safe, and I push it to the right, further than I need to but nothing obvious. Coquine taps me on the bum. 'Don't worry about it. The next one.'

Within five minutes I have another chance. This time it's easier, about thirty-five metres out, fifteen in from touch. Well within my range. I push it wide again. The crowd murmurs. I get another bum tap, Jacques this time. 'It doesn't matter. Don't worry about it.' Coquine doesn't say anything. A couple of minutes later I put a kick to touch out on the full. Rich grins: 'Silky skills.' A penalty for them from the lineout. Mercifully, they put it over.

A few minutes later we are deep in their half. Lineout ball off the top for me. I have called a crash ball on Xavier. I throw it on his hip, making it almost impossible to catch, and he knocks it on. 'Am I too flat?' he asks, knowing that he wasn't.

'I'm sorry. My fault.' I am starting to think that I am pretty crafty. If only these muppets could get their game together, this could be relatively painless. They seem to have stage fright.

I am conscious of not being able to do too much, otherwise — baby on the bench or not — I will get subbed. Everyone will be hoping that I come right. I need to be patient. There's an injury break for one of their players. Coquine brings us in. 'Jacques, just get us down there. Back three, same thing — just kick us down there. We want to play in their half. This is our game — it's there for the taking. When we hit contact down there, stand up in the tackle, try to keep it up, pull them in around the fringes, that'll create the space.' He hasn't looked at me. As we break up, he comes over, dropping his voice as the others take up their positions. 'Come on, Mark.' He looks me straight in the eye. 'You're better than this. Get it together. Get us down there.'

'I'm sorry.' I shake my head. 'I'm doing what I can. It'll come.'

He smiles. 'I know. It'll come.' A pat on the head. 'I trust you.' Another smile.

Jesus. Is it that obvious?

Rich trots past, gives me a worried look. 'You're good, mate. Don't sweat it.'

For the next few minutes I try to play my normal game. Find a weakness, exploit it: their fullback was the man who went down injured, so I hoist a bomb on him and he fumbles it when he is challenged in the air. We recover the loose ball and press into attack. They are caught offside. A simple penalty chance for me, and I tap it over. I couldn't miss. 3–3. Twenty-two minutes gone. Still plenty of time. Thomas gives me a wink as we run back. 'Nice one.' They're all so fucking supportive, and I'm stealing from them. Moose ruffles my hair, the big lunk. Harden up, Mark, this was never going to be that simple. Like Rachel said, it's nothing they'll really notice. Sweat in my eyes. Christophe is waving his arms and shouting on the sideline. Yes, I get it, play down their end. Jacques, sensing I'm not at my best, takes the pressure off me and starts kicking himself. Soft-hearted bastard.

* * *

Half time. 10–6 to them. Not going too badly. Just another forty minutes, and I'm home free. The doc nods at the ankle as I walk past him into the changing room. 'All right?' I lift my eyebrows, grimace a little, play the martyr.

'It's not all right?'

Don't overcook it. 'I'll make it.'

He holds my look and I drop my eyes. 'You're sure? It's not the match of the century. Don't go screwing yourself up for this. Seriously.'

I keep moving. 'It's fine.' I sit down, and out of the corner of my eye I can see Christophe telling the kid to warm up. Fuck. Christophe sits down next to me. 'You're not right, are you?'

'I'm fine.'

'We're not going to push it. I'll take you off.'

'Just give me ten minutes. I'll tell you how it's going. If it's not right I'll come off.'

'You're sure? The young guy is ready.' I can see from his expression that he thinks I'm a stand-up bloke, taking one for the team and all that. Ah, shit, now he develops a conscience. It's a bit late in the piece for that. I give him a curt, heroic nod. 'OK. Ten minutes. But you let me know.'

We'll have to go to Plan B.

* * *

I've never had a red card in my life. I've only ever had a handful of yellows: a couple for technical infringements, a couple for head-high tackles, just one for a fight and that was after I got eye-gouged. I have already thought this through — I can't just walk up and lamp someone. Well, I suppose I could, but I'd probably get suspended for the rest of the season and rule myself out of another contract. It has to look like I got a bit carried away with retaliation, lost my cool, got frustrated. An English referee should help — he'll be harsher on punches. A head-high tackle is more dangerous for everyone concerned. A couple of slaps won't do any real harm. That said, I'm not all that keen on getting the crap kicked out of me, so I'd better pick the right guy. Ten minutes. For the first time in my entire life, I wish I was a forward.

We receive the kick-off, set and Jacques kicks from the base despite my calling for it. Their throw-in just our side of halfway. They win the ball, maul forward a couple of yards before passing. I rush their ten hoping to catch him but he's standing too deep and gets his kick away well before I arrive. Lineout. I have to get on with this. Two minutes gone already. A penalty against us at the lineout. Three minutes are up by the time he kicks it.

Kick-off: they kick back, we run it. Finally, a chance. Pierre is tackled near halfway; I go in to help him. The first support there is a lock — a bit big for my liking. Patience. Their winger who made the tackle, looks young and small. Perhaps a little too young and small, but I don't have time for a Goldilocks routine so I bounce to my feet, wait for him to stand — I can see droplets of sweat on the end of his long curly hair — and then pop him. Not a king hit, just a crack that glances off the side of his temple. He looks startled. That was lame, I thought about it too much, didn't really want to hurt him, so I give him another just to make sure. His eyes narrow. 'What? You want to fight? Come on then.' He's more into this than I expected, his chest puffed out like a rooster's. Referee, now would be a good time to notice this and take the necessary action. The ball has left and play continues elsewhere but the crowd has seen what has happened. They are booing. I look across at the touch judge, who only now seems to pick up on the little drama. Pierre, last up off the floor, stands by my side. Their lock, who was trundling off, has been alerted by the crowd and starts to return to the scene. I think I've done enough, but walking backwards now would be humiliating. The touch judge, his flag out, arrives at the same time as the lock; the winger snaps out an arm, pushing me. Jesus, he's got small-man syndrome — probably been picked on forever and has adapted by becoming punchy. I grab hold of his jersey, pull him in and land a sneaky uppercut. He bends his legs slightly, then launches his head into my face. The loud crack of bone on bone. I let go of his jersey and stagger back a step. Pierre slides in front of me, his arms moving, blocking my vision for a moment. My ears are ringing. The touch judge and the lock separate Pierre and the winger who is looking at me, smiling and mouthing off: 'Watch your back, my friend.' I put my hand to my chin. Blood. The ref is here now, pushing the winger and me back into our corners along with our respective seconds. He checks upstairs with the video ref but there's nothing, the cameras have followed the ball apart from one wide angle that is indecisive. We're not live, this is too small a game for a full quota of hardware. After a brief interview with the touch judge, he calls the two of us back and produces a yellow card, holding it above his head pointed first in the other guy's direction, then in mine.

* * *

My head is a swirl of ideas and yet nothing will stick, like a bicycle chain that has come undone from its gear, a whirring waste of energy taking me nowhere. I am sitting on the physio table. The doc's fingers, encased in rubber gloves, purse the wound on my chin closed.

'Four stitches should do it.'

'No anaesthetic.' I want to feel it. I deserve some pain. I disgust myself. First treachery, then incompetence.

'You're sure? There's no rush — you've got ten minutes. And I think Stephane is going to replace you anyway.'

'No. Let's get on with it.' Nico is watching. 'Nico, tell Christophe I'm fine. I have to play.'

He doesn't budge. 'Don't worry. Let the kid have a run. It's the perfect game for him.'

'Nico, please, tell Christophe I'm going to finish. I'll be fine.' He looks doubtful, waiting for a second opinion.

The doc shrugs his shoulders. 'I think it's a cock-up, but there's no reason why you can't. I can stitch it again.' A cheer from outside rises to a crescendo, followed by clapping. 'That doesn't sound great.'

Nico leaves. The doc has the needle, trailing fine blue thread, in his hand. 'OK, lie down. Hold still.'

Josh, subbed off, is at the door. 'You all right, slugger?'

'You should see the other guy.'

'I love what you do, mate. You work hard, you come home hungry.'

The doc is fidgety. 'This isn't going to work if you talk. You, out.'

'Don't mess up his looks, doc. It's all he's got.' I can hear his footsteps click away. The bite of the first puncture is a relief, focusing my attention. I look at the white squares on the ceiling. 'Don't move.' He pulls the thread through until the knot at the end tugs on my skin. 'Number two, coming up.'

I don't believe in God, or fate. This is not a sign. I don't really believe in anything, except myself. I have no grand scheme, just my instincts. And my guilt: 'Look after the girls.' And my mates. I should have got Rich in on this. He would have thought it was a laugh: it would have felt more normal, justifiable. We could have egged each other on.

'Number three.'

And Rachel. Maybe. And that money and the freedom it gives me. That it will give me. Freedom from guilt, from pain, from worry. Assuming I am the same person afterwards as I was before, that I want to be able to step over myself to get there. Oh, Jesus, I'm having a moment. Just when I need to be hard I go soft. One way or another, I'm going to let somebody down. I already knew that.

'We might need five, just to be safe.' Another bite of the needle through my flesh. 'If you're going to go out and play . . .'

This is the course of action I have decided on, and I have good reasons for doing it. I should just sit back now and see what happens. Wash my hands of the whole thing. I don't have to go back out. I feel tired. I close my eyes. I can see Sasha in the uniform of her new school, a huge grin on her face. What the boys don't know won't hurt them. They'd probably understand even if I told them. They'd want a taste, though.

'Last one. Just let me tie this off. Do you want a bandage? If you get hit there again it will split and there's nothing I can do about that. We'd have to strap under your chin right round like a bonnet. It's still no guarantee.'

Nico is at the door. 'Two minutes. If you're not ready Christophe is sending Stephane on.'

So it comes to this. The stubbornness that kept my grandfather alive in the trenches. The pigheadedness that kept my father running around on a windswept field where no one was paying attention, even when his knees might give out at any second. Now I, who have been handed the keys to the palace and an easy life, am looking for an even easier one. Fuck it. All right, all right. I'll have a go. Even if I play my guts out now I wouldn't flatter myself that I can turn it around on my own. But that way I will avoid sleepless nights further down the track. I can have it both ways. I don't have any more time to think about it. 'Don't worry about the bandage.'

Chapter 33

'A horse walks into a bar. The barman says—.'

'Why the long face? I dunno.' I would like to confide in someone, but it won't be Rich. Or any of the boys. I am tied to Rachel now. And I don't feel like talking to her at the moment. She isn't going to be pleased.

'Come on, we won, dickhead. Here, go out to the bogs and stick some of this up your nose. Don't worry, be happy.'

'Where did you get that from?'

'It's sweet. My man here got us a couple of grams.'

'Your man?'

'Saffa dude I used to play with has set up here. Wasn't keen on going back to the homeland. He dabbles a little and I asked him to bring something along. It ain't so bad. Why are you down? Yoko on the rag or something?'

In the end, it was a perfect result. At least, that's what I'm trying to tell myself. A one-point win for us. I came back on, threw a few miss passes, kicked a goal and that was that. OK, it was a bit more complicated than that but I'll spare you the details. The kid, Stephane, even came on and kicked the winning points, so I can blame that on him. We still beat the spread. They — we? — will have lost something on the straight win but Rachel said the occasional loss would help their credibility. My winnings will be less than what they might have been, but I'm not going to lie on my deathbed weeping about having sold my mates short. Now we're in a nightclub, and the Fibber, intoxicated by a last-minute away win, has put his card behind the bar. Fluorescent light, faceless dance music and a table in front of us crammed with bottles and black plastic jugs full of ice and mixers. Girls hover, shimmying, trying not to look interested. And Rich wants to palm me a folded piece of paper whose contents could bring a swifter end to my career than even I had contemplated until now.

'You're such a badass. When did you turn into Tony Montana?'

'You're the high-roller. Just a little tourism in the lifestyle for me.'

'I'm not sure it's such a good idea.'

'Look, it takes three days to get out of your system. Tomorrow is Sunday, and we're off until Thursday. There's no way we're getting tested before then — and we've never been tested for this anyway. Loosen up and live a little. You ever done this? Here, I'll come with you.'

The route to the toilets is crowded and we jostle past faces I recognise from the field this afternoon. Eric is coming out of the toilets as we arrive. 'Whoops, that was close.' There are a few other men; no one I recognise. We squeeze into a cubicle, giggling. Rich extracts a mangy-looking five euro note from his pocket.

'You can't do it with that. Jesus, Tony Montana? You're more like a crack whore. Here.' I pass him a crisp fifty.

'Now you're talking.'

There is a knock on the door. 'Police. Open up.' We both stiffen. For a fraction of a second — the amount of time it takes for your brain to work out whether an injury is serious or not, or whether you can make it through a hole in the defence — there is a swoop of fear in my bowels. Then we realise that the accent is Canadian.

'Jesus, Moose.' He must have spotted us coming in.

'You guys having a good time in there? Who's pitching, who's catching?'

'It's a private party. No offence, but fuck off.'

'You guys . . .'

I know what you're thinking. That I'm making bad choices here, that this is going to end in tears, that I'm an idiot for doing something that could jeopardise my career, my reputation. Yeah, well, maybe. Probably not, though. Anyway, let's face it, my career is on its last legs. And the sort of people who talk about sportsmen being idiots for doing this kind of thing because they would have given their right arm to be in our situation never got close to being here in the first place because they didn't have the character to stick it out. Really, they arranged not to be here, quietly — perhaps not even so they'd notice — making little compromises with themselves when it mattered, avoiding risks, refusing to implicate themselves too deeply. They weren't demanding enough of themselves or of life to get a chance at the big time. 'I could have, should have, would have.' Mediocrity is a shitburger and if that's what's on your menu, then it's your fault — don't bring me down. I've been living clean for so many years I'm knocking on the door of middle age, and I'll be even more settled soon. If I don't try this sort of thing now I never will. All right, it's not the first time, but it's the first time in season, and the first time for a while — and I've turned it down a lot more often. Every time I go to see friends in London it's a fucking snowstorm. It's a calculated risk, and I like to take calculated risks. The act of transgression is pleasurable in itself. We hardly get a chance to make decisions for ourselves: we wear what we're told, eat what we're told, do what we're told. This is a little treat just for me. I'm not about to get hooked on a couple of lines on a Saturday night once every couple of years. Jesus, Barack Obama used to do it, and it doesn't seem to have done his career any harm. ('A little blow' anyone? Yeah, I read the papers.) If I get busted, I get busted. Who wants to live life by other people's rules? I did the right thing this afternoon, didn't I? So maybe I deserve a break. And why am I bothering to justify myself anyway?

Sorry. It's been a long day.

Rich has chopped out a couple of lines on the wonky black plastic lid of the toilet with his card. Somehow I always imagine this being a little more glamorous and it never is. Errol Flynn used to sniff it off the back of his conquests, apparently. I wonder if Rachel would be into that? I think she probably would. The dragon tattoo would make for a nice backdrop. She isn't going to be pleased by what happened today. I had almost managed to forget about it.

Rich, kneeling, goes first. He hoovers up half of his line, then switches nostrils for the second half. 'Ah, fuck. It won't go up.'

A burst of laughter from outside. Moose. 'What the hell are you guys doing?'

'My nose is broken, you big bloody lumberjack. Stop being frisky.' More giggles. He finishes off with his good nostril. 'Mm-hmm. Fine as May wine. Sweet like something really sweet. Candy. You *know* what I'm talking about.' Cleans up, then it's my turn. By now we are both laughing so much that some of the powder blows away.

'Don't! Stop it.'

'You stop it, you jackass. You're so uncool. Oh, man . . .'

There is the familiar, bitter taste at the back of my throat as it hits, and my gums turn numb from the wipe-up. Then we are striding past the urinals, sniffing. 'Moose, you're too young for this shit. It wouldn't be right.' Moose is the same age as Rich: twenty-seven.

I feel better already. 'Drive it like you stole it.' Rich heads to the bar. By the time I get back to the table I feel like a one-man army. Coquine limps up, takes a seat next to me so that I can hear him speak over the music and looks straight at me, seriously. He puts his two fingers up to his eyes, then points them towards mine: 'I saw you today. Good job. You were there for us when we needed you.'

I grind my teeth without even thinking about it.

* * *

Coke was a bad idea. I can't sleep. Again. I'm exhausted. I've got the fear. My heart is bullocking at the inside of my chest, trying to get out. Curled into a ball, I keep running the day's events through my head. Why didn't I just take a seat like everyone wanted and ride it out? No one would have known. I had done my bit. As a boy I could look my mother in the eye and tell her a lie without feeling any the worse for it. Now everything is complicated. What is Rachel going to say? What am I going to say to her? I keep thinking about the kitchen knives. Jacques leans over and swats me with a pillow: 'Hey, shut up. You're talking in your sleep.' I realise that I have been swearing out loud for some time. I feel like I've got Tourette's. I want to cry. How could I be so stupid? And then drugs, to top the whole day off. Fuckwit.

I went out to the bogs again later on, this time to use them for the normal reason. A slender, dark-haired bloke a few years younger than me was there, doing his hair in the mirror. '*T'es un coquin, toi, hein?*' It took a while for me to compute — *coquin* is the masculine version of *coquine*: he thought I was a flirty boy. Or something stronger. He turned and looked me over. His smile was his way of showing me that he liked the idea of my being a *coquin*. I suppose my polo shirt was quite tight. 'I think there's been a misunderstanding.' He shrugged and sauntered out.

When, finally, I drift under, I dream that I am on a barge travelling on a river through the middle of a city. I have a wheel in front of me and am supposed to be steering, but while I can see the tops of high-rise buildings on either side, I can't see where I'm going. The walls are too high. The barge is filled with old-model cars that are obviously used. They look like they still work, but from the way they are piled carelessly on top of each other it's clear they are going to be junked anyway. A long, thick snake slithers in and out of the cars then wends its way towards me. It rears up in front of me. I can't move. The snake's tongue flickers and I wake up, sweating and shivering.

Chapter 34

I am unravelling, run-down, vulnerable. Pathetic. On the upside, I'm approaching the point where I'm too tired to care. I thought about checking into a hotel to avoid facing Rachel in this state. But there's no point in putting it off. I did warn her that it might not work out. Attack is the best form of defence. 'I told you so' probably won't be the best opening line, though. I like to think that running a game is like playing chess or driving or just living: to do it well you need to take in what's happening now and act, at the same time as seeing what is about to happen, the dangers and opportunities that may arise, anticipate how you can make them work for you. This is the kind of moment where that skill is useful, only I have no idea how this is going to play out, and I haven't the energy to try to think through my options.

I haven't heard from her since the game.

I turn the key in the door. With Sarah, I used to be able to tell what kind of mood she was in just from the sound of her footsteps. I don't know Rachel that well yet. Now I'm not sure that I'll get the chance. There is no noise. Perhaps she's not here. I drop my bag at the entrance, walk through to the living room. She's here, curled up catlike on the sofa reading a book. I can smell stale tobacco smoke. The ashtrays are full. She looks up. 'The conquering hero returns.'

'So you saw the result.'

She uncoils and stands in a liquid movement. I walk towards her. 'I'm sorry it didn't work out.'

Out of the corner of my eye, I see her hand swinging up. I don't flinch. A full-blooded slap stings my cheek. The skin of my face tightens with the contact, pulling at the fresh, still very tender wound on my chin. My eyes water. Embarrassed, I laugh to cover the discomfort. The hand swings again, but this time I catch it. 'I get the point. One is enough.'

She pulls her hand away. 'It's quite obvious that you *don't* get the point.' She lights a cigarette. The flame quivers in her hands. I wanted to see her unsettled. Not like this.

'He can afford to lose money. I can afford to lose money — I could even cover some for him — as long as it's not too much. At least you haven't lost anything.'

'You idiot. You boy-scout idiot. You really don't get it, do you? We told him, *I* told him, that you were going to do something, and you didn't do it. You could have done it, but you didn't. I don't know how much he will have lost. That doesn't matter. You have principles — so does he. And his are not as high-minded as yours. We are in trouble.'

'I'm in trouble. It's not your fault.'

'Do you really think he cares?' She is shouting now, waving the hand with the cigarette for effect. 'You can't possibly be so naive as to think that he is going to say, "I know it wasn't your fault, never mind"? Philip is not a nice man. And he has some very unpleasant friends. You can't just shake hands with him and tell him it's bad luck.'

'What do you mean, "unpleasant friends"?'

Very slowly, as if to a slow-learning child: 'He works with people who are criminals.'

'Oh.' I plump down onto the sofa. 'Shit.'

'Oh, I think the boy scout is starting to get it.'

'I had no idea. You should have told me.'

'I thought you knew. I really thought you knew. Until yesterday afternoon.'

'All right. What can we do about it?'

'There's nothing we can do about it. I tried to call him yesterday but he didn't pick up.' A sharp look. 'You understand that that is not good?'

'Yes, OK, I get it. Neither of us is covered in glory. So he hasn't made contact. Exactly who are we dealing with here?'

'I told you we were introduced at a party. It turned out he had some useful contacts for a story I was doing. I saw him a couple of times to follow up, then again socially. I mentioned I was going to do a piece on rugby in France and he said that he would talk to people he knew and came back with your name and another guy.'

'Who was the other guy?'

'I can't remember. You were in Paris, you're well-known, you kick. It fitted the profile I was looking for.'

'So I was set up from the start?'

'Your eyes were open, Mark. No one forced you to do anything.'

'You can be quite persuasive.'

'I'm not a whore. That was for fun.'

'Was' is not lost on me. 'We' no longer seem to have a present or a future. But I still want to believe that she has been telling me the truth, on this at least. Until now I have believed what I wanted to believe. It hasn't served me very well. I get scratchy when I haven't had enough sleep, and I feel anger welling up inside. Anger at myself for going along with this stupid idea, and anger with her for tempting me. Anger at the corrosion of my body that now goes hand in hand with the corruption of my soul, and my impotence in the face of it all. Testosterone and self-loathing. Not a good mix. It breaks too fast for me to control and I am possessed by a desire to hurt this woman I love, to wreak vengeance, to break something so it can never be put together again.

'Is it still fun enough for you?' I grab her hair, sleek and black and vital. Twisting it into a rope I yank her head back and towards me. The red wetness of her mouth is half open. I can see her teeth and the smooth delicacy of the tongue that has given me so much pleasure as she catches her breath, holds it, waiting for what might come next. This is the only power that I have left and I relish it, reasserting myself on her by ugly, unsophisticated brute strength. Without thinking I force my left hand up her skirt, my fingers pushing aside the flimsy material at the junction of her legs. Eyes that were wide with fear and surprise narrow and glitter with fury. Now I can force the moment to its crisis. 'It's just the way the world works.'

But instead of pressing on, I hesitate. Again. And the danger passes. I find that I too have held my breath, and after releasing her we both spend a few seconds panting, eyeing each other warily as my anger seeps away to be replaced by more self-disgust. I don't seem to be able to do anything right.

'*Que frouxo*.'

'What?'

'There are a lot of things you don't understand.' She walks into the bedroom and pulls out a big black suitcase from underneath the bed and starts throwing her clothes into it. I go into the spare bedroom, flop down and roll myself in the duvet. I can hear her moving around next door, high heels clicking on the parquet. I was wrong: I can tell her mood by the sound of her footsteps. A few minutes later the door slams. Shortly afterwards I fall into a dreamless sleep.

* * *

The ringing of a telephone pierces the blackness. When I open my eyes I am lost for a moment, disconnected, looking at surroundings that are familiar yet not what I am used to seeing first thing. That's right, the spare room. It is dark outside. I stagger to the phone in the living room, favouring my ankle, but by the time I get there it has rung through to the answer service. As I pick it up it starts ringing again, vibrating in my hand. Ali. It's been a couple of weeks since we've spoken. By my calculations it's six in the morning at home. What is she doing calling at this time? 'Sis.'

'Jesus fucking Christ, Sparky, what the fuck are you doing to us?' She is sobbing and shouting at the same time.

'What are you talking about? Calm down, sis. Deep breaths. Now, what are you talking about?'

'I'm sorry, I'm so sorry. Darrin will pay you back for the jetski. No, he'll buy a new one. I told him not to, I said you'd be mad as hell. You never use it, though. It's been sitting in the garage for years.'

'What?'

Her voice rises to a shriek. 'Don't burn us down, you bastard. You've had all the luck. What would Mum and Dad say? What about the girls? You can't do this.'

'Tell me what you're talking about. You're not making any sense. Is everyone all right?' She's a hard case, Ali. She wouldn't be like this without reason. Interesting that Darrin has flogged my jetski, the thieving prick. She's right, though — I never use it. It was second-hand anyway.

'No thanks to you.'

'For fuck's sake, Ali, talk sense. I haven't done anything. I'm in Paris. What do you mean by burning you down? Is the house on fire?'

'Your goons, they poured petrol everywhere.'

'What?'

'The guys in the black balaclavas.' Her breathing is still broken.

'Some guys in black balaclavas came to the house and poured petrol everywhere — is that what you're saying? What makes you think it had anything to do with me? Has Darrin been doing some dealing on the side?'

'No, Darrin has *not* been doing any dealing.' Now she is calming down. More focused, anyway. 'They told me to call you.'

'The guys in the balaclavas told you to call me? What did they say, exactly?'

'They didn't say anything. We were all asleep, and I heard the sound of breaking glass — they smashed through the ranchslider on the side of the house — and I went into the living room and this guy was pouring petrol onto the carpet. It's fucking everywhere, the whole place reeks, I can't even have a ciggie, it's killing me.' Back to her old self, or close enough.

'Jesus, that's terrible. We'll get it fixed, don't worry. Is everyone all right? The girls?'

'We're all a bit shaken up. Jesus, I hate Monday mornings as it is.'

'You're all right, then. But what does it have to do with me?'

'You really don't know? Well, I shouted at them, told them to leave, and the other guy, he had a gun. He had a gun, Sparky, and Sasha was up by now, wondering what the hell was going on, as you do. She was standing next to me, Sparky, and the guy with the gun pointed it at me, then he pointed it at Sasha, and he came up to the window that wasn't broken and put a piece of paper up against the window. And the piece of paper said 'CALL YOUR BROTHER'. So don't tell me you have nothing to do with this. Why would they do that if you had nothing to do with this?' Her voice has risen towards the end.

It hits me. Philip. Rachel. I mentioned them to her, she must have passed it on to him. It can't be that hard to find the right family. I recognise the tactic: find a weak point, exploit it. Monday morning at home, Sunday night here — he must have done that this morning, or perhaps last night, in anger. Twenty seconds on the internet, a phone call to the right person, a second phone call, a couple of local thugs take a ride: an hour's work, two hours, tops.

'Are you there, Sparky?'

'Yeah. OK. Hold on for a second, let me think. Listen, Ali, I didn't have anything to do with this. I'm not responsible. I mean, I didn't make this happen.'

'So why did they want me to call you?'

'I don't know for sure, but I think someone is trying to force me to do something that I don't want to do. Dad wouldn't have wanted me to do it either.' I think about adding Granddad as well, but he doesn't seem to swing a lot of weight with Ali.

'Well, I'm pretty sure he wouldn't have wanted the house burned down with his grandchildren inside either. What have you got yourself mixed up in? These bastards are serious, Sparky.'

'Just let me think. Can you go to Auntie Rita's for a bit? No, scratch that, stay out of the family. I don't suppose Darrin has any money left over from the jetski? Anyway, this is just a warning, they won't do anything more until they see what I'm going to do, so you've got a couple of days at least. I'll call the bank now and send something through. Take the girls away for a holiday somewhere for a week.'

'School is back. Holidays are finished.' She's looking to turn this to her advantage.

'Come on, sis, be reasonable. A few days off school won't do any harm.'

'You're the one who's always going on about bringing them up right.'

'So take them somewhere interesting. Go to the museum, I don't know, just avoid being a target for a week or so. Keep your mobile on, and I'll let you know when it's safe to go home.'

'All right. Make sure you send through some money for the cleaning, though. The carpets are going to cost a bomb. And the window.'

'Fine. Talk soon.'

'Listen, Spark, what *is* the story? Are you going to be OK? You're my little bro, you know. It sounds like you're in some deep shit. I haven't always been crash-hot at looking after you, but if you're in a hole, give me a shout. I don't know what I can do, but if these dickheads are giving you trouble, I know some guys who might be able to help. You know what Dad would say: we don't take this kind of shit lying down.'

'Thanks. I'll let you know. But the problem isn't your end. It's at mine.'

'What's going on then?' She giggles. I imagine her wiping away tears. 'Have you been sticking your wick somewhere you shouldn't have?'

'Something like that. But more complicated. I'll tell you about it later. You just get those girls somewhere safe. Tell them someone made a mistake and you're going away while everything gets cleaned up. And make sure you use cash when you pay for the hotel. Use cash for everything.'

'I know how it works. I watch TV too.'

'I owe you one.'

'You know it.'

I call the bank at home, send five grand through to Ali, then eat. Afterwards I spend a couple of hours making a couple of phone calls, formulating various plans and mulling over them before discarding all but a couple. I keep coming back to the one involving guns, but there's no way that will work. I have to grow up. I need Rachel, which won't be easy. I feel strangely happy about this new development. Philip has shown his hand, and I have to beat him. I may have struggled to act, but I'll be able to react. Ali is right: we don't take this shit lying down. I wonder what Granddad would have done.

I have no problem sleeping.

Chapter 35

I didn't set an alarm but I wake up at nine, feeling fresh. We have nothing on until Thursday, and with a bit of luck this will all be over by then. I have breakfast, reassure myself that last night's thinking was along the right lines, then call Rachel. No answer. Only to be expected after what happened. I send her a text: 'Philip has made contact.' I give her a couple of minutes to digest this little nugget, then call again. I can't do this by text.

'You're bluffing. Philip would never contact you.'

'Listen, I'm sorry about the way I behaved. I really am. I was out of control.'

'I don't want to hear it. This is strictly business. For the moment we have a common interest so I'll hear you out. But don't do the tearful boyfriend routine. You'll be wasting everyone's time.'

'Ali rang last night after you left.' It only now occurs to me that she might have been in on this, that Philip wasn't acting on his own. I console myself with the fact that I can always fall back on Plan B. 'Two goons broke in and threatened to burn her house down.'

'And you think this has something to do with Philip?' Chillier than I had hoped, but she's probably not directly involved. Unless she knew exactly what happened, and is playing me.

'They told her to call me.' A pause.

'They didn't really want to burn the house down, otherwise

they would have. I've heard of the technique. It's a warning. I guess we can assume it's Philip.'

'Bloody right we can assume it's Philip. I can't think of anyone else, unless it's you. So you told him about them?'

'He wanted to know where to apply pressure if it was necessary. I told him that you were a bad bet because your boy-scout tendencies would oblige you not to back down, and you're no use to anyone if you're hurt or dead. You don't seem to have a lot of time for your sister, but you're quite attached to your nieces.' So she had consciously worked out the best way to get to me for her master. I have to stop myself from shouting at her. Just as well we're doing this on the phone. Still, if she was trying to play me, wouldn't she try harder to be nice?

'Yeah, I see. So what he's saying is that I should go along with the next fix or there's a family barbecue?'

'Let's hope it doesn't come to that.' That's my ice-cream girl — sweet and cold as you like.

'It won't. I'm going to the police.' A pause. I can almost hear her brain whirring. Between you and me, the cops are Plan B.

'That sounds like you. Honest and stupid. You don't solve any of your problems. In fact, you're just creating more for yourself.'

'What would you suggest?'

'That you do what he wants. You don't have anywhere else to go. If you're very lucky he may still give you some money.'

'I don't care about the money any more.'

'Then you're more of a fool than I thought, and I can't help you. If you go to the police you'll have to incriminate yourself. Your career will be over, you'll be fined and you might go to jail.'

'You always said I wasn't doing anything wrong.'

'You were talking about morality. I didn't say it was legal.'

'All right, let's avoid the philosophy angle. We should try

to find a solution together.' I would like this to come from her. People who think they're smart always prefer to believe they found the answer themselves. I've had any number of coaches like that.

'Let me think about it for a while.'

'No. I don't want you calling Philip.'

'You don't trust me?'

'Don't sound so surprised.'

'You know he hasn't been picking up my calls.'

'Maybe he will this time. Where are you?'

'In the hotel on the corner.'

'Meet me in reception. I'll come round now. Stay on the phone — I want you with me all the time until this is over.'

* * *

We go to the café down the street: neutral territory. 'I'm not going to take a dive, so that's out. You think the cops are a bad idea, presumably because you would go down as well. What does that leave us with?'

'If you're not going to do what you said you would, the easiest solution as far as Philip and I are concerned is for you to quietly disappear.'

That's a bluff, I'm sure of it. She's not that ruthless. Or is that just what I want to believe? 'I'll assume that's Brazilian humour. What I think is that we should find a way to keep Philip quiet. To leave us alone, at least. Personally, I'd prefer that it was him that quietly disappeared, but I don't think either of us are capable of that.'

'Why are you so convinced that I am going to help you?'

'Because you're not the hard bitch you're trying to make out.

Because you're in a corner as much as I am, if not more, because you're more expendable if Philip is as bad a guy as you think he is — and his methods so far would suggest that he's not shy about putting the shit in. And because guys like Philip are the ones who screw people like us over. There must be a way out that doesn't involve anyone disappearing.'

'I'm listening.'

'Try doing some thinking as well. I can't do it all on my own. What has Philip got on us? What does he control? And what can we get on him?'

'This isn't going to work.'

'Let's just see what our options are.'

She sighs. 'He controls the money, and I imagine he can take it out as easily as he put it in. I haven't checked yet to see if it has already gone. He knows who we are, and how to get to us. You more than me, but spending a life on the run, looking over my shoulder every day, doesn't appeal to me. He could probably pass on information about us to the police as well, though I don't think that is his style and it would be too dangerous for him.'

'What does he fear?'

She laughs, a husky, breathy noise that combines with the crinkle in her eyes to hit me in the guts, or a bit lower. I'm not over her. 'He doesn't fear us, that is for certain.'

'That's good.'

'He's not a fool, Mark. He doesn't fear us because we can't hurt him. If he even starts to think about us as a threat, we're halfway dead. If he is afraid of anything, it would be his associates. He may have lost them some money, and if he did he will have lost face with them, which is worse than losing money in their world. He would be afraid of losing his own money, but it would have to be a lot of money and we don't have any way of getting to it. If he is going to bet on you again, he will need to be one hundred per cent certain you don't let him down again, and you don't want to suffer the consequences of that.'

'So we could go to his, what did you call them, associates?'

'Don't be idiotic. There's no way they'll trust us, and I wouldn't even know how to contact them. We're not getting anywhere.'

'Yes, we are. We have to go through all the possibilities. He'll have a weak point. We just need to find it.'

'It's not a game, Mark. You're not evenly matched.' She says this surprisingly gently. There's hope yet, son. 'You're just going to have to do what they want.'

'That's not on the table.' It's true. Money no longer enters into the equation. I would like to think that I'm doing this to protect Ali and Sasha and Steph, but if that was the case I'd go along with what Philip wants. So now it's about pride, or self-respect, or vanity, whatever you want to call it. It feels like a refreshingly clean motivation. I haven't looked too closely, though. I prefer to trust my instincts. I'm hoping it's the same sort of thing that got Granddad and his mates out of the trenches. Maybe not the right reason, but honest at least. Perhaps not everyone wants to be a hero, but I don't want to have to think of myself as a coward. In a way, I'm glad Philip has forced me to dig a little deeper. That is, I'll be glad if this turns out all right. 'You don't think there's a way of exposing him, or threatening to expose him, that might work?'

'First of all, it would blow up in your face because you would be exposed as soon as he was. Second, your family would be dead within hours.'

'He doesn't know where they are. And anyway, what would that prove?'

'I imagine it would be a question of principle. They'll find them, sooner or later. Your sister can't go on the run with a couple of little girls and a few hundred bucks.'

'So where does that leave us?'

'You just have to do what he wants.'

'Let's go see him. Maybe we can come to an arrangement.'

Rachel weighs it up. 'OK.'

Chapter 36

Here we are at the Gare du Nord again. In theory we could make the necessary arrangements long-distance, but I want a resolution as soon as possible. The longer the standoff drags on with Philip, the greater the chance of harm coming to Ali and the girls, and I don't need that on my conscience. I spoke to her on the way over in the taxi — they're down in Wellington in a flash hotel. Things almost got sticky when she couldn't provide a credit card but she paid cash for three nights up front and that seemed to go all right.

Rachel has been wearing a guarded look since we met this morning. Her phone rings as I finish buying the train tickets. 'It's Philip.'

'Put it on speaker.'

'He'll hear.'

'I don't care. Do it.' She presses a button on her phone, twice.

'Hello.'

'Can you talk?' She gives me a nervous look. I push her towards a corner, and huddle close.

'Yes.'

'You sound distant.' I don't know England well enough to get all the accents, but his voice has that rich, fruity sound that I associate with expensive schools. And Scar in *The Lion King*. I watched it with Sasha.

'I'm in the street.'

'Your boyfriend let me down.'

'What do you want me to do?'

'Tell me what happened.'

'He told me he couldn't go through with it.'

'What is his state of mind?'

'He's angry about what happened to his sister.'

'Ah!'

'He doesn't know what to do next. I think he's frightened, but it's hard to tell. He's angry with me as well. He knows I told you about them.'

'Tell him, tell him that no one wants anything bad to happen to his family. This is true. I am still prepared to be generous if he does what is required of him. But there won't be any more chances. And I suggest that you use all the powers of persuasion that you have at your disposal. The stakes are high for you as well.'

'I've done exactly what you told me to. I can't be responsible for his actions.'

'Of course. I understand. I'll be in touch. Goodbye.' The line beeps dead.

'Sounds like a nice bloke.'

* * *

As the train curves round a bend on the final few kilometres of its journey, the taller buildings of the London skyline come into view. In the town I grew up in, houses stood separate, with their own chunk of land and a low running fence shared with neighbours on three sides. Even with the trees you couldn't help knowing everyone else's business, the late-night shouting match, the state of the garden, the weekend occupation. In Paris I know, vaguely, some people on my staircase to smile at and the concierge who probably gossips about me. My building has three staircases, eight floors, three flats on each floor, averaging say three to a flat: two hundred lives being lived on a footprint that would be half the size of a family section at home. I wonder what it would be like to grow up here. When I first went to Wellington, aged about ten, the car followed the road round a similar curve at the bottom of a gorge and I was looking at a city for the first time. I was struck by the immensity of the place and the accumulation of effort required to build it, how long the process must have taken and the sheer sweat that must have gone into it, beam after beam, brick after brick, until the whole unstoppable growth arrived at that particular day's tally of created space. The cluster of high-rises that stretch back from the waterfront of New Zealand's capital and the houses that pepper the surrounding hills are dwarfed by the sprawl of a metropolis like London or Paris, yet this is the image that always comes back when I think of the scale of a city and the number of man-hours that go into their creation. Perhaps it's because I know some of the men who built the place. Perhaps it's just more manageable.

Beneath the buildings and the streets and the parks and the squares there always lies another, invisible construction, the guts that make it work, carved out of dirt and rock: sewers and tunnels and cemeteries. Not far from where I live in Paris are the catacombs, the old stone quarries of the city converted by necessity into an ossuary. The entry point is at the old Porte d'Enfer: the gate to hell. The Resistance used the catacombs to meet and hide and travel undetected. The Germans used them as well. Now they are given over to tourism and underground parties. Sarah and I walked through there one damp Sunday afternoon when we couldn't think of anything else to do, unsettled by the piles of bones and skulls in every room and the fine white dust that accumulated on our shoes that presumably wasn't chalk. I shouldn't have been so squeamish. One way or another, every civilisation is built on the bones of its dead.

* * *

The train slows as we arrive into London. Rachel looks out the window as the city slides past us. She has no enthusiasm for what lies ahead. Understandable. For her, this is damage control. At best, once it's done, she will be able to limp away and start again. She deserves better than desperation. We're all terrified of falling back. But pity allows me distance, and I find the spell that she had cast on me worn off. Somehow she is a lesser being, whereas I have always liked the idea of pitting myself against an opponent. After finally asserting myself I find it gratifying to have such an impact on the strange world that rolls on beyond my own small existence, unknown wheels that have been set in motion only to come juddering to a halt.

There are any number of reasons for not playing by the rules: my own was the lazy hope of a slate somehow wiped clean — as if that would even work — without the need for sacrifice, imagining living up to one ideal not realising that I was wrecking another. Vague, unsayable, but there, inside, hooked on to something. A conscience tapeworm. Why can't my genes be more selfish? There would have been a big cherry on top as well — two, three hundred thousand pounds? Given their enthusiasm for games that were likely to be lost, I could have tried for a gig with some really lowly outfit and made a packet walking out the back door. Or if I'd got Rich in on it we might have rationalised the whole thing away, talked it out, convinced ourselves that because the Fibber and others like him rig the game so should we, that we would be idiots not to enjoy our special status. Perhaps this corruption of reality, this arrangement with the truth, this ability to step over should be welcomed as a gift. If you can manipulate it, nudge it towards becoming a useful driver, then slowly assimilate it into who you are, you become a justifiable sinner.

I don't need that.

I can't be that.

Chapter 37

London is already dark by the time we get out of the station. We don't talk in the cab. Even though she signed up for this, Rachel is sending out waves of disapproval. We take such a series of sharp turns down empty suburban streets that I lose all sense of direction and wonder if the driver is having a laugh. I send Ali a text, and she replies immediately: 'All good.' Then I slide the partition across, hope like hell that the driver is listening to his radio, and call the Bamboozler.

I explain the situation, giving the names and making sure he writes them down. When I have finished, there is no reply. 'You there?'

A long pause. 'Fucking hell. You're a hidden gig, aren't you, Spark? Yeah, I've got it. I've got your back. We're in the trust nest now. How're you doing? Can we keep this neat? This baboon isn't going to do a number on you?'

'I'm about to find out.' I like hearing that he's got my back, and that he says 'we'. I don't know that it will make any difference to Philip, but it feels good to me. 'I'll let you know how I get on.'

'What have you got? A plan so crazy it just might work?'

I can't help grinning. Rachel looks at me like I'm unhinged.

The taxi pulls up by a house opposite the river. The cabbie pulls the partition back. 'Here you are then. Number twenty-seven is the one with the lights on downstairs. Fifty-two quid, thanks.' Behind the grand-looking living area visible through the windows, the house stretches back into darkness. On our left, a vast lawn leads down to the water. The property has been cut in half by the road. 'Summers by the river.' We haven't even talked about how to approach this, and we're already here. I like to know as much as I can about an adversary, how he's likely to react in any given situation, his strengths, his weaknesses. I look at the house. I don't have much. A plummy accent and the hope that he doesn't know how to play this either. Unlikely to be enough. We're here now, anyway.

He will have had spooked, sleepless nights at some point. Everyone wings it.

'Can you stay here until we get back?' I pass the driver two fifties. The ends of my fingers are tingling.

'I'll wait for half an hour.' I pull out another fifty and hand it to him. 'An hour, then.'

'Don't worry about it. If we're not out in an hour, call 911.'

'You mean 999?'

'Just call the cops.'

'You're not in any trouble?'

'I hope not.'

'I'll park just a little way down the road. Just over there, y'see?'

'Are you coming?' I say to Rachel.

'Try to stop me. Just don't expect me to do any talking.' She looks half-amused. We clamber out onto the street.

'Wait up for a second, will you?' I try to take a mental step back, get some perspective on the different ways this might work out, on how I should play it. On tour with the All Blacks after beating the Poms here in London we had a bus trip across to Wales. The old heads briefed us on the journey, and as we crossed the Severn Bridge everyone stood up and on the count of three shouted 'WE DON'T FUCKING LOSE IN WALES.' And so we didn't. The memory warms me for a few seconds — pride, competence, solidarity, an obvious shared goal. Then the moment passes, and I feel emptier than before. There is no one else to rely on, no example to follow and I barely even know what I'm trying to achieve. A peace treaty with a scumbag, apparently. Until now I have assumed that Philip would be unlikely to do me any harm on the basis that either he wants me to play or too many others know about him for him to risk topping me. Standing thirty metres from his front door I start to think that I have been overly optimistic. No bright ideas present themselves. I may not know that much about the real world but I understand that confidence in your ability to meet what's coming needs to be earned — otherwise you're a fool, or drunk. Ahead of me, the outcome is already decided. I just can't see it; the millions of factors that have fed into me and the opponent I face are, for the moment, unreadable to me. Whatever happens, it will be my responsibility. I own this.

A damp, chilled mist comes off the water and goes straight to my bones. Might as well get it over with. Rachel has lit up a cigarette while she waits. Now she grinds it out beneath the two-inch heel of her boot as I catch up with her. I open the gate and we walk up the couple of steps, feet crunching the concrete in the now silent street. I knock at the door.

We can hear movement inside. A woman answers the door. She is blonde, petite, mid-thirties, handsome in a healthy, rosy-cheeked, horsey way. She is wearing jeans and a powder-blue V-neck sweater that looks like cashmere. Her face is neutral. 'Oh, Rachel. Hello.' The door remains narrowly open, her body blocking entry.

'Hello, Joanna. We're here to see Philip. It's about work.'

'It's a bit late, isn't it?'

A voice from further back in the building. 'Who is it, darling?'

The woman relays the information with a shout. 'Rachel. It's about work, apparently.' She gives way, opens the door wider. The man who must be Philip comes through a door off a long corridor and makes his way down to us. His age is hard to place but the woman who answered the door is too young to be his first wife.

'Rachel. Good to see you. And Mark. How do you do?' He sticks out his hand, and I am so stunned that I shake it. He hesitates for a millisecond, then kisses Rachel formally on both cheeks. Given half a chance, no straight man can resist coming into closer contact with her flesh. He turns. 'Thanks, darling. This won't take long.' The domestic aspect is a surprise. I suppose I was expecting hookers and coke. Now I start to wonder if there are teenagers skulking in bedrooms over their computers upstairs — but we were right to come. It's a nice pad, but it's hardly a lair. And there is plastic sheeting on the floor in the hall. They've had a leak. Beautiful. I wonder whether he dresses down slightly, or whether the original Mrs got the big payoff for keeping her mouth shut about her ex's shadiness. Anyway, I enjoy the knowledge that he's not such a big deal. There will be weaknesses: there always are. Joanna trots upstairs obediently, or perhaps in a sulk. 'Can I get you something? Tea, coffee, something stronger?'

All right, maybe I wasn't expecting hookers and coke, but I wasn't expecting tea.

'Coffee would be lovely, thank you, Philip.' I gape at Rachel as she walks past me, apparently oblivious. It's a front, has to be. I follow her into the kitchen.

'Thanks, I'm fine,' I say.

'So you got the message?' He presses a button on a chrome

machine that looks like it was wrenched from the guts of a spaceship.

'The one about killing my sister and her kids? I think so.'

'Yes, it does sound a little . . . overwrought when you put it like that.' At least I know we have the right house. 'Here you are.' He hands a cup and saucer to Rachel. She looks as if she is enjoying herself.

'Under the circumstances, I might have a little snifter. Come through to the study. You're sure I can't tempt you, Mark?' I shake my head, regathering. Time gloops forward, unknowing. A picture on the wall inside the door of a vast, ancient building attracts my eye. 'Durham Castle.' In smaller writing, beneath this: 'Philip Sangster. From his friends. June 1981.' A small, yellow, metal lamp curls out from the frame over the top of the painting, highlighting its subject. There are rugs on the polished wood of the floor that is dotted with artfully mismatched ageing leather furniture; three canvases with slashes of red and black dominate the three walls around the room; the fourth wall is the vast picture window that looks out on darkness punctuated by the watery light of the streetlamp, which doesn't stretch far enough to illuminate the river view.

Philip pulls a bottle of a pale-yellow, syrupy liquid from an antique sideboard and pours it up to near the halfway mark of a brandy balloon. That's good: he needs a drink, and he drinks more than he should. Or perhaps he's just enjoying the moment, so in control that he can afford to drop his guard and celebrate. 'Shall we sit down?'

Rachel is already moving towards a chair.

I take a seat, mesmerised.

Chapter 38

'You shouldn't have come here.' Philip says it quietly, looking at me. He has blue eyes in a pink, fleshy face. His hair is so blond that his eyelashes are almost invisible.

'You pushed me into a corner.' I had rehearsed some lines. That wasn't one of them.

'Our arrangement was working very well until you let us down.'

'I'm sorry.' Is that me apologising? He lights a cigarette, throws the match into a cut-glass ashtray the size of a brick on the long, low table in front of him. The ashtray might come in handy.

'It's rather late in the piece to say that now.'

'Look, it didn't suit me. It wasn't me.' I have to hold myself back from blurting out a story about my grandfather. Trenches, death, stubbornness. Honour. It would sound too earnest. Laughable, given the context.

'That is unfortunate. But you understand that I operate as part of a wider organisation. And my colleagues take a dim view of people who don't do what they say they will. Particularly when that loses them money. And they are quite ruthless. I am not really inclined to kill anyone, but the people above me couldn't care one way or the other. And they do not make empty threats. You will have appreciated that from the way in which we acted this weekend. Incidentally, I believe your sister is at the James Cook Hotel in Wellington? A double room. For Sasha and Steph.'

He settles back in his chair, swirling his liquor then taking a sip. 'So now the question is, what happens next. Are you prepared to resolve the problem? You know what is at stake. You've had time to think it over. We are prepared to let this go. We're only just beginning to look at this market, and it won't do anyone any good to draw too much attention to the situation — but you need to make it up to us quickly. What I would suggest, and I'm prepared to talk about the practicalities, is a red card in your European quarter-final. Early on is best, wouldn't you say?'

'I'm not going to do that. I won't be doing anything like that.'

'Don't say that, please.' His mouth smiles; his eyes don't. 'You don't appear to realise how lucky you are to have this chance. I suppose I shouldn't blame you for trying, but I do have to tell you that you need to come around now.' He leans forward and lowers his voice to a stage whisper. 'I would be prepared to look the other way, but others will not. It really is in your best interest. And those poor little girls . . .'

Fuck him. I'm not losing to this bastard.

Winning or losing. As if it were enough to simply wish it. Sport magnifies the glory of youth, growing it under the glass of observation until its beauty becomes other-worldly, grotesque and magical, its actors capable of anything: if they want it enough, they can have it. Which makes you think that perhaps if you want it enough, you can have it. The page still unwritten. The promise of limitless potential.

There comes a moment when you realise that you're not going to win if you continue to play according to the rules. After that you're kidding yourself if you think it's going to get better while you continue along the same track. Either you submit and let go, give yourself up to all the untellable factors that it turns out were against you, shake hands and tell the other bloke that he played well — or with a fine disregard for the rules you were supposed to be playing by, you step over them and look for an advantage wherever you can find it.

The ashtray looks heavy enough to strike a blow.

I stand and lean over the table. Philip stands, knees slightly bent, side-on to present a smaller target. He doesn't flinch. Bullies aren't always cowards. Taking the ashtray in my right hand, I throw its contents out on the floor and bend down to lay the tips of the fingers of my left hand on the edge of the thick plane of the wood. I bring the edge of the ashtray down as hard as I can between the knuckle and the first joint.

A satisfying crunching sound. I hold my hand up. The index and the middle finger are bent back at a ludicrous angle. Crimson seeps into the whiteness of bunched flesh. I can see bone. I force a smile. 'Eight weeks. At least.' The pain takes a second to arrive but when it hits it makes me want to throw up. Pinpricks of sweat break out on my forehead. My hand shakes. A ruby-red bead drops to the white carpet, holds its spherical shape for a second, then sinks and spreads across the colourless surface.

Philip's mouth forms an oval. I can't look at Rachel. Seconds pass. Then he recovers, sits back and laughs, before remembering his responsibilities as a host. I am still holding my mangled hand out in front of me. 'I'll get you some ice.' He rummages around in the freezer while Rachel grabs a tea-towel. She pours water on the package before bringing it over. She won't look me in the eye. I think I can see a tear on her cheek, but my own eyes are squeezed tight trying not to bleat, so I might be imagining it. She wraps the ice around my hand. I might have whimpered a little. It doesn't feel so bad now I know I haven't lost.

If there is a tear on her cheek, I don't know if it is for me or for her.

Philip shakes his head. 'You're a determined bugger, aren't you? Shall I get you a whisky to go with that ice?' He brings me a glass, looks at the hand and barks another laugh. 'You should really get to a hospital.'

I can barely think any more. Philip does it for me. 'I suppose we could come to an arrangement.'

Epilogue

Six months later

It feels strange to watch the team training and know that they're not waiting for me to come back. The Bamboozler reckons that something will crop up for me in the next month or two. Maybe. I'm not that fussed any more. The girls will get to their new school. I'll get through this, one way or another. The broken fingers kept me from playing for the rest of the season. I had to get screws in both of them, and by the time I was ready to play at the end of April the club wasn't that interested in having me back. They weren't happy that I got injured in the first place, weren't satisfied with the explanation, and by that point we weren't going to win anything anyway so they said they were building for the coming season and I could put my feet up. They could have got a bit sticky about pay, but the doc fudged the forms and made out it was a work injury so in the end it wasn't a problem.

I haven't seen Rachel since that night down by the river in west London. She went out of my life in the dark, the same way she came in. She'll be all right. I think of her sometimes at night. The Bamboozler is a rock, making me wonder what other dark secrets he might have buried behind his eyes. Rich sniffs around. Then we go out and get hammered. If I blurt anything out, he doesn't bring it up.

I head north on the battlefield tourist trail. The grainy black-

and-white films that run on a loop in the museums are surprisingly raw. 'The Last Post' at the Menin Gate plays to an easy, lump-throated crowd; tastefully preserved ranks of crosses and rows of names on monuments serve as a blank canvas for projected emotions. I guess everyone goes with the intention of being moved. The names etched on white stone are too many and their stories too fragmented to enlighten me any more than a packet of tapes and some hundred-year-old newsprint already have. It is impossible to think of our generation sacrificing ourselves on the same scale, and that might be some kind of progress.

In the Belgian bars, English-speaking pilgrims sip thoughtfully at their beer, stare into space and hold discreet, knowledgeable conversations.

I think of a curtain whipped aside for a moment so that I can look in on a great secret.

When practice breaks up I'll go down and see the boys. It's the second game of the championship this weekend. I've got a package here from Philip for the ten from Toulouse who replaced me. It's a Rolex. I've sneaked a look at it and I'm pretty sure it's more expensive than my one was. I'm not going to take it personally. It's just the way it goes.

I wonder how he'll play it?

Acknowledgments

First to Michael Gifkins, whose good cheer and excellent advice is sorely missed. Lucia Rae at Curtis Brown, who made me think about this in a whole different way. Kevin and Warren at Upstart Press who have given me a home. KR, who encouraged me with useful kicks in the arse, accommodation and launch points.

My grandfather, Len Daniell, who left us when I was only two but whose writing — taken word for word in chapter 13 — from the Somme is so much better than mine that the first publisher to see it hoped that I could replicate it across an entire book.

In addition to LTD's letters, my reference books for the World War I material were *Mud Beneath My Boots* by Allan Marriott, *In the Shadow of War* (oral histories of WWI veterans compiled by Nicholas Boyack and Jane Tolerton) and Jane Tolerton's *Ettie: A Life of Ettie Rout*, as well as the extensive online archive at the Alexander Turnbull/National Library of New Zealand.

DA Smith and Charlie Matthews for reminding me how to kill a sheep. Andrew Mehrtens for telling me how to kick goals. Pascal Guidicelli for telling me about ankle injuries. Vanessa and Mathieu Perez for the 'Recipe for Love'. Mark Alderdice for telling me my first draft was 'Jackie Collins for boofheads'; Max Duthie for being slightly more encouraging with the second draft.

My father for providing my grandfather's letters. My mother, for obvious reasons. My daughter, Chloé.

Noelle just for being Noelle.